STORMW

BOOK I

OF

THE SWORD OF LIGHT TRILOGY

Aaron Hodges

Written by Aaron Hodges

Edited by Dynamik Kulture Editing

Proofread by Laura Harnden

Cover Art by Roltirirang on Devianart

The Sword of Light Trilogy

Book 1: Stormwielder

Book 2: Firestorm

Book 3: Soul Blade

The National Library of New Zealand
ISBN: 0473319705
ISBN-13: 978-0473319700

Aaron Hodges was born in 1989 in the small town of Whakatane, New Zealand. He studied for five years at the University of Auckland, completing a Bachelor's of Science in Biology and Geography, and a Masters of Environmental Engineering. After working as an environmental consultant for two years, he now spends his time traveling the world in search of his next adventure.

Thank you to my family, friends, and teachers for all the support you've shown over the years. This has been a work in progress for half my life.

Thanks also to the community at Writing.com, who helped make me the author I am today.

A big thank you to my brother Michael Hodges for the awesome map.

For all the people who have changed my life.
Always keep fighting.

THE THREE NATIONS

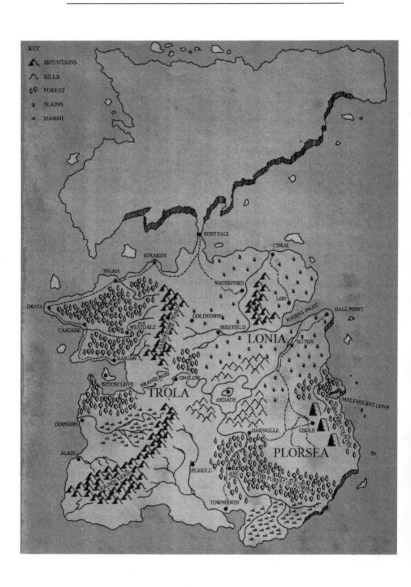

PROLOGUE

Alastair stared into the fire, letting its heat wash through his damp cloak. The autumn storm had caught him in the open, drenching him before he could reach the shelter of a band of trees. The sudden violence of the storm was a grim warning of winter's fast approach.

Thunder rumbled in the distance. Alastair shifted position, groaning as his old joints cracked in the cold. He added another stick to the fire. A greedy tongue of flame licked up the tender wood. Wind rustled the dark branches above. The fire flickered in the breeze and blew smoke into his face. Its feeble light cast dancing shadows across the clearing.

A head appeared in the trees nearby, its long face staring at him. Alastair gripped his sword and fought to control the pain in his chest. His horse snickered at his fear and retreated into the shadows. It was only Elcano, his constant companion for almost a decade. Shivering, he released his sword hilt. He knew all too well the dangers of the night. Once he had been one to stand against such things. Now, though...

He shook his head to clear the morbid thoughts. He was

still a warrior, and creatures of the dark still feared his name. Yet lately doubt had crept into his mind. It had been a long time since he'd fought the good fight, long before the ravages of time stripped away his strength. The old man shivering at autumn shadows was but a spectre of the Alastair who had once battled the demons of winter.

"If only..." he whispered to himself. The words haunted him, carrying with them the weight of wasted decades. If only he had known, if only he had prepared himself. Instead the great Alastair had settled down and put the dark days behind him.

Then two years ago, Antonia had come. She shattered the peaceful world he had built for himself and dragged him back into a life he had thought long buried.

"Find them," she ordered, and he had obeyed.

If only it were so simple. Things were never as they seemed when *she* was involved. Two years of searching and he was now farther from the truth than when he started. The trail was ancient, his quarry adept at disappearing without trace. He himself had taught them the skills, but for generations they had perfected them. Alastair had tracked them as far as Peakill but there all trace vanished. For all he knew they were dead. He prayed to Antonia it was not so.

The wind died away and the chirp of crickets rose above the whisper of the trees. The fire popped as a log collapsed, scattering sparks across the ground. He watched them slowly dwindle to nothing and then looked up at the dark canopy. Through the branches he glimpsed the brilliance of the full moon.

Alastair gritted his teeth. She would come tonight. His hands began to shake; he had dreaded this moment for weeks. The sickly taste of despair rose in his throat. The world would feel the consequences of his failure.

"Not yet, there is still time," the soft whisper of a

female's voice came from the shadows.

Antonia walked from the trees. A veil of mist clung to her small frame, obscuring her features. Her violet eyes shone through the darkness, making the firelight seem pale by comparison. Those eyes held such power and resolve that he shrank before them. The scent of roses filled the grove and cleansed the smoky air. Her footsteps made the slightest crunch as she glided towards him.

"It doesn't matter. They're gone and I don't have the strength to continue. Find someone else to fight this battle, I'm done!" he lowered his gaze, unable to meet her eyes.

"There is no one else like you. You know that," there was anger in the girl's voice. "Look at me and tell me you would abandon everything we have worked for!"

Alastair glanced up. "I abandoned my *family* for your cause," he forced the words out, struggling to hold back tears. "I have given *everything* for you, and it has all been in vain. It's over, they're gone."

He stared at Antonia, expecting anger, scorn, disappointment. She smiled. "It has not been in vain, there is still hope. Elynbrigge has found them."

A rush of strength surged through Alastair. "Where?"

Antonia laughed. Absently she flicked a strand of hair from her face. "The trail was years old, but they are alive and well in Chole. Look for them there. He will watch over them until you arrive."

Alastair jumped to his feet, scattering firewood into the flames. The blaze roared and leapt to devour the fresh meal. He ignored it. The fire be damned, *they were alive!*

"Wait," the tone of Antonia's voice gave him pause. "First you must go to Oaksville. There is someone there who needs you. When you find him, take him with you. Be quick; Archon won't be far behind."

"Who is in Oaksville?" the town was close, but the

detour would cost precious time.

"*Eric.*"

Before he could reply, she was gone.

For a long time Alastair stood staring at the space where she had vanished. Her words spun through his head. His anguish was gone, replaced by a fragile spark of hope. Despair still prowled at the back of his mind, but for now the spark was all that mattered.

He did not sleep that night and the sun was approaching noon as he neared the town. As he cleared the last of the trees he saw the sickly pillars of smoke curling up from the city. He kicked Elcano into a gallop.

ONE

A pillar of smoke rose from the burning house. The roar of the flames was deafening. Heat scorched his eyes but he could not look away. The blaze lit the night, chasing the stars from the sky. Amidst the fire the silhouette of a boy appeared. He stumbled from the wreckage, clothes falling to ashes around him. Sparks of lightning leapt from his fingertips, leaving scorch marks on the tiled street. Soot covered his slim face, marred only by the trail of tears running down his cheeks. The wind caught his mop of dark brown hair and revealed the deep blue glow of his eyes. He wore an expression of absolute terror.

"Help me!"

Eric sat bolt upright, the nightmare tearing him from his sleep. He gasped for breath, eyes darting around in search of escape. A wall of vegetation loomed above him. The dark fingers of branches clawed at his clothing. He scrambled for his dagger but it tumbled through his hands. He dove for the falling blade.

His knees hit the dirt and with a sudden rush he remembered where he was. Eric took a deep breath; slowing his racing heart as he rose to his feet. The clearing had not changed while he slept. The trees still stood in a silent ring, their leaves speckled with the red and gold of early autumn. Where the canopy thinned above he could make out the blue sky, but below the dark of night still clung.

Eric shivered and wished he had more than a holey blanket and worn leather jacket to ward off the cold. Reaching down he stuffed the blanket into his bag with the rest of his measly possessions – dried meat, a water skin, and the steel bracelet his parents had given to him as a child. The familiar dream clung to him, the boy's face lurking in the shadows of his memory. He knew that face. It was his own.

A tremor ran through his body. He flung the bag over his shoulder with a little too much energy, determined to forget the bad omen. Just through the trees was the Gods Road and about a mile west was the town of Oaksville. There he planned to make a fresh start for himself.

Eric paused long enough to pull on his travel worn boots and brush the leaves from his hair, then he was away through the trees. Excitement quickened his pace – this was it. Today he would end his exile. In the two years since his fifteenth birthday he had wandered alone through the forests and plains of Plorsea. In that time he had kept his own company. It had very nearly driven him insane.

The trees either side of the Gods Road soon began to thin, giving way to the grassy steeps of a valley. Eric squinted into the rising sun, straining for his first glimpse of Oaksville. A layer of fog clung to the slopes, but it was quickly fading in the rising sun. Buildings began to take shape – wooden houses with tall smoking chimneys, the three-pronged spire of the temple, an old castle set in the centre that towered above the town walls.

Eric's spirit leapt at the sight. Then the first gust of wind reached him on the hilltop, carrying with it the clang of hammers and clip clop of hooves. His nose twitched at the tang of smoke and humanity hanging in the air. The image of a burning house flickered into his mind.

He paused mid-stride. A voice whispered in his mind. *Go back – it's too dangerous!*

Fear gripped him. *What if I'm not ready?* His knees shook. His heart pounded like a runaway wagon on a cobbled street. His vision swam and he felt the warmth of tears on his cheeks.

Eric turned his head and looked back up the hill. The long grass rippled in the wind, the trees beyond shadowing the movement. The forest could offer him nothing more. He drew a breath of air and faced the town. He took a step forward. The terror returned. His chest constricted until he could hardly breathe, but this time his nerve held. Eric walked down the valley towards the gates.

Soon the outer wall loomed over him, its great stone blocks casting the path in shadow. Ahead a gaping hole in the stonework swallowed the road whole. A guard stood to either side of the gates, dressed in the chainmail and crimson tunic marking the Plorsean reserve army. Each held a steel tipped spear loosely at their side and a sword on their belt. The one to the right spared Eric a glance as he passed by, then returned his eyes to the road. Until recently Plorsea had enjoyed decades of peace. But now bandits had moved down from the mountains and were plaguing the countryside. At first they had only targeted travellers, but lately raids had been launched against some of the smaller settlements.

Eric passed between the open gates and into the darkness of the tunnel. Moss covered the giant slabs of rock on either side of him. Iron grates peeked from the ceiling, once used to pour burning oil on invaders who breached the outer gates. These walls dated back to darker times, before peace had come to the Three Nations.

With a deep breath Eric stepped from the tunnel and back into sunlight. A bustling marketplace spread out around him. The air was heavy with dust and the stink of human bodies. The buzz of a hundred voices assaulted Eric's ears. To his left bakers stood at their booths waving loaves of bread in the faces of passers-by. Elsewhere he could see others plying their wares; butchers and jewellers, fishermen and carpenters, all chaotically crammed into the small square before the city gates. Each was doing their best to draw the early morning crowds to their stalls.

A jeweller caught Eric's eye and began motioning for him to look at his array of golden necklaces laid out on the table. Eric smiled and shook his head, but suddenly the jeweller was out of his stall and moving through the crowd towards him shouting, "Sir! Sir!"

Eric shrank back towards the cool comfort of the tunnel. His feet stumbled on the uneven surface and sent him tumbling to the ground. His head struck the cobbled pavement. His ears rung. Groaning he looked up, straining to see while his vision spun.

A face appeared overhead. "Careful there, mate," the man offered a hand. Eric immediately recognised the western twang of a Trolan accent.

Eric took the hand and the man hauled him to his feet. He stumbled for a second, trying to regain his balance.

"That looked like a nasty fall," the Trolan offered. "You okay?"

The man wore a dark brown cloak and towered over Eric's own five feet and seven. A poorly trimmed beard and moustache matted his face, while a broad smile detracted somewhat from the twisted lump serving him for a nose. His hazel eyes looked down from beneath bushy eyebrows. Silver streaked his black hair.

Eric nodded. "It was my fault," he stuttered.

"Everything is so… overwhelming."

"A country boy then?" the man gave a booming laugh. "I remember my first time in a town like this. They stole every penny I had, not the pickpockets, those crooked merchants! Bought a dagger that snapped the first time I dropped it. These townsmen prey on the weak. Well don't you worry mate, us country folk look after our own. The name's Pyrros Gray, what can I do for ya?"

Eric grinned. The man reminded him of the warm manner of people in his old village. "I'm Eric. Is there some place quiet I could sit for a while? My head is spinning."

"My pleasure, Eric. There's a tavern not far from here, it's usually quiet at this hour. I know the owner; he won't mind you sitting down for a bit. Just follow me and we'll have you there in no time. Only try not to catch the eye of any of these vultures, or they'll soon convince you to trade everything you own for one of 'em statues that grants luck with woman."

Pyrros set off through the crowd. Eric followed close behind, afraid to lose him in the press of bodies. His legs felt unsteady and his head throbbed with each step.

A big woman stepped between them and thrust a wet trout in his face. "Cheapest fish in town! You buy!" she demanded.

Eric shook his head and side stepped the merchant, trying to avoid any further contact. She shouted after him but he ignored her words. He scanned the crowd, searching for Pyrros.

"Didn't think I'd leave you behind, did you?" Pyrros' voice came from behind him.

Eric spun around, relieved to see the bulky man right beside him.

Pyrros laughed. "So what brought you to Oaksville, mate?"

Eric shrugged. "I wanted a fresh start."

"Well we'll have to see what we can do about that. Now come on, we're almost there."

They slipped into a narrow alleyway which twisted away from the marketplace. Tall brick walls hemmed them in on either side, casting the alley in shadow. The drone of the markets died off as they rounded the first corner. Dead wood and discarded garbage lay in piles along the alley, but someone had maintained a trail through the mess, leading deeper into the town.

Eric wrinkled his nose as they passed a pile of decomposing fish heads. He stepped around it and hesitated. "Are you sure this is the way?"

Pyrros turned and grinned. "It's a short cut. The streets surrounding the marketplace tend to get so crowded you can hardly move. This way goes around."

A chill breeze blew through the alley. The hairs on Eric's neck stood up. He did not like the way Pyrros was grinning. The man no longer seemed so friendly; suddenly the way he towered over Eric was threatening and a strange glint had appeared in his eyes. Eric's gut churned in warning.

"I think I'd prefer the crowd to this mess, thanks," Eric turned to leave.

Two men blocked his path. One spun a wooden baton in his hand and the other held a heavy club. Each stood a head above Eric. They were dressed in plain clothes, but the smiles they wore lacked any trace of warmth. A coil of rope was slung over the baton wielder's shoulder. They spread out to block Eric's escape.

"Don't bother running, mate," Pyrros' voice was menacing now. "You'll make this easier on everyone if you come willingly."

Eric half turned, keeping the other men in sight. "What do you want?"

Pyrros shrugged. "Fair trade's not the only business that's booming. Slaves have grown popular in southern Trola. So long as we're discrete, take the ones no one misses, people turn a blind eye. You're one of those, aren't you mate?"

He shook his head. "No, my parents are waiting–" he was interrupted by a harsh cackle.

Pyrros scratched at his beard. "So you were lying earlier? About starting a new life?"

Eric clenched his fists, tense as coiled wire. He glanced at the men behind him, gauging the distance between them. Fear made his breath come in short, ragged gasps.

"No, I think you're lying now, mate. I don't think anyone is out there waiting for you. I don't think there's anyone in the world who will miss you."

This cannot be happening!

Pain pounded at Eric's head, but he fought it down. He glanced at Pyrros, and then leapt at the man with the club. Grinning, the thug lifted his weapon. A moment before he swung Eric dived sideways, twisting for the gap between the men. He almost made it.

A club to his chest stopped him cold. For the second time that day he found himself flat on his back. Winded, he choked for air, the faces of the two men spinning above him. He could feel his anger taking hold. Overhead, thunder clapped. Drops of rain began to fall.

Footsteps came from nearby. Pyrros appeared above him, a frown on his face. "The first thing a slave must learn is obedience. You disappoint me, Eric. I took you for a quick learner."

The man's boot came up and crashed down on Eric's stomach. The breath exploded from his lungs. Pain constricted his chest and he gasped, eyes watering, desperate for air. Inside, Eric felt the embers of his fury take light.

"Stupid boy," by now the rain was bucketing down, soaking through the clothes of his attackers. Pyrros' foot lashed out again, smashing into his ribs and head.

Eric curled into a ball as the assault rained down. He choked back his tears, fear and rage battling for control. There was a sudden roar as something within snapped, giving way to the chaos of his emotions. A terrible power exploded through his mind, slipping from the darkest recesses of his conscious. He no longer felt the blows, or the rain, or the dirt beneath him. All that remained was an all-consuming hate; a need to lash out. A scream of torment echoed through the alleyway. The last barrier in his mind shattered.

Eric opened his eyes. Blue light lit the stone walls of the passageway, freezing the men in a sudden blue glare. He saw the hate in Pyrros' eyes turn to terror, saw the men beside him glance up, heard the crackling and smelt the burning as it came. Then the lightning struck.

The men vanished into the blue light, their screams cut short by the roar of thunder. There was no chance for escape. One second the three were there, the next the lightning had consumed them. But it did not stop there.

With a deafening crack the sky tore asunder, unleashing a hail of lightning. The screams of the villagers rose above the crash of thunder, as destruction rained down on the defenceless village. Splinters of wood and stone flew through the air as the blue fire tore buildings apart.

Eric struggled to his feet. His anger had vanished, his hatred spent. He stumbled towards the marketplace, mouth agape. Horror clutched his soul.

No, no, no, this cannot be happening – not again!

Eric watched the lightning burn a deadly trail through the marketplace. Booths exploded before its wrath, filling the air with smoke and debris. Dozens had already fallen, their clothes blackened and crumbling, their bodies broken. Gusts of wind swirled through the square, picking up tiles and rubble and flinging them into the air. The rain poured down, but even that could not wash away the smell of burning. Eric stumbled amid the chaos, powerless to save his hapless victims.

There was no escape from the storm's fury. It tore through the market, an unstoppable force of nature. Eric fell to his knees, his tears mingling with the torrent of rain. Lightning struck his frail body but he felt nothing. Bolts of energy danced along his skin, raising goose bumps wherever they touched. Yet he remained unharmed. He buried his head in his arms.

Why?

The thunder died away, leaving a devastating silence in its wake. Eric could hardly summon the courage to look. At last he opened his eyes. His gaze swept the wreckage with growing shock. There was not a stall left standing. Burnt beams and canvas covered the square and flames were already beginning to spread. Bodies lay scattered amid the ruin, at times half-buried by the rubble. Eric choked at the sight, His mind rebelling against the truth.

This is my doing.

Movement came from his right. He looked across as a man struggled to his feet. Their eyes met. Eric saw the horror grow in the stranger's eyes. He looked down and saw that lightning still played across his chest and arms. Noise came from elsewhere now as more survivors rose to view the shattered remains – and to see the boy with lightning dancing on his skin.

Eric watched them, heart filled with despair. The faces of those around him wore only hatred. He had to say something, but could not find the words. His body ached and his muscles burned but he struggled to his feet. A surge of blood rushed to his head. He swayed. Then, determined, he opened his mouth to speak.

An angry buzz of voices assailed him. To his left a man drew a dagger from his belt. He started towards Eric. Another quickly followed suit, ripping a makeshift club from a pile of rubble as he approached. The broken ground crunched beneath their booted feet. Each wore a grim mask of determination. When they were a few feet away they hesitated, eyeing him with caution.

Eric struggled to find some words of explanation. He wanted to tell them it had not been him, that he could not control this curse. Yet he knew in his heart it would be a lie. He had known his presence brought a terrible danger to all around him. A heavy weight settled on his shoulders. There was nothing he could offer these souls but his life.

More survivors joined the first two men, arming themselves with whatever makeshift weapons were within reach. Each sported burns across their arms and clothing, and dark bruises on their faces. A fire burned in their eyes, fuelled by the horror they had just witnessed.

Eric trembled, staring at the blades and cudgels held by men and women alike. His heart pounded in his chest. He clenched his fists, struggling to ignore the hollow feeling in the pit of his stomach. His rib cage ached where the club had struck him earlier. Bruises from the beating were already starting to swell on his arms and legs. His mind shuddered at the thought of the pain still to come.

Cautiously the survivors edged towards him, numbers fuelling their courage.

Eric backed away, his own courage fading with each step. The villagers moved faster, sensing his fear. He stumbled backwards over the rubble, unable to tear his gaze from the madness in the eyes of the crowd. He stumbled over a pile of rubble and crashed to the ground. The shock lifted the spell. Eric scrabbled to his feet and ran for his life.

TWO

Eric sprinted down the burning streets. The roar of angry voices and pounding footsteps from behind drove him through the downpour. He dodged past the wreckage of shattered homes, squinting through the rain, searching for a path. The whistling wind whipped across his face and sliced through his waterlogged jacket.

His eyes watered as he ran through clouds of acrid smoke. Lifeless bodies lay scattered across the flooded streets. Thick droplets of rain splattered around them.

Eric ran on. Soot clung to his skin, mixing with the torrents of water washing over him. He passed a hand through his filthy hair, struggling to think, gasping for air. His muscles burned and great shivers ran through his body. He was at the end of his endurance.

The light of approaching torches flickered in the lengthening shadows. The day was dying and Eric could only pray the darkness would come soon. He drove himself on; the freezing autumn wind buffeted him, his footsteps splattering in the flooded streets. Water filled his boots. His leggings squelched with every stride.

A shout came from behind, followed by the clang of steel-tipped arrows as they struck the wall a few feet to his right. Eric ducked, glancing back to see a crowd of people sprinting towards him. He slid into a nearby passageway before the bowman could fire again.

Why? The thought chased itself around his head. He scrambled through the alley, scarcely able to make out a path through the shadows. A jagged piece of tile tore a slice of skin from his arm. Blood gushed from the wound and ran down his side. Eric winced, fighting down the pain.

He burst from the alley into a broad avenue. The sun had finally set, leaving only dying tongues of flame to light his way. They cast the world into a realm of shadows. Curses came from the alley behind him. Eric did not stop to wait for them.

Voices chased after him. He glanced back to see the first of the townsfolk emerging from the alley. Flaming torches lit the murky gloom and exposed the gaunt faces of his hunters.

Eric weaved through the rubble strewn street, listening for the telltale whistle of arrows. Water flicked up in his wake and mingled with the drifting smoke. An arrow shot past his shoulder. The shriek of its passage raised goose bumps down his neck. He looked back without breaking stride and saw two bowmen hurriedly nocking new arrows. Then the smoke closed in, the wind driving it down into the street, and they vanished.

He ran on through a world twisted by his destruction.

****

The darkness was finally complete, the last flames snuffed out by the blanket of night. The rain had ceased and the clouds parted to reveal the star-studded sky above.

The moon had yet to show its face, yet to cast its pale glow on the devastation below.

Eric huddled among the ruins of an old building, listening carefully as the footsteps of his pursuers passed him by. A chill breath of air sent a violent shiver through his body. His clothes were soaked, ruined. His teeth began to chatter. He clamped a hand over his mouth, terrified of being overheard. The stench of his own body filled the small space, an overwhelming mixture of soot, sweat, and death.

At last Eric allowed himself a deep breath, satisfied for the moment he was safe. He sat back, his hand pressing against something soft and cold. A shiver ran through him and his eyes slid down to where his hand rested. The glassy eyes of a dead man stared up at him. Terrible burns blackened the man's shoulders and face. His skin had turned a pale grey.

Eric threw himself back from the body. He scrambled to his feet as his stomach swirled. With a gut wrenching heave, he emptied the pitiful contents of his stomach onto the cracked floor.

He fell back, holding his face in his hands, fighting back tears. Choking, he turned away and returned to his spy hole to check if anyone had noticed the noise. All was silent. How he wished he'd had the courage to give himself up. By now the torment would be over. He deserved what they had in store. No torture could match what he had wrought on these people.

Through the broken roof he watched a full moon rise into the sky. Its cool light offered no warmth, yet the sight gave him comfort. Eric glimpsed his soot streaked face in a nearby puddle. Leaning down, he cupped a handful of water and tried to wash the dirt from his face. It clung to him, rasping along his skin. Finally he fell back on his haunches, defeated even by this simple task.

The soft sound of a footstep on gravel carried to him from outside. Another followed, barely audible over the thudding of his heart. Eric swallowed hard, struggling to dislodge the lump in his throat, and peered out into the street. His keen eyes searched the darkness. The silhouette of a man shifted in the shadows, coming closer.

A pale brown cloak billowed out in a gust of wind, revealing the gold embossed hilt of a short sword strapped to the man's waist. The man moved faster, emerging from the shadows and making straight for Eric's hiding place. Lines of silver embroidering wove an intangible pattern across the arms of the man's cloak. The same designs had been worked into the black leather of his boots. A grey hood obscured his face but Eric could feel the man's eyes as they searched the wreckage.

Eric crouched in his hiding place, muscles tensed, ready to spring. He fought to control his breathing, told himself he was hidden, concealed by the shadows. Fists clenched, he watched as the man made straight for him.

"Come out," the man whispered in an old, crackling voice. "I'm not here to hurt you."

The man pulled back his hood to reveal long grey hair and a clean-shaven face. His lips curled into a frown that sent a shiver down to Eric's stomach. Piercing green eyes stared straight at where Eric hid. The man continued to advance.

Eric found his gaze trapped in the heat of the old man's glare. For a moment it seemed time stood still. Eric felt as though his mind was an open book; that this man could stare into his very soul and read his every thought. Staring into those awful eyes, Eric felt the shame well up within, felt the crushing weight of guilt crash down on him. Suddenly he wanted nothing more than to curl up and die.

The old man blinked and Eric shuddered as the spell broke. He sank to his knees, staring at the muddy ground. Fresh tears welled in his eyes and streamed down his face. Sobs racked his body. The man stood over him, sword in hand.

It took a long time for Eric to regain his composure. Finally he stood. Taking a deep breath, he met the old man's eyes. The moon lit the space between them, turning the world to black and white. Eric spoke in a whisper. "What do you want?"

"To help you," came the reply.

Eric could have laughed. "Why? Who do you think I am? Look around you," Eric threw out his arms. "This is what I create. This is my existence – chaos and destruction. Are you some demon, come for an apprentice in murder?"

The man's eyes hardened. "I am no demon, boy. I am a man who understands what you are, a man who sees the good within you. And I am perhaps the only chance you have to control that power inside you. If you want to live, I suggest you come with me."

Eric stood rigidly in front of the old man. His mind was spinning, trying to make sense of what he had heard. "Who are you?" he whispered.

"My name is Alastair. Now come, before the others find us."

Alastair. The name had a familiar ring. Regardless, he was not prepared to trust so easily; not after what had happened in the marketplace. Who knew what this man planned. Then again, what had he to lose? If he wished him harm, he need only to swing his sword.

Still he hesitated. "I don't trust you, Alastair."

Alastair frowned down at him, a hint of anger in his eyes. Then with a heavy sigh and shrug of his shoulders, he offered a small smile. "Fair enough," he flicked his sword into the air and caught it by the blade. He handed it hilt first to Eric. "You hold onto this for now, if it makes you feel safer. You can give it back once I've earned your trust."

Surprised, Eric took the sword. Still hesitant, he gave Alastair a quick nod. Alastair nodded back and took off down the road. Eric followed, moving as silently as he could through the debris strewn across the ground. His senses probed the gloom, but the streets were deserted. The mob had moved on.

Ahead Alastair slipped off the road and into another alley. Eric followed close on his heels. He held the sword close to his body with the tip pointed down. He had never used a sword before. It felt strange and awkward in his hands.

The old man moved on, drawing Eric deeper into the gloom. The alleyway grew narrower as they went, and with a shiver Eric realised the buildings on either side of them had collapsed. The walls of each building now leaned out into the alley, forming an unstable tepee above their heads. Streams of moonlight flooded through the cracks above them.

Eric swallowed hard at the thought of the unstable stone and wood perched above him. Swallowing his fear, he picked his way further into the alley, following the silver streaks of Alastair's cloak. The man moved with a confident stride, seemingly indifferent to the danger looming above.

The scuff of leather on stone echoed off the walls. They froze. The shuffling sound of someone moving down the tunnel followed. Then a dark figure stepped forward into a column of moonlight. Brown eyes locked on Eric.

"*You*," it hissed.

THREE

G abriel knelt in the mud, head bowed, and let the grief wash over him. Pain wrapped around his heart, its thorny tendrils robbing him of strength. Sharp stones cut through the fabric of his pants. He no longer cared. Agony twisted through his mind, burning away all other sensation.

The night's chill seeped through his rain-soaked clothes and sucked the warmth from his body. He could almost feel his life fading away, but he could not muster the strength to care. At least in death he might finally be free from this all-consuming grief.

Until this morning he had lived a simple life, toiling alongside his father in the family forge, surrounded by the love of his parents and soon-to-be wife. Their faces flew through his mind, smiling and full, and then as he had last seen them – twisted in death.

There had been no warning, just a flash of light and clap of thunder. Then death had rained from the skies. There was no defence, nowhere to run. Lightning danced through the streets, its fiery touch tearing through flesh and mortar. The wind had followed, ripping up roofing tiles and flinging them down on the streets below. Debris hurtled through the air to smash the fragile bodies of those caught in the open. Death was indiscriminate, claiming young and old alike, leaving the few survivors to stare in shock at the tattered remnants of their lives.

Somehow Gabriel had survived with only minor burns and bruises. He had stumbled through the shattered streets towards his home, each step bringing a growing sense of dread. By the time he rounded the final corner he had already known what he would find.

Everything looked the same through the howling wind and rain, and at first he was unable to process the sight that greeted him. Then with sudden realisation, he recognised the remains of his home. The two-storey villa was gone; all that remained were broken walls and scattered roofing. Flames flickered amid the wreckage, already growing.

Gabriel plunged into the ruins, ignorant to the danger. He called out for his family, desperate for a response, for any sign of life. His father, mother, fiancé, they had all been home when he left.

He found them in the back of the house where they must have gathered to wait out the storm. Tears ran down Gabriel's cheeks. He collapsed to his knees, fingers reaching for the bloody beam impaling his father. Empty eyes stared up at him, frozen in terror. Partly sheltered by his father's body lay Gabriel's mother. The same beam had stolen her life. Blood still seeped from the gashes in her arms and face.

The final blow came as Gabriel found his fiancé. She lay behind his parents, buried beneath heavy tiles, only her loving face left untouched.

A sharp moan escaped Gabriel. At the noise, his fiancé's eyes fluttered open. He was at her side in an instant, heart racing with sudden hope.

"Gabriel," she whispered. Blood ran from her mouth.

"I'm here, it'll be okay," as he knelt beside her, he

started to sob. So close he could not ignore the horror. The collapsing wall had crushed her chest. It would not be long.

He stroked her hair, whispering soft comforts. He didn't know whether they were for her sake or his own. He had cherished this girl, and to watch helpless as her life faded away… Her breath came in rugged gasps, until slowly her eyes closed and with a long sigh, she was gone.

Gabriel stood, fists clenched. He looked around the room one final time, gathering himself. Scrunching his eyes closed, he left the ruin. His mind was in shock. It begged him to run, to escape, to hide where the pain could not find him.

He walked out into the pouring rain, searching for some sense or reason for this nightmare. He cursed his luck, cursed the Goddess for sparing him.

Then he heard the whispers of the other survivors. He listened as they told of the boy who danced with lightning, of the demon who had wrought this madness. So he had joined the mob in their hunt, driven by hate, by the need to escape his pain. He no longer feared the powers such a demon might unleash. His own life meant little to him now.

The gates were sealed, but their prey had vanished. Exhaustion soon quenched his anger and, without it, grief returned to overwhelm him. Soon the day was coming to an end and Gabriel felt the last of his energy slipping away. Despair took hold of his heart and with the last of his strength he dragged himself into an alley. Cracks riddled its walls. It would not be long before they crumbled.

Gabriel stumbled through the growing darkness, moving deeper into the alleyway. In the dark he sank to his knees, closed his eyes, and waited for death.

Yet death did not come. Hours passed and at some stage he had fallen asleep. Still the alley stood strong. Every so often the bricks would groan and Gabriel would brace himself for the end. It never came.

Others had come instead. It began with the scrape of boots in the distance. He lifted his head, eyes struggling to pierce the darkness. He stilled his breath and listened. Someone was in the alley, coming closer.

Two figures shifted in the shadows and then stepped into a patch of moonlight. Gabriel glimpsed a tall man with greying hair before the boy beside him drew his eyes. A mop of dark brown hair hung across his face, but beneath he could see the bright blue of the demon's eyes. Thick eyebrows and a small nose appeared when the boy looked around. His gaze passed over where Gabriel sat hidden in the shadows.

The boy held a short sword gripped tightly in one hand. Mud and ash covered his clothes and his tunic was dotted with holes that revealed the pale flesh beneath. Cuts and grazes marked his arms and blood ran from a gash on his cheek. Yet there were no burn marks.

Gabriel stepped into the light. "You!"

FOUR

Eric froze as the voice hissed from the shadows. A young man stepped into a shaft of moonlight sparing from the fractured roof. He towered over Alastair, shoulders heaving, eyes ablaze with rage. Soot covered his clean-shaven cheeks, and tears and burns marked his cloak. Deep lines of exhaustion crisscrossed his face. "*You?*" he repeated.

Alastair stepped towards him. "Step aside, boy."

"They're all *dead!*" the stranger sobbed. "My parents, my fiancé. *Gone!*" he screamed the last word. Eric could hear the accusation in his voice. "*Why?*"

The old man did not reply. Silence fell. Eric found his eyes locked with those of his accuser. His chest grew tight with guilt. He licked his cracked lips, his mouth dry as sand, and felt the terror inside him grow.

The man snarled and took a step forward.

Alastair threw out his arm, blocking his path. Eric shrank from the man's rage, his feet betraying him to take an involuntary step backwards.

"Stop," Alastair ordered, his voice laced with authority.

"You protect him?" the villager challenged. "He is a murderer, a demon. You must know this!"

Alastair ignored the question. "What is your name?"

"Gabriel," he swallowed. "I will not let him escape. Now out of my way, old man. He must die!" he made to push Alastair from his path.

"No," Alastair's voice rang with command.

Gabriel clenched his fists, for a second frozen with indecision, and then with a snarl launched himself at Alastair.

The alleyway echoed with the thump of fists on flesh. Alastair moved with shocking speed, spinning on his heel to sidestep Gabriel's charge. Then as his heavily built attacker stumbled past, Alastair struck. Reaching out he grasped the young man by his coat and with casual ease threw Gabriel headlong into the brick wall.

There was a harsh crunch and A second later Gabriel lay slumped on the ground, unconscious.

"Come, Eric, we are running out of time," Alastair said over his shoulder.

Eric nodded, struggling to peel his eyes from Gabriel. *How had the old man moved so quickly?*

"He'll be fine. Come!" he moved off. Eric followed, his not-so-silent shadow.

They emerged into an empty street. Above them towered the bulk of the city's outer walls, the brick and stone forming a silent shadow on the night sky. Beyond, the stars glittered and the cold moon had taken its place above.

Alastair took the lead again, crossing the road and picking his way through the rubble of an old building until they reached the foot of the city walls. Eric stared at the giant blocks of stone that made up the thirty-foot wall. Each rock had been worn smooth by the passage of time, their surface slick with rain. He placed a hand to the cold stone. The ramparts of this wall had overlooked Oaksville for centuries. In all that time they had stood as protection against the dangers without. Today they had witnessed the fall of Oaksville.

A knotted rope trailed down from high above, flapping in the night's breeze. Alastair took the rope in one hand. Eric's legs trembled and fear rose in his chest. His heart began to race. He was terrified of heights; the thought of clambering up that rope was horrifying.

Alastair held out the rope. "They had already barred the gates when I reached the city, so I had to make my own way in. I left this here in case I needed to leave the same way. You'll need to climb first and wait at the top for me. There is another rope on the other side, but I've hidden it well. If you hear a guard while you're up there, whistle. But I imagine most are busy elsewhere."

Eric struggled to keep his fear to himself. His breath came in quick, short gasps and a cold sweat trickled down his brow. Hands shaking, he slipped Alastair's short sword into his belt, walked forward and took the rope.

You can do this, he repeated the mantra to himself.

He looked up. The wall towered thirty feet above his head. Gritting his teeth, he began to pull himself up hand over hand. With each lunge he planted the tips of his feet firmly in the shallow cracks of the wall before moving on.

At first the going was relatively easy; the knots gave him something to grip so he rarely slipped. Yet as he moved upwards the stones became more worn, the cracks between them finer. His old boots struggled to find grip.

Twenty feet above the town his feet slipped on the slick surface. He grasped desperately at the rope and slammed into the cold wall. His muscles ached from the strain and his hands burned where the coarse rope had slipped between his fingers. He scrambled to find purchase with his feet, the desperate seconds seemingly like hours. Finally the tips of his boots found a crack and he was able to relieve his arms of some weight.

Eric took a deep breath, struggling to regain his composure, acutely aware of the open air beneath him. His arms shook with the effort.

It took another five minutes to reach the top. With the last of his strength he threw himself over the battlements. In that moment he did not care whether a guard waited for him or not. All that mattered was escaping the yawning chasm beneath him.

Head spinning, chest heaving, Eric peered over the side. He could hardly believe he had made it. After a few seconds he drew back again. He shook his head, trying to free himself of the fear lodged there. He finally thought to look for guards. The bright moonlight illuminated the empty ramparts.

Eric managed a grim smile. Boot scuffled on stone and then Alastair was settling himself beside him. A hint of sweat shone on his forehead but otherwise he showed no sign of exertion.

He nodded to Eric. "I'll go down first, you look exhausted." He crossed to the other side, reached between two crenulations and pulled up a rope. He vanished over the edge.

Eric gazed back at the town. He had dreaded this moment, knew he shouldn't look, but the pull of his conscience overwhelmed him. He needed to know, had to see what he had wrought.

Oaksville stretched out beneath him, the dim remnants cast in grey by the light of the moon. In places the flames still burned but the rain had tamed the worst. From the wreckage rose the distant cries of the desperate and dying. A cloud of smoke hung low over the town, an embodiment of the evil that had cursed the place.

With misty eyes he turned away. This was far worse than

he could ever have imagined. Oaksville would never recover. He had been its doom; if evil had come to this place it was Eric who had brought it. He thought of the thousands of lives that had been shattered and swore he would somehow make things right.

The rope went slack beside him. It was time.

Eric grasped the rope tight in both hands and leaned back over the side. He closed his eyes, the fear rising up inside him and threatening to overwhelm him. His head throbbed. A dull wind brushed against him.

He began to make his slow way down. His hands clung to the rope while his feet sought tiny cracks to support his weight. His arms burned already, not used to the strain and still exhausted from the climb up. Every movement seemed to knock another bruise or scrape. Inch by inch, he descended towards the ground.

A sudden gust of wind knocked his feet from beneath him. He slammed face first into the hard stone, arms struggling to hold him. The metallic taste of blood ran across his tongue. He spat it out and looked down.

The rope trailed away beneath him, curling towards the ground far, far below. His vision swam, blurring and fading until it seemed his head must explode. The fear froze in his chest. He could not draw a single breath. The ice in his chest slowly spread to his arms and legs, freezing his entire body with fear.

The wind came from nowhere, a sudden gale kissed with the deathly chill of the far north. It ripped at his wet clothing, sucking the little warmth remaining from his body. The temperature plummeted. Eric shivered and clung desperately to the rope. His teeth began to chatter.

He sucked in a breath, using a hand to wipe the cold sweat from his forehead. Ice cracked and fell away into the darkness below. Eric stared at the bare stone of the wall, struggling to control himself. As he watched, the rain-soaked surface began to glisten, the freezing wind turning the water to ice.

"*No*," Eric whispered, fighting to control his terror.

He closed his eyes and struggled to slow his panicked breath, to calm his rampant fear. It was no use. He watched, helpless, as the creeping ice reached his feet first, then the rope. His boots slipped from the wall, leaving only his tenuous hold to keep him aloft.

The rope grew colder in his hands. He clung tighter, gritting his teeth as the cold burned his skin. His eyes watered, tears freezing on his cheeks. Eric choked on the frozen air and pulled himself closer to the rope, bracing himself on the icy threads. He fought to hold on. He could not give up now, not when he was so close.

It was impossible. Bit by bit the feeling in his fingers faded away, until, as if by a will of their own, they released his last hold on life. He fell away into the darkness.

****

Gabriel hauled himself to his feet. His sight blurred and began to spin. He placed a hand against a wall to hold himself steady. The stone groaned, the sound an agony to his aching head. At least it would be over soon.

He stood motionless, eyes closed, ready to embrace his death. His heart called for his family, for the comfort of their loving embrace. The makeshift roof gave another groan. Dust filled the air. A crash came from nearby as the first piece of wall gave way.

Soon.

His thoughts returned to the boy and the old man. *Damn*

them! If only he could have reached the boy, he would have been able to rest in peace. But the demon had escaped.

Gabriel reached up and touched the gash on his forehead. He felt the sticky moisture of his own blood. He grimaced. Soon the pain would be gone.

But was he ready to die? Did he not have something more to do now, something more important than this lonely death?

Revenge.

A twisted smile crossed his face. He walked slowly towards the street. As he emerged from the alleyway there came the strangely muted crunch of falling rock, followed by a whoosh of air.

Gabriel did not care. There was only one single, tangible thought left in his mind. The demon would die. He would die for Oaksville. He would die for his fiancé and his parents. And most of all, he would die so Gabriel could watch the horror in his eyes as life fled from his broken body.

FIVE

"*Come closer, let me see your face,*" *the voice whispered, snaking its way deep into the cracks of his shattered conscious.*

Something deep within him shrank from the voice, fought against the darkness creeping through his mind.

"*Do not be afraid. You have a gift, one that could offer you the world.*"

He could feel the defences of his mind beginning to crumble. The dark silhouette of a face began to take shape.

"*Ahhhh,*" *the voice let out a long sigh.* "*I can almost see you now. Almost....*" *the voice was eager now, filled with hunger and greed.*

His instincts screamed danger. With a wrench of effort he tore himself free.

An ungodly wail echoed through the confines of his mind. There came a flash of light, and the dream ended.

"Wake, Eric! We have to move. They have found us," a rough hand clasped his shoulder and shook him. Pain jolted down Eric's back.

He jerked awake, instinctively reaching for his knife. For a moment the world was cast in red and he saw only a tall figure towering over him. He lashed out with a fist, his other hand drawing the dagger from his belt.

Calloused hands caught his wrists. "Stop. Remember where you are, Eric. I have carried you as far as I can, but my strength is running out."

The red faded from Eric's vision and he began to remember the night. The storm, the destruction, the climb, *the fall!* He ceased to struggle, searching his memory for the man's name. "*Alastair*," the old man nodded. "Who *are* you?"

Alastair shook his head. "There's no time. We must move, *now!*"

Eric could hear the urgency in his voice but was not eager to leap at a strangers command. He glanced around, noticing now the dense wall of trees surrounding them. He lay in a small clearing, the ground all churned mud and scattered leaves. Above the light of the morning sun shone through the branches. He heard the first calls of the dawn chorus over the dripping of water on fallen leaves. Eric sat on the cold earth, the damp seeping through his thin clothes. The scent of fresh rain toyed with his nostrils.

Alastair stared at the trees on the far side of the clearing. He glanced back at Eric. "We need to move, they can't be far behind by now. Can you walk?"

Seeing the panic in the old man's eyes Eric gave in and nodded. He took Alastair's hand and the old man pulled him to his feet.

A crash came from the forest behind them. A streak of emerald flashed past Eric's head; a parakeet fleeing the coming danger. Others followed and the clearing filled with the thumping of wings and the screech of panicked birds. A breath of wind touched his cheek, carrying with it the stench of smoke.

"*Run!*" Alastair hissed, making for the trees.

Eric sucked in a breath and followed. A whirlwind of questions raced through his mind. *Where were they? How had the hunters found them? What had happened after the fall?*

He chose one and shouted it at Alastair's back. "How did they find us?"

He thought the question had been lost in the wind. Another crash came from behind, closer this time.

Then Alastair answered. "They've been on our trail since the wall. A couple of guards heard your scream as you fell. At first I managed to outpace them, but there was no time to disguise my trail."

They were moving downhill now and Eric struggled to keep his feet on the muddy ground. He grasped at seedlings and low hanging branches as he ran, struggling to control his descent on the slippery slope. Ahead Alastair slid between the trees with ease.

Suddenly the old man slammed to a halt and shouted a warning. He spun, cloak whirling around him. His arm slammed into Eric's chest and knocked him flat on his back. Air exploded from his mouth at the impact. Eric fought for air, unable to draw breath. But his keen eyes did not miss the black shaft that flashed through the space he had just occupied. A sharp crack followed as the bolt smashed into a nearby tree.

Now the forest filled with the shouts of men. Still gasping in pain, Eric watched from the ground as three armoured guards appeared between the trees. Twigs and stones littered the ground beneath him. They stabbed through his clothing and scratched at his skin. Two inches to his left lay a fallen branch. Wincing, he reached out and wrapped his fingers around it. The rough bark stung the cuts on his palm but its weight felt reassuring in his hands.

Alastair stepped across him. Reaching down he drew his sword. Its cold metal shone in the streaks of sun which speared through the canopy above. Silver streaks of hair hung across his face, masking his expression. Eric could sense his anger; he saw it in the hunch of the old man's shoulders as he marched towards the guards.

Pulling himself to his feet, Eric took stock of the men who faced them. The foremost was a small man, clean-shaven with short black hair. He was edging backwards with one eye on Alastair as he frantically wound his crossbow. The other two stepped past him, their eyes locked on Alastair. Both were larger than the first with bulging arms and necks as thick as tree trunks. One held a long sword in an easy grip. The other raised his own crossbow and took aim. Each wore the blackened burns of the storm.

The crossbow twanged. This time Alastair had no time to react. The metal bolt flashed through the space between them and buried itself in his left shoulder. Alastair stumbled back, face twisted with pain. Then with a roar he straightened, arm swinging out at his attacker.

Eric watched with shock as some invisible force caught the archer and flung him through the air. There came a sickening crunch as the man plunged headfirst into a tree. Alastair had not moved a step, had not come within ten feet of him.

Magic! The word spun through Eric's head.

The swordsman charged. He moved with shocking speed for such a giant, his footsteps making muffled thuds on the leaf litter. Before Alastair could raise his arm again the man had closed the distance between them. With a scream of defiance, he swung his sword at the old man's head.

The clash of steel on steel rang through the trees. Alastair pulled back his sword and stepped sideways as the man charged past. He spun to stab at his foe's exposed back but the soldier had already righted himself. Sparks flew as their swords clashed again.

An overhanded blow forced Alastair back a step. The

old man's face clenched with pain, his movements disjointed. Yet still he managed to fend off his foe's unrelenting attack. Eric clutched his club at his side, unable to see an opening in the deadly dance of steel.

Colour was slowly draining from Alastair's face, turning his skin a paled grey. The bolt remained imbedded in his shoulder. Blood stained his cloak.

The guard pressed his attack, eyes narrowed with determination. His strength seemed to grow with every swing of his sword. His blade struck like a snake, tip darting out, only to be narrowly blocked. Each attack drew closer to the killing blow.

Beyond them, Eric saw the first bowman raise his reloaded weapon and then lower it again. Alastair was at least succeeding at keeping the swordsman between them, denying the archer a clean shot.

The man's eyes slid to where Eric stood in indecision. He raised his crossbow again.

Eric threw himself to the side as a bolt flashed towards him. He felt the blood flee his face and his heart stop. Fists clenched, he silently swore to himself. *Too close!*

Shaking his head he scrambled to his feet. The bowman had vanished. He raised his club before him, eyes searching the trees for the dark-haired man. The clashing of swords seemed to die away against the harsh clanking of the rewinding crossbow. Eric felt a sliver of ice trickle down his neck.

Eric's back began to itch as he imagined the hidden archer taking aim. He spun left, then right, eyes searching for any flicker of movement. His gaze took in Alastair and the swordsman, lingering on the old man's limp left arm. With every blow the wrinkles on his face deepened. It seemed as though whatever trick or magic he had used earlier had run out.

The cranking click of the crossbow ceased. Then something sharp pressed into Eric's back. He froze.

"Drop the club," the archer growled into his ear.

Eric's legs began to shake. He tossed away his feeble weapon.

"On your knees, slowly now! Hands behind your head."

Eric obeyed, kneeling in the mud and placing his hands over his head. The crossbow point followed him down. He could almost feel the man's finger on the trigger and knew he might be only seconds from death.

"Stay where you are." The pressure on his back vanished as the man walked round in front of him. The crossbow point never wavered from Eric's chest.

A bead of sweat trickled down Eric's forehead. The huntsman's clothes were charred and streaked with mud, and the air around him reeked of soot and smoke. Raw hate twisted his face.

"Do you know how many died last night, *demon?*" his voice shook with emotion. "I should kill you now. But no, that would be too good for you. You deserve the same suffering my people have felt. Your death will be slow and painful."

Eric could feel his eyes begin to water, hopeless guilt welling up inside him. He deserved this, deserved this hate, and whatever terrible punishment they devised. Yet still he shook with terror.

"But your friend, he'll die quick, magic or no. Sammy's no amateur. The old man doesn't stand a chance."

****

Alastair's arm shook with the weight of his short sword.

His muscles screamed but he drove on through the pain. He struck out with a short stab, but too slow, his foe blocking with ease. Pain shot down his arm as their swords met, the power in the guard's swing almost knocking the weapon from his hand.

The man twisted his sword away and came again, forcing Alastair backwards. His blade slid beneath Alastair's guard, followed by the tearing of fabric as the tip sliced his cloak.

Alastair forced his weary body forwards, stabbing upwards as his foe closed. The guard blocked but Alastair was expecting it and lashed out with his foot. He struck the man a heavy blow to the chest.

His opponent stumbled back and if Alastair had possessed the strength, he might have finished the fight then and there. As it was he barely stayed on his feet. His muscles burned and his heart raced. Pain radiated from where the bolt was buried in his shoulder. He felt as though he had aged ten years in the last five minutes.

The man he faced recovered, sneering as he saw his opponent had not moved.

Alastair cursed his hesitation when the men had first appeared. He should have used his magic then but he had held back, knowing he faced only mortal men. How arrogant he had been.

"Stupid old man. You will regret helping the demon by the time I'm done with you. You may have destroyed our town, but I will not let your evil prevail."

Alastair sighed, summoning the last of his strength as the man made to renew his attack. They both knew the fight was drawing to an end. One way or another, one of them would soon be dead.

Alastair drew on the last of his energy, preparing himself for one final, underhand move. He watched his opponent closely, saw his boots shift slightly in the litter of the forest floor. It was all the warning he needed.

The man leapt towards him, sword raised high to deliver a mighty blow to Alastair's head. He surged across the six feet separating them, a battle cry on his lips.

Just as it seemed the blow would land, Alastair flicked the near limp fingers of his left hand. A surge of energy rushed through his mind and along his arm as he summoned the last dredges of his magic.

With a cry of shock the guard toppled forwards, his feet tripped by some unseen force. His arms windmilled as he tried to right himself.

But it was too late. Alastair stepped forward and drove his short sword through the guard's chest. An explosive gasp escaped the man as his weight drove the sword deep into his body. His eyes widened in shock and a gurgling noise began deep in his throat. Convulsing, he sank to his knees and toppled to the ground. The sword slid free with a horrifying sucking sound.

Alastair stared at the lifeless body. A hot tear ran down his cheek. He had not wanted this. What was Antonia playing at here? A good man lay at his feet, just one more to add to the ruin of Oaksville, to the curse of runaway magic.

****

There was silence as they stared at the dead man. Then a scream of rage pierced the air. Eric looked at the bowman in horror. The crossbow was no longer pointing at him.

The man's voice was shrill. *"Die, damn you!"*

Eric did not hesitate. He drove himself forwards, tackling the man from behind. The two of them went down in a heap, rolling across the muddy ground. The crossbow twanged as they hit. Eric prayed it had not still been pointed at Alastair.

The larger man quickly recovered from his attack and surged back against him. An elbow slammed into Eric's stomach, winding him for the second time in ten minutes. The villager regained his feet, a knife appearing in his hand.

"Move and you die," Alastair's voice was as cold as frost.

The old man walked into view, his sword never wavering from the man's throat. His face twitched with pain but his eyes were determined.

"Drop it," Alastair nodded at the knife.

The man threw his weapon into the bushes and raised his hands, mouth clamped shut. A bead of sweat trickled down his forehead.

"What is your name?" Alastair demanded.

"Tacus," the guard spat the word.

"Well, Tacus, you can return to Oaksville. The city needs every man it can get. The boy is in my custody now."

"And who are *you?*"

"Alastair," as he spoke the word he slammed the pommel of his sword into the man's head. The archer's eyes rolled up and he crumpled without a sound.

Shaking, Eric pulled himself to his feet. He brushed the mud and leaves from his face and clothes with trembling hands. He could not remember a worse day in his life. In the past twenty four hours he had almost died a dozen times. Closing his eyes he tried to dismiss the determination in the archer's eyes as he had raised the knife. Another few seconds and he would have driven it through Eric's heart. Slowly the image faded and the trembling slowed, until at last he opened his eyes.

Eric looked around for any new surprises. The silence of

the forest was profound. The local creatures had fled the sounds of the fight long ago. The only movement now was the waving of the leaves in the wind. They were alone in the forest.

Eric's gaze slid to the dead and unconscious men.

He tore his gaze away from their fallen foes, turning his concern to Alastair. "Are you okay?"

Alastair shook his head. "No, but there's no time to worry about that now. We have to move. There may be more yet. We don't have too much further to go though."

Alastair turned away before Eric could question his last statement, leaving him no choice but to follow. He did so without complaint. Now Alastair's pace was slower, his exhaustion obvious in the heavy tread of his feet and slump of his shoulders. He would not make it far without help.

A surge of despair threatened to overwhelm Eric. There was no one out here to help them, and without treatment Alastair would surely die of blood loss – or worse. Eric barely knew the man, but in the last few hours Alastair had risked his life, and more for him. It was a gesture unlike any Eric had experienced and one he doubted he would ever understand.

"Alastair, are you sure we shouldn't take a look at your shoulder? How much farther–"

Alastair raised a hand. "We're here," there was relief in his voice. He gave a short, sharp whistle.

Two horses appeared from the trees and walked over to join them. The first stood sixteen hands tall and wore a glistening black coat and a brown leather saddle. It watched them with intelligent hazel eyes. It was a horse fit for a king. It wandered across and nuzzled at Alastair's shoulder.

The second was a similar build to the other, although its chestnut coat did not glisten with the same magic. It stood slightly smaller at fifteen hands and stared at Eric with glistening blue eyes. Four saddlebags and a water skin hung from its saddle.

Alastair tightened the straps of each saddle and turned to Eric. "The black is Elcano; he has been my horse for a long time. You can ride Briar. He's a packhorse, but a good gelding. I hope you've ridden before."

Eric hesitated, his tongue tied in embarrassment. He had not been near a horse since his banishment, and even then his family had never been rich enough to own one. He had certainly never *ridden* a horse. He gave a short shake of his head.

A slight smile added colour to Alastair's face. "Very well then, a quick lesson will have to do for now. There's no time for more than that. Come here."

Eric moved cautiously to where Alastair stood with the horses.

"Quickly now, stand on Briar's left side."

Eric hurried to comply, though the horse seemed to tower over him. Shivering, he placed a hand on Briar's silky coat. He felt the warmth of the horse beneath the thick hair and drew some comfort from it. The cold of the forest had long since seeped into his bones. He breathed in the scent of mud and straw and horse, the rustic smells bringing memories of his former life. Pain rose in his chest and he quenched the thoughts from his mind.

Looking up at Alastair, he caught the old man's emerald gaze. Alastair nodded and began to instruct him. "Place the toes of your left boot into the stirrup and grab the saddle horn."

Eric complied, listening as Alastair continued to speak. "Now push off with your right leg. As you push, straighten your left leg and swing your right over the saddle and into the other stirrup."

In one smooth movement Alastair demonstrated with

Elcano.

Eric tried to copy the movement. He made it halfway before he lost his grip and fell to the ground. He rose with a groan, mentally adding another strike to his tally of bruises. But he refused to quit. Stabbing his foot into the stirrup he half climbed, half scrambled onto the horse's back; inhaling a mouthful of horsehair in the process.

For a few seconds he sat doubled over in the saddle, his body racked by a coughing fit. When he finally recovered, he looked up to see an amused grin on Alastair's face.

The old man gave a weak chuckle. "There's no time to adjust the stirrups properly, they'll have to do for now."

Eric nodded, feeling awkward in the saddle.

"Now, horses are generally trained to obey a few simple commands. To make him move forward, give a small kick with your heels. If you want to stop, pull back on the reins. Gently mind, you don't want to hurt his mouth. To change directions, give a small tug in the direction you want him to turn. Got all that?"

Eric nodded silently. The instructions sounded simple enough but he had doubts as to whether that would transfer into reality.

"All right, let's get out of here then," as Alastair spoke Elcano spun beneath him and started into the forest.

Eric gave Briar a short kick. The horse bent its head back to look at him, snorted, and followed the black stallion. The heavy footsteps of the animal beneath him immediately sent jolts up his spine. He grimaced and tried his best to ignore the fresh waves of pain. Gritting his teeth, he focused on keeping himself in the saddle.

After a few minutes he found himself growing used to the heavy trot of Briar's hooves. His body slowly settled into the rhythm of the ride and the pain in his spine began to fade. A wave of weariness swept over him, his body finally giving way to exhaustion. His eyelids felt unbearably heavy.

Eric closed his eyes and breathed in the sweet smell of horse and forest. He listened to the snort of the horse's breath and the thump of Briar's footsteps. Within minutes he found himself slipping into a deep sleep.

****

Eric snapped awake, suddenly aware that something had changed. He no longer felt the constant thud of Briar's footsteps beneath him. They had stopped. Sitting up in the saddle, he looked around in astonishment.

They had left the tiny animal track in the depths of the forest. Instead, they now found themselves on a wide road cutting a straight path through the thick forest either side of them. The hard packed earth beneath them was free of roots and potholes. There was no mistaking it; the horses had found the Gods Road.

"What are we doing here? They'll be patrolling the road for sure!"

There was no reply from Alastair. Eric glanced across and saw the old man slumped on Elcano's back. He nudged Briar towards the other horse and was pleased to feel the horse respond immediately.

Eric gulped as he came alongside Elcano. Alastair was unconscious, his breathing weak and rasping. His face was grey and paled, and seemed to have added a hundred extra wrinkles in the last hour. He reached out to shake Alastair – and froze.

From the distance came the thunder of galloping hooves.

SIX

It had not taken long to sift through the shattered remains of his family home. There was little left worth keeping – an old cloak and dagger of his father's, his fiancé's silver necklace, a few gold coins that were his family's life savings. And in the ruins of the forge, a short sword an old soldier had once given his father in payment for repairing his wagon wheel.

Gabriel smiled as he lifted the sword from the rubble, its weight satisfying in his hand. He gave a few practice swings, the blade hissing as it cut the air. He had never used a sword before but hoped his strength would suffice.

Pleased with the small collection, Gabriel clipped the sword sheath to his belt and left the house. He had studiously avoided the room in which his family lay. No force on earth could compel him to face what waited there.

He made his way out into the broken streets of Oaksville, glancing around at the other homeless souls wandering in the darkness. It was time someone gave them purpose. Gabriel had found his in the grim determination to bring justice to his family's killer. He knew there would be others who felt the same.

His first recruit was a large man who wore the tattered

cloak and chainmail of the city guard. From the slump of his shoulders and blank expression there looked to be little fight left in him. He did not look up as Gabriel walked over, did not even register his presence until Gabriel reached out and grabbed his arm.

"What's the matter with you man?" he asked.

The guard blinked as though waking from a deep sleep. Finally he looked down at Gabriel. "What's the matter with me? They're all dead. Everyone I ever knew – gone!"

"Ay, they are," Gabriel held his gaze. "What are you going to do about it?"

"Do about it? This was the work of a demon, haven't you heard? There's nothing us mortal men can do to fight the likes of that. No one but the Goddess could stand against such darkness. And she isn't exactly easy to reach these days."

Gabriel shook his head. "The Goddess be damned, if she cared she would have stopped this. No, it's up to us *mortal men*," he stared hard at the guard. "We may not have magic, but I have a sword and last I heard a demon still dies when you stab it."

The guard looked down at Gabriel, a strange look on his face. "You're just one man."

"Join me and there will be two."

The silence stretched out but Gabriel held the man's gaze.

With a grim smile, the guard nodded. "You're a tough little bugger. Ay, but you're right, someone's got to stand against this evil," he held out his hand. "The name's Tom."

After that, two quickly turned to twenty, and then fifty, then a hundred. All across Oaksville the word went out of the young man gathering fighters to hunt the demon. Many brought horses and weapons to spare. Gabriel soon found himself surrounded by a small army – an army of desperate men with nothing left to lose.

Word came at dawn the old man and boy had been spotted fleeing east through the forest. Several soldiers had followed but so far none had returned. That had been hours ago; there was no telling how far they could have travelled in that time. But sooner or later the forest to the east would run out and they would be forced to return to the Gods Road or risk crossing the Wasteland.

By sunrise Gabriel had sixty mounted men and almost two hundred footmen. He gathered his cavalry at the eastern gate, himself riding a horse one of the recruits had provided. He left orders for the rest to follow down the Gods Road while the cavalry rode ahead to cut off their quarry.

Gabriel waved to his foot soldiers at the eastern gate, then turned his horse and led the horsemen through the tunnel beneath the wall. His mind was already preoccupied with the chase, obsessed with bringing death to the two they hunted.

The clatter of hooves on the cobbles were deafening in the darkness of the tunnel. Ahead the bright light of the world outside Oaksville beckoned. Gabriel kicked his horse into a trot, eager to return to the light and begin the chase in earnest.

As they emerged he kicked his horse again, forcing the beast to a canter. The wind picked up around him and pulled at his clothes and hair. Within minutes they had reached the forest, and Oaksville had disappeared behind them. Trees towered either side of the road, their branches stretching overhead to blot out the sky. The rising sun flashed through gaps in the canopy as they raced onwards.

The iron-shod shoes of their horses tore the damp ground, the fury of their passage sending leaves whirling into the air behind them. Gone was the stench of the burning city. Gabriel found himself enveloped by the earthly scent of the forest. His horse snorted beneath him, not used to the hard pace he set.

Gabriel was not concerned about the health of their horses. There was only one thought on his mind now. To get ahead of the two they hunted. If they could do that, their quarry would be trapped between his cavalry and the men who followed. They would have them – and if it cost a few horses, so be it.

Gabriel smiled at the thought of victory. He could almost see the fear on the demon boy's face as he plunged his sword into that black heart, almost smell the blood, taste the thrill of revenge in his mouth.

Yet the memory of their previous encounter still gave him pause. Tom had been right about one thing; the two they faced were no mortal men. He had no doubt it would cost lives to bring an end to them. He prayed the sixty men at his back would be enough.

Ahead the bend in the road straightened. Gabriel felt his heart stop and then start to race. There, not thirty feet away, two horses stood in the middle of the road. Each bore a rider, one lying slumped over his saddle horn. On the second sat the boy – *the demon*. His face was stark with terror, his eyes widening in shock.

Gabriel licked his cracked lips, rethinking his comments to Tom about the Goddess. Antonia had sent them a blessing after all. *We have them!*

He kicked his horse into a gallop. Their prey sat frozen as they raced towards them.

****

Eric could only stare as the horses charged towards them. They had come so close, were almost in the clear, only to be undone by one stupid mistake. The crash of hooves had silenced the forest. He glanced at Alastair, amazed the old man was still unconscious despite the roar of the approaching men.

Eric found himself glued to his saddle, unable to summon the strength to flee. Surely this was his destiny, surely this meant his death was the will of the Gods. He could only watch now as fate raced towards him, chasing all hope from his mind.

A gust of wind rustled the branches above and a light rain began to fall. It was only the remnants of yesterday's storm. There was no welling of energy within him now. He would sooner die than allow his curse to run rampant again. He shivered as the water began to trickle down his back.

The horses slowed as they approached, the men realising their quarry had given up all thought of escape. Eric saw many had drawn their weapons and held a collection of swords, spears, and crossbows pointed in their direction. He saw the odd uniform of the city guard sprinkled through the crowd but most seemed to wear the plain clothing of the townsfolk.

The reek of smoke reached his nostrils. With it came images of the burning city he had left behind. He stared at the men who had come to avenge their city, whose lives he had forever changed. Each now carried a darkness in their heart, a sadness and hate that would never leave them.

Briar shifted beneath him, slowly turning to face the oncoming horses. His ears lay flat against his skull. He began to snort, tremors rippling through his muscles. Eric could feel the strength in the horse beneath him but they could not flee now. Not with the condition Alastair was in.

Now the hunters were close enough to make out men's

faces. A tingle of shock ran through Eric as he recognised their leader. It was the man from the alley, his face tight with hate, his eyes touched by insanity. Their eyes met and a slight smile appeared on the man's lips. He kicked at his foam-flecked horse, eager to close the distance.

Then they were there, weapons drawn, crossbows pointed, surrounding them in a circle of death. Their leader – Gabriel, he remembered – lay a short sword across his saddle horn and stared at him.

"I didn't think it would be so easy."

The rest of the men did not speak but Eric could feel their silent hate. The air was thick with unvoiced tension. Eric gripped Briar's mane, struggling to control his fear. A tremor ran through his body. He squashed it quickly, determined to stay strong.

The silence stretched out, punctuated only by the heavy puffing of the horses.

Gabriel spoke again, his voice rough but calm. "Don't you have anything to say, demon? Some last trick to play?" He gestured at the circle of men. A few held crossbows carefully trained on the two of them. "Go ahead, see which is faster. An arrow, or magic."

Eric swallowed, mouth dry. Magic? He had considered the idea before. Yet Magickers were discovered at a young age and born to the noble families. Magic for commoners was the cheap parlour tricks of the circus, never anything of note.

He shook his head. Either way it did not matter. He measured his life now in hours, if not minutes.

Gabriel's lips twisted into a cruel smile. Suddenly his fist lashed out across the space between them and slammed into Eric's ear. Eric rolled back in the saddle, teeth rattling, and only the saddle horn stopped him from tumbling to the ground. His ears rang and tears leapt to his eyes.

"There will be far more where that came from, *demon*," Gabriel spat. "You will be granted no mercy from *us!*"

Eric looked around the circle of men and knew Gabriel spoke the truth. It was pointless, but he spoke anyway. "I cannot bring back the ones you have lost. But I swear to you, I did not mean to bring this destruction down on you. And if I have the chance, I swear I will dedicate the rest my life making up for this terrible –"

Eric broke off as Gabriel's fist smashed into his face again. He made no effort to deflect the blow – he knew any sudden movement would leave him dotted with arrows.

"Do not speak any more lies, demon. You would have us believe that *that*," he gestured in the direction of the unseen town, "was an accident? No, you must be some servant of Archon himself to wield such horror."

Eric trembled at the mention of the evil name. Archon was the ancient foe of the Gods, who had brought war and darkness to the Three Nations over a century before. A spell had banished him before his conquest was complete, though the legends still debated over whom had cast it.

Eric's anger ate away his fear. "How dare you –?"

A horse's scream tore the air. Gabriel's mount reared up, a black shafted arrow materialising in its chest. With a dying cry it tumbled backwards, throwing Gabriel into the midst of his men. Then the air filled with arrows. The shrieks of dying men and horses rang out and madness descended on the hunters.

Eric could only stare in shock.

War cries came from behind him. He turned and saw armed men rushing from the treeline. Most sported thick, matted beards and long, unkempt hair. All wore a terrifying scowl on their faces and the black leather armour of roving bandits.

The host emerging from the trees seemed beyond count.

A black tide of death engulfed Gabriel's men. They caved before its onslaught.

A horse crashed into Briar and drove him from the centre of the road. Eric pulled on the reins, struggling to control the horse's sudden movements. With his free hand he reached for his dagger and swung to face the horseman.

"Come on!" Alastair's gruff voice shouted over the clashing swords.

The old man now sat straight in the saddle. Colour had returned to his face, although his left arm still hung limp at his side. He nodded his head towards the forest on the side of the road opposite from which the bandits had appeared. Eric nodded back. He kicked his heels and felt Briar leap beneath him. The horse was just as desperate to escape the scene of battle.

Briar charged through the scattered men and horses, Elcano racing beside him. Bodies bounced off his shoulders but he did not slow. A wall of greenery loomed ahead. Eric ducked his head against Briar's broad neck, terrified a stray branch would knock him from the saddle. He caught a glimpse of Alastair's face and swallowed hard – his eyes had lost focus and his skin shone with sweat. He looked ready to pass out again.

Then they were charging through the trees, unwilling to slow down yet coming horrifyingly close to the tree trunks. Branches struck at Eric's face and arms, tore at him, threatening to throw him from the saddle. His ears throbbed with the erratic beat of his heart. Nothing mattered now but keeping low in his saddle.

The forest briefly opened out and Eric risked a glance back. He glimpsed a single pursuer through the tree trunks. He thought it looked like one of the townsmen. The man rode like a maniac, his eyes locked on their fleeing horses. He raised a crossbow, somehow managing to hold it steady as his horse crashed through the forest. Eric barely caught the telltale twang as it fired. The bolt whistled as it flew, but the shot went wide and struck a tree off to their left. The man tossed the crossbow aside and bent low over his saddle. He spurred his beast faster, eating up the short distance between them.

Grimacing Eric did the same and urged Briar to draw alongside Alastair. He wobbled in the saddle as they drew opposite, then recovered and looked over at the old man.

Alastair had his good arm raised above his head, his fist clenched hard. The veins on his forehead seemed to leap from his skin as he strained to attempt some fresh feat of magic. A brilliant flash of light burst from his fist, forcing Eric to look away.

A cry came from behind them and Eric looked back in time to see their pursuer knocked from his saddle. Timber crunched as the man dropped into the dense undergrowth while his horse galloped on without him. then Briar carried him out of sight.

A few minutes later Eric drew in a breath of relief and pulled back on the reins. Alastair did the same and they drew to a stop. Still gasping for air, Eric slid from the saddle. His feet crumpled when they touched the soft earth. A swarm of insects rose up to meet him. He ignored them, his mind still reeling with the shock of the attack, of their escape.

The damp ground felt reassuring beneath his hands, an anchor to reality.

Finally, he looked up at Alastair. "Who were those people?"

There was a sick feeling in the pit of his stomach. He already knew the answer but could not bring himself to believe it.

"A raiding party – Baronian bandits I'd guess from the

black leather. A lot of them too. Gabriel and those men didn't stand a chance, not after being taken by surprise."

"And Oaksville?" Eric croaked.

Alastair shook his head. "That's no doubt what drew them here – the smoke from the town. I don't know. The town's walls are high, but if the gates are open…"

A shiver went through Eric. For a pack of bandits to descend on Oaksville after the disaster last night – the chances were small the town would survive. Baronians were not known for their mercy. They were more than just outlaws; they were a godless, landless people. Some groups were peaceful, but most were ruthless killers who made their living from the misfortune of others. Patrols kept them from the main roads and cities but lately they had grown bold. Still, it was unheard of for them to attack a town the size of Oaksville.

"Is there anything we can do to help them?"

Alastair grabbed the bolt in his shoulder, grimaced, and tore it out. He groaned, wavering on his feet, then opened his eyes and stared at the bloody thing. The puckered skin of his shoulder was bruised and swollen, stained by the blood that had scabbed around the wound. Fresh blood began to flow from the tear the bolt had left. Alastair grunted and threw the piece of metal away.

His gaze returned to Eric. "No. I'm sorry, Eric, but their fate lies in their own hands now. There is nothing either of us in this state can do."

Eric stared up from the ground, eyes locked on the blood oozing from Alastair's shoulder.

"You should do something about that," he snapped.

Alastair glared back. Eric let the silence stretch out, unable to put words to the pain and horror he felt at this final blow to Oaksville.

Muffled by the forest around them, the dying sounds of

the battle being fought on the road was an all too vivid reminder of Oaksville's fate.

****

The air exploded from Gabriel's lungs as he struck the ground. Pain shot through his chest and he struggled to draw breath. Beside him his horse kicked and screamed in agony, the black shafted arrow still sticking from its chest. His men stampeded around him, their formation turned to chaos. Leaderless and taken by surprise they were unable to fight back against whoever, or whatever, had attacked.

Gabriel scrambled in the mud for his sword. The press of horses threatened to crush him but he finally managed to scramble to his feet. Body aching, heart racing with fear, he looked around at the cacophony of men and horses. The rain of arrows had ceased but now men streamed from the trees, launching themselves at the panicked townsfolk. Each wore the black leather armour of the Baronians.

A shiver ran down Gabriel's spine. There were too many. Already half his horsemen had fallen to arrows and the rest were quickly being dispatched.

Gabriel swore. *How could this be happening?* They had been so close, had the boy within their grasp. Now their quarry had disappeared in the chaos and his followers were dead, dying, or fleeing for their lives. At least the footmen they had left behind would be warned of the coming raid. They could retreat back to the town and close the gates. Oaksville may still survive – if there were enough men left to man the walls.

The scream of a dying horse interrupted Gabriel's thoughts. He turned in time to dive from the path of a battle-axe. He slammed into the ground and rolled, springing back to his feet with his sword at the ready.

The axeman grinned, his face black with soot to match his armour. He raised his axe and with a scream of rage, charged. Gabriel leapt backwards as the axe carved an arc through the space where he had stood. There would be no blocking such a blow with his short-sword.

As the axe swept past, Gabriel rushed forward, sword stabbing out to disembowel his opponent. The axeman met him with a fist to the face that knocked Gabriel flat on his back. His vision swam. Instinctively he rolled and heard the thunk of the axe blade as it embedded itself in the soft ground. He kicked out at his foe's legs and heard a satisfying grunt as the man fell.

Ignoring the pain throbbing from his nose, Gabriel threw himself atop his attacker. His sword had been lost when he fell so he smashed his fist into the axeman's face. The man surged against him, but he was no match for the strength Gabriel had built as a blacksmith.

Grimacing, Gabriel gripped his black-garbed foe by the throat and began to squeeze. He saw panic flash across the man's coal speckled eyes. Arms flailed at him, struggling to break his iron grip. Veins bulged on the man's forehead and his eyes began to turn red.

Gabriel clung on, determined to destroy this man who had thwarted his revenge. His vision swept with red and his ears filled with a wild cackling. A madness swept over Gabriel, and he was suddenly sure it was the laughter of the demon boy, taunting him with his freedom.

When the laughter finally died away, Gabriel found himself strangling a dead man. Tears streamed down his face. He swallowed hard and stood, running his hands through his thick hair. *What is happening to me?*

He looked up at the crunch of nearby footsteps.

Another axeman approached, a grim look on his face. Rust speckled the blade but it looked as sharp as any he had seen.

Gabriel swept up his sword and regained his feet. He sidestepped the man's first blow but this time was more cautious with the counter attack. Their weapons clashed, sparks leaping between them. The sounds of the battle faded away until there was only the ring of their weapons, the crunch of their boots, and his opponent's laboured breath.

The axeman raised his weapon again and Gabriel caught the flash of blue eyes staring out from beneath bushy eyebrows. He ducked forwards without thought and the decapitating swing passed over him. His shoulder struck the ground but he rolled forward and regained his feet.

His opponent's eyes widened in surprise. He struggled to bring his weapon about to defend himself, but Gabriel's blade was already in motion. It plunged through the man's leather armour and deep into his chest. A rattling sound grew in the man's throat. The axe slipped from his fingers as he fumbled at the blade impaling him. His legs gave way beneath him and he slumped to the ground.

Grabbing the hilt of his sword with both hands, Gabriel tore the blade free. He stumbled as his vision swam again. Now, the dark ghost of a man seemed to hover over him, hands reaching out for him. The spectral mouth opened and the soft whisper of words touched the air. The language was strange and foreign to him. The figure leaned closer, and then vanished.

Gabriel shook his head, trying to shake the apparition. The battle had moved on without him. The Baronians had forced his remaining men farther down the road towards town. There were only a dozen or so left standing. They fought hard but they were on foot now, their horses long dead. It would not be long before the Baronians trampled the last of them into the ground. As he watched, another villager died, a sword spearing through his chest.

The dead and dying covered the road, most his own men. Far too few of their black cloaked enemy lay amid the fallen. Riderless horses wandered aimlessly amid the corpses. There was no trace of the boy or old man. They had vanished and so must he if he wanted to live. if he wanted to catch them.

Gabriel slipped away into the forest, casting one last glance behind him. Through the press of bodies, the raised blades and falling leaves, he saw his last man fighting against the tide. Across the distance their gazes caught.

Gabriel choked and looked away. He had not missed the accusation, the question. *Why are you alive, while we are dead?*

When he looked again there was only the black and bloodied Baronians. Other than the few who had fled, his men were all slain.

He moved further into the forest. For now he would hide. Later he would return to the road. There was only one direction his quarry could run now. And he would be waiting there for them.

****

Gabriel sat on a cool stone pedestal amongst the trees, the rain falling around him. It had long since soaked through his coat and filled his boots. Yet still he sat here. The strength and determination that had driven him this far had fled, leaving a dull emptiness within him.

The patter of rain on leaves grew stronger. Water had begun to gather in the small dips of the pedestal on which he sat. With each drip ripples raced across the puddle, reflecting and multiplying in on each other.

Gabriel watched the ripples with detached curiosity. His hands were pale with cold and every few seconds an involuntary shiver would shake his body. His sword stuck from the ground a foot away, in reach if the need arose.

Gabriel shivered again, but not from the cold. There was a voice in his mind. *Beautiful, aren't they? So complex, yet so predictable. Each path can be tracked, followed, foreseen.*

Gabriel groaned. He shut his eyes and put his head between his hands. The voice hissed through his mind, slivered into his every thought. It had started as a whisper as he fled from the road – now it filled every recess of his conscious.

His head ached, throbbing with each new word. *What would make it stop? What did it want?*

"To help you."

His eyes shot open. This time the voice had not come from within. *It was real!*

Gabriel reeled back as he took in the shadowy figure towering above him, tumbling from the pedestal in his panic. He opened his mouth to cry out but no sound escaped. Shaking with fear, he looked up, praying he had imagined the apparition.

The thing loomed – not just over him but the whole clearing. The great trees of the forest shrank before it, the dark presence withering their ancient strength. The rustling of leaves, the shrieking wind, the sound of the rain – all seemed to flee before this being's presence. Dark silhouettes raced about the spectre's body, clothing it in a cloak of living death.

It's not there, he insisted to himself.

"You are correct, but that does not mean I am not real," its voice was a roar now, deafening.

Gabriel's mouth opened and closed. Finally he found his voice. "What do you want with me then, evil one? Out with it!"

A shrieking laugh filled the clearing. "Evil? Who are you to judge me of that? You know not who or what I am."

Gabriel swallowed hard but did not reply. He knew what he felt, *what he saw.*

"*What do you want?*" he demanded once more.

"To help you on your quest."

"Why? Why would you want death for your fellow demons?"

"My reasons matter not. Why do you care? Is not the death of these demons all that matters to you now? I ask nothing in return, nor will I take anything from you."

"And why would I need your help?" Gabriel found courage in his anger.

It laughed again, now a soft, crackling sound that reached through the air and clawed at his sanity. There was a creeping corruption in the laugh that sent tendrils through his very soul. It called to him, begged him to join the rancid laughter. He had never been so glad as when it stopped.

"Look around you. Your men are dead. Your town a ruin. And here you sit, freezing in the rain while your quarry draws ever farther away."

Gabriel shook his head. How could this creature help him? And even if it could, he was not so naïve as to believe there would be no cost.

"What help could you possibly offer me?"

"Immunity from their magic, and the means to track them down."

Uncertainty gripped him then, for what it offered would guarantee his success. Without their magic they were only mortal men, and he had already proven he could handle them. They would not escape justice this time.

He looked again at the source of this gift, at the demon towering amidst the clearing. What would it gain from their deaths?

Their deaths! The words rung in his head. Suddenly his choices were clear; if he accepted this offer he would at least be able to rid the world of one evil. If he declined, both evils would continue unchecked.

It was a simple decision.

"I accept your gift," he whispered.

Darkness descended around him.

SEVEN

Eric stared across the empty fire pit. A cool autumn breeze had picked up as the sun began to set, encouraging him to prepare a fire before realising it would be a beacon to their hunters. Now he sat shivering in the lengthening shadows with nothing but Alastair's snoring for company. When they had finally stopped Alastair had dismounted, propped himself up against a tree, and promptly went to sleep.

Wincing, Eric shifted into a more comfortable position on his log. The day's ride had left his body hurting in places he had never dreamed. Even his knees hurt – Gods only knew how that had happened.

To his left Alastair slept on. He half wondered if the old man would succumb to his injuries and never wake again. Yet after what he had witnessed in the last twenty-four hours, it would not have surprised him if Alastair were to wake fully recovered.

The birds had fallen silent and twilight had now settled over the forest. The last glow of the setting sun lit the sky red, reminding him of the savage flames from the night before. Only now the world seemed at peace.

They were not far from the God's Road now. Alastair

wanted to be away before the sun rose, which would be almost impossible without the road to follow. He reasoned the Baronian threat meant there was little chance the hunters could continue the pursuit. The silence from the road seemed to confirm the old man's suspicions.

Eric's mind was alight with an endless loop of questions. Alastair had promised answers when he woke. Until then Eric was left to stew in his thoughts.

A chill gust of wind swept through the tiny clearing. Eric shivered, looking up in time to see a last flash of sunlight through the branches above. His breath steamed in front of his face. It looked like a cold autumn was on its way.

"Good evening, Eric."

Eric jumped, almost tumbling from the log. He looked across to see Alastair awake and raising an eyebrow in his direction. The spark of life had returned to his eyes.

"Anything happen on the road while I slept?"

Eric shook his head, watching as Alastair stood and stretched his arms. His bones creaked with the movement and Eric again found himself wondering how old the man truly was.

Alastair took a moment to inspect the wound in his shoulder. The bleeding had stopped beneath the makeshift bandage he had applied.

"How is it?"

"Better. There shouldn't be any infection. It'll heal, eventually."

Standing himself, Eric walked across to where they had tied the horses. "Hope you don't mind, but I explored Briar's saddle bags. I got hungry."

Reaching into the bag strapped to Briar's side, he retrieved a strip of beef jerky. He tossed the lump of dried meat across to Alastair and fished out another for himself.

"There wasn't much in there but beef jerky and dried

fruits."

Alastair smiled. "I was planning on buying supplies in Oaksville. Although I don't generally carry much anyway."

Eric hesitated. "Is that why you were in Oaksville, for supplies?"

The old man looked up at him. "Starting with the questions already? Can't you let an injured old man finish his meal?"

Eric scowled. "Not after listening to him snore all afternoon."

Alastair laughed. "I was in Oaksville for you, Eric. And before you bother asking, no, I cannot tell you how I knew you were there."

Eric stared at the other man, slowly chewing the salty strip of meat. Eric had guessed some things had been left unsaid in Oaksville. Someone, or something, had sent Alastair to find him. The question of who was burning on his tongue, but Alastair's expression made it clear there would be no headway there.

He asked the other question consuming him. "*Why?*" he tried to keep his tone neutral, but his desperation still seeped into the question.

"Because you have magic."

Eric heard the words Alastair spoke but his mind refused to process them. Suddenly he was struggling for breath. His head throbbed. He felt a sharp pain in his palms and realised he was clenching his fists so hard his nails had punctured the skin.

Finally, he shook his head. "That's impossible. Only nobles have magic…"

"No. While it's true most of those with magic are powerful people, the gift is not limited to royal families or the rich. It is passed down bloodlines from generation to generation."

"But neither of my… parents… had magic."

"Magic can lie dormant for generations, until it is all but forgotten, before reasserting itself," Alastair paused for a long moment. "Such situations often have horrifying results."

Eric closed his eyes, unable to face the truth. *No, it's not possible!* A trembling began in his arms and slowly spread until his whole body shook.

"I… I thought it was a curse," a curse was beyond his control, but magic? People could control magic.

"I'm sorry, no. The power you possess is far too great for a curse. No one has such power they could waste so much on a curse."

Eric sank to his knees and felt the mud begin to seep through his trousers. A gurgling, growling sob rumbled up from his chest. His fingers dug into the soft earth, grasping for something solid to cling too. His eyes never left Alastair's.

"Could I have stopped it? Could I have saved those people?"

He regretted the question as soon as the words left his mouth. He was not strong enough to face the answer.

It's all your fault, a voice whispered in his mind.

Strong hands clasped his shoulders and shook him. "Look at me, Eric!"

Eric stared at the old man. "Tell me, Alastair."

"You could not have saved them, Eric. You could not have stopped the magic. Without training, magic responds to emotions like an extension of yourself, but once released there was no way to stop it. Only proper training would have allowed you to do so."

"It was still me though."

"It wasn't your fault, Eric. Magic is a wondrous thing, when properly controlled. Yet it also has a mind of its own.

It will do what it wants, when it can – especially to preserve itself. And a threat to you threatens it."

"It is a part of me though, and I could not control it," he paused. "I need to learn how."

Silently he prayed Alastair could teach him. He had pledged to make amends for the deaths in Oaksville. If he could control his magic, perhaps he could take his first step on that journey.

Alastair's eyes bored into his own. At last, he nodded. "Very well, I will teach you."

Eric felt a rush of elation. He sat back against his log, a smile tugging at his lips. For the first time in years he felt a touch of hope. "Do you think it's safe to light a fire, before we get started?" The night had closed in; he could barely make out Alastair's silhouette in the faint light. Somewhere in the darkness an owl began to hoot. Soon other creatures would begin to prowl the night.

"I think that's a good idea," he shrugged his wounded shoulder. "I'm still too weak for an encounter with some of the animals that stalk these woods and a fire will keep them at bay. I think both the Baronian's and villagers will be occupied with each other tonight," he moved over to the horses. "It's a good thing you collected the firewood before night fell."

A few minutes later they had a merry fire crackling. Eric stretched out his hands towards the blaze, feeling the chill flee before its heat. The fire cast the tiny clearing in a warm glow.

"How old are you, Eric?"

"Seventeen. A man for two years. Why?"

Alastair chuckled. "Just curious. So young, but yes, you are by rights a man."

They fell into silence. Eric stared into the fire, deep in thought. When he finally spoke his voice was soft. "What *is* magic? It's not the cheap potions and gimmicks of the street venders. So what is it?" he flicked another stick into the flames. Sparks rose up, drifting for a moment on a gentle breeze before fading.

"No, magic is not a human creation. It is a part of nature. It comes from the forces that move us, the energy that drives the weather, the light of the sun. It is the harnessing of the energy stored in everything on this planet. Only a lucky few have the power to tap into this energy, and even then, there are limitations. For starters a person can only be connected to one of the Elements."

"What do you mean by the Elements?"

Alastair frowned. "Sorry, I'm getting ahead of myself. The forces of magic are divided into three Elements – the Light, the Earth, and the Sky. Most people control just a small part of an Element. For instance, I am able to manipulate the forces of attraction between objects. That comes from the Light Element. But I cannot control fire, or light itself, which are other aspects of the Light."

"And mine?"

"Your magic is different. From what I have seen, it seems you may control all facets of the Sky. And while it is the weakest of the Elements, that is no laughing matter."

"It didn't seem weak when I created that storm," Eric replied bitterly.

"No. But you should also understand, our magic cannot create. Only the Gods can create something out of nothing."

Eric tilted his head. "What do you mean? That storm certainly seemed to come from nowhere!"

"Yes, but that is because it came from somewhere else! Your magic manipulates the weather, Eric, but it does not conjure it from nothing. The magic within you drew that storm to Oaksville and made it larger by pulling in other weather systems. But it was not *createa.*"

Eric ran his hands through his hair, trying to process the new information. The magic was a part of him, a part of everything, but only certain people could control it. Magic could manipulate the world but could not create new forces. His head still ached from the beating Gabriel had given him.

"…night," lost in thought, Eric only caught Alastair's last word.

"Sorry?"

"I think that it would be best if we stop for the night. A good night's rest will do you good. As I said, magic comes from within you – and when you use it, it draws on your life force. That can be exhausting, in fact I'm surprised you've lasted this long. I'll keep watch, since I slept all day. We'll leave before first light."

Eric nodded, struggling to contain a yawn. His questions had kept him alert through the day but now a wave of exhaustion swept over him. His eyes were drooping and his thoughts had grown fuzzy and confused. It would be useless to continue their discussion now.

He grabbed a blanket he had taken from Briar's saddlebags and curled up in front of the fire. Closing his eyes, he sought sleep. Thoughts drifted through his consciousness. Images appeared, some as clear as day, others just a blur, as if viewed through a cloud of smoke. Then as it so often did, his mind turned to his parents and his fifteenth birthday.

The day was still clear in his memory. Clearer, in fact, than much of the two years that had followed since. The time he had spent on the road seemed a dream compared to the clarity of that fateful day – and the horror the night had brought.

It haunted him still.

"Eric, catch!" the nectarine tumbled towards him.

Eric reached up and plucked the fruit from the air. He wiped it clean on his shirt before sinking his teeth into the soft flesh. His friend sat in the branches of the tree above him, munching on a second nectarine. Juice ran down his young face. Behind him, an autumn sunset lit the sky blood red.

"So how does it feel to be old, Eric?" Mathew asked.

Eric shrugged. "No different really, only I think it could mean a lot more work from here on out. My father's already talking about getting me in the fields!"

Mathew laughed. "That's too bad. Maybe you should just forget about this birthday thing. Stay young forever."

Eric grinned back. "I don't think it works that way."

"Eric" a voice shouted from down the hill. "Come help set the tables. Just because you're a man now doesn't get you out of your chores!" he swore sometimes his mother's voice could carry across mountains.

"It begins," Mathew mocked in an ominous voice.

"At least I get presents," Eric retorted as he started down the hill.

Eric heard his mother's voice again and began to run. The ground was muddy from rain, but his sturdy boots carried him easily along the slippery trail.

Covered by uncut grass and scraggly trees, the hill led down to his parents' house on the edge of town. Half a dozen other houses also neighboured the hill but his family's was easily the smallest. Over its thatched roof and smoking chimney he could just make out the rest of the farming village. It spread across the rolling plains, around fifty houses in all. In the aistance green mountains towered over the valley, hedging them in to the west.

Puffing, he ran up to his back door and pulled it open. Leaning down, he was sure to scrape the mud from his shoes before entering. His mother's fury would be something to behold if he trekked mud into the house again.

"There's the birthday boy – or should I say man!" His father greeted him with his booming laugh and welcoming grin.

He moved across the room and scooped Eric up into a bear hug. His strong arms crushed the air from Eric's lungs before releasing him.

Eric looked up into his father's dark amber eyes. They were edged by wrinkles, with grey hairs streaked through his jet-black hair. They reminded Eric his father was no longer a young man.

His mother's voice echoed from the corridor. "Sounds like it's dinner time, we'd better not keep your mother waiting," his father said, still grinning.

"Better late than never I guess," his mother greeted them as they entered the dining room.

Her hazel eyes locked on Eric from across the room. Despite her grey hair, his mother had lost none of her strength or will. She wore a dark blue dress and a smile, despite her scolding tone.

Eric bowed his head. "Sorry mum, I came as soon as I heard you!"

His mother shook her head, laughing softly. "Oh don't worry you; it's your day after all. Come here!" She too drew him into a long hug.

They sat down at the small table then. The sweet aroma of roast lamb filled the room. Its source, a haunch of lamb, sat centrepiece on the table surrounded by potatoes, broccoli, and an assortment of other vegetables. It was a feast unlike any Eric had seen in his youth.

They spent the evening talking of his childhood and dreams for the future. The past and future intermingled freely, both bright and full of life. Finally his exhaustion overcame him. Yawning, he bid his parents good night and headed to his room.

There, the darkness entered his dreams. He watched as an army of demons marched across the valley of his hometown. The villagers fled before them but were overrun, dying by the hundreds. His village burned, but the destruction did not stop there.

The demons spread across the land, entire cities burning in the night. People ran screaming from their homes, clothes ablaze, human torches lighting up the darkness. Rivers turned red with blood and then overtopped their banks to drown the land. Through it all Eric could *hear the soft cackling of laughter.*

With a scream of terror Eric wrenched himself from the dream, awakening in his house, his bed. But the dream had followed him. His room was burning. Flames clung to the walls and lightning leapt across the ceiling above, leaving scorched timber in its wake.

Eric screamed again, throwing off his blankets and leaping from the bed. The lightning caught the covers and suddenly the wooden floor was alight as well. Eric fled the bedroom, heat swamping him. The house was already ablaze and smoke filled the corridor. He held his breath and sprinted for his parents' bedroom.

He yanked open the door and was met by a blast of heat that forced him back a step. His eyes burned but he pushed forward again until he could see what lay within. Through the heat and smoke he made out the burning bed and its occupants. Nothing living remained in that room.

Eric stumbled backwards, tears boiling from his face. Shrieking in horror he turned and ran from the nightmare. His heart hammered in his chest as he ran through the falling rubble, the house collapsing around him.

When he burst through the front door a crowd had already gathered outside. He staggered a few steps towards them, and then collapsed to his knees. His hands clawed at the ground, seeking something solid at which to cling. He swayed, felt the hot tears streaming down his face.

The crowd surrounded him, staring. No one spoke, no one approached to help him. Their eyes were wide; their mouths open in shock and fear. Some sported burns and ash covered faces, as if they had tried and failed to enter the house.

The whispers of the watchers began to race around their circle. Eric looked around at them, reaching out, unable to form words but silently begging for their help. The crowd drew back as one.

It was then he noticed the lightning. It crawled along his skin, jumping between the raised hairs on his arms. Sparks leapt from his arm as he moved. Yet he felt nothing.

Eric fell backwards, scrambling to brush the horrible stuff from him. Lightning burst from his arm and struck the ground. Thunder cracked and the crowd screamed. Eric looked up at them, terror in his eyes.

"Help me," somehow his burnt throat managed to croak the words. It felt as though he had inhaled the flames.

The crowd stared back at him. No one spoke a word.

Then he saw Mathew in the crowd and turned to him. "Help me, Mathew!"

Mathew stared at him. His face was a mask of terror but still he took a step forward. He had always been brave, always been the one to leap from high cliffs into the river where Eric had been too scared. As he walked towards Eric the crowd shifted. The inferno lit the expressions on their faces – anger, fear, agony, sorrow.

Eric reached out to his friend. "Help me, Matthew."

Mathew ignored his outstretched hand. Instead he drew his dagger. Eric had seen it many times. His own parents had given it to the boy last year, as a birthday gift. It was a good blade, although nothing expensive. Now it glowed red in the light of the flames.

"Leave now, Eric, or I swear by Antonia I will plunge this blade through your heart."

Beside the campfire, in the forests near Oaksville, Eric found himself once again crying at his friend's words, at the death of his parents. If only he had known.

Finally, he slept.

****

Gabriel sat up. His head burned and his muscles ached. Yet somehow he felt rejuvenated, filled with a strange energy that throbbed just beneath his skin. Already the pain was fading. Closing his eyes he searched his body, looking for a change.

Nothing, and yet *something* felt different.

He looked around for the demon but the clearing was empty now, the trees silent. Standing, he walked across and pulled his sword from the soft earth.

As he turned in the direction of the road, movement came from the bushes. He watched as a wolf walked from the forest. Eyes bright as a full moon locked on his. It bared its yellowed teeth, jet-black fur bristling. A growl rattled deep in its throat. It took a step towards him.

Gabriel stepped back as the huge beast approached. He held his sword out, ready to strike, silently cursing the demon for his useless gift.

Sudden laughter echoed in his mind and the wolf halted.

Relax, Gabriel. I am here to track the two you seek.

EIGHT

They were a long way from Oaksville by the time the first rays of sunlight announced the start of a new day. As the light grew, Eric turned in his saddle to check the road behind them, searching for the first signs of pursuit. The trail remained empty, but in the distance smoke from the hidden city still stained the horizon.

Alastair was confident the hunters would have returned to protect the city, leaving them in the clear. Eric was not so sure. Gabriel was obsessed with revenge and if he had survived the battle, nothing would stop him from following them. Alastair had proven in Oaksville that, alone, the man was little threat, but they still needed to be wary.

They rode hard down the well-kept road. Eric bounced along in the leather saddle for most of the morning, unable to find the rhythm of his horse's trot. By lunchtime, his backside felt as though it had been beaten black and blue.

Beneath the canopy of branches the air was still, but the wind whistled through the upper treetops. The higher branches swayed in the breeze and a rain of copper leaves drifted slowly in the air. The cool grip of autumn seemed to have arrived overnight.

The two had barely spoken since they had risen in

darkness. Eric's mind was racing; terrified Alastair might have reconsidered his teaching. At last, he summoned his courage and turned to the old man. "Do you still want to teach me?"

"Of course, why should I not?"

"The reason of daylight?"

Alastair laughed. "No, daylight will not change my mind. A cowardly man might leave you, but I have never been a coward. Besides, without training, you would remain a danger to all you encounter."

Eric smiled. "Then tell me about the Elements. I thought they sounded familiar, and this morning I realised where I had heard of them before. They are the same powers the Gods possess, right?

"Exactly. Each of the three Gods is a master of one of the Elements. In fact, they are the embodiment of those forces. That is why, unlike us mortals, they have the power to create. It is also why, together, there is no force on earth capable of defeating them."

Noticing Briar beginning to pull ahead, Eric gave a short tug on his reins. The horse snorted before slowing. "And what exactly does each Element control?"

"A good question," Alastair scratched his chin. "Well, let me think. The Light is the simplest to explain, although it is the most powerful. The Light allows wielders to control raw energy, although usually only one particular type. For instance, a Magicker might be able to control fire, or light, or even another person's magic. As I said last night, it gives me the ability to manipulate the forces of attraction between objects."

"Then there is the Earth, which controls nature – animals, plants, even the earth itself. Humans too, in rare cases. Healers also fall under the Earth Element."

"Finally, there is your Element. The Sky is a wild and

unwieldy force, Eric. It is the most uncanny and tricky of the three Elements."

"I see," Eric paused a moment to digest the new information. "Where does that leave dark magic?"

"Dark magic is the opposite of all that magic comes from. As I said last night, magic is a part of the natural world. Dark magic is wholly unnatural. To wield it, one must ignore the Elements and give themselves to their magic. It takes someone whose thirst for power defies all reason to walk that path, for it will change you in ways you cannot imagine. Magic is a perilous force, and when given free will, it incites only ruin. Allow it free rein and you may become a puppet to the very force you would control."

Eric shivered in horror. The more he heard the more perilous magic seemed to become. Before, he had feared the unknown. Now that he knew its name, his terror was only growing.

As morning progressed to afternoon the trees around them began to thin. Light streamed through the canopy above, the tree trunks on either side of the path shrinking to pale mimics of those near Oaksville. Dust rose from the road with each thump of their horses' hooves and hung in a cloud behind them. A dry, stifling heat set in with the afternoon sun.

"We are close to the edge of the Wasteland now. It rarely rains here. The trees that survive have deep roots to tap the groundwater deep below the surface," Alastair explained.

They pressed on. Eric wiped sweat from his brow, sweltering in the beating sun. The forest dwindled, turning to scraggly bushes and outcrops of rock. sweat left his clothes sticking to his skin. The carcasses of ancient trees littered the forest around them.

Eric could hardly believe the change he was witnessing.

He had heard of the Wasteland during his two years on the road, but he had steered well clear of it.

"Why are we heading towards the Wasteland?"

"The hunters did not give us much choice of direction, but fortunately I had already planned to head for Chole."

"The Dying City? Why?"

"There is someone there I must meet."

"Who?"

"I cannot say, but there is little time to waste. We'll have to travel through the Wasteland itself."

Eric's chest constricted in fear. "I thought the road went around the outskirts of the desert."

"It does. But there is an old road that crosses the desert, it leads straight to Chole."

"That's insane. If even half the tales I've heard are true…"

"Relax," Alastair shrugged his injured shoulder again. "Most of the tales *are* exaggerated. Plus, I heal quickly; my shoulder will be greatly improved by tomorrow. And of course, you are forgetting you now travel with a Magicker. I have crossed the Wasteland many times without incident."

Eric fell silent, only partly reassured. He realised something else was still weighing on his mind. "What about the city? What if I lose control of my magic again?"

"We will work on that. I cannot make you a master overnight, but I can help you to at least gain some control over it by the time we arrive."

Eric fell silent. Alastair had not allayed his fears. So far he had learned nothing to help him control the horrific force inside of him. To enter another city seemed like madness, especially so soon after Oaksville.

They reached the end of the treeline as the sun dipped towards the horizon, lighting the sky on fire. The trees either side of them gave way to cracked brown earth, as if sliced away by the axes of men. The Wasteland stretched into the distance, where three volcanic peaks rose from the skyline. The plain was devoid of life; only the petrified corpses of the old forest remained. Dust coated their lifeless trunks. The air smelt of baked earth and old rock, and the only sounds were the whistling of the wind and the snort of their horses.

The road veered away to their left, but a thin gravel path continued into the arid land.

Alastair spurred his horse onto the path. He turned back as Eric directed Briar to follow. "Keep your eyes open. We're in a different world now; these are not safe lands. Tell me if you see anything. Dark things hide within these crevasses."

Eric nodded, an involuntary shiver running down his spine. It did not take much imagination to fear a place like this. Suddenly the hunters from Oaksville almost seemed preferable to whatever nightmares stalked here. He prayed Alastair knew what he was doing.

He stared at the three volcanoes stabbing up into the red sky. The middle one, he knew, was Mount Chole; the others remained nameless. They had erupted from the earth a hundred years ago, at the apex of the war with Archon. The great Magickers of the time saved the city from the lava flows, but the mountains still stood not a mile from the city, and the magic had not stopped the shadow the three peaks cast across the land. The drought that followed had all but destroyed the once great city of Chole.

Eric hoped his magic would not be the final nail in the city's coffin.

****

Flames crackled in the darkness. Eric and Alastair sat huddled close to the fire, its warmth warding off the chill that had fallen over them with nightfall. Above, a tapestry of stars crowded the sky.

Eric shifted uncomfortably on his log, body aching from the long day's ride. They were a long way from Oaksville now. He felt almost relaxed. Almost. His neck tingled. He could feel the unseen eyes of unknown creatures peering at him from the darkness.

Alastair was not doing much to allay his fears. He sat staring into the night, as if his eyes could pierce the veil of darkness surrounding them. The silence ate at Eric. In his head, thoughts and worries vied for attention until he found himself jumping at every pop of the fire.

"Do you think Gabriel could still be out there?" he asked, remembering the insanity in the man's eyes. It was not something he wished to face again.

"I do not know. It seems unlikely he could have survived the attack on the highway, but the man was driven. He has been pushed past the brink; there is not much that could bring him back now."

"I think he is still alive. I think it would take more than a few bandits to stop him. He terrifies me."

Alastair nodded. "With good reason. There is much to fear from someone with nothing to lose. But there is more to it than that, isn't there?"

Eric stared into the fire. "I can't defend myself against him. Whatever he has become, my actions created him. To hurt him would be the greatest hypocrisy."

He fell silent, waiting for the old man's reply. It was a long time coming. "There is nothing you can do to change the past. All you *can* do is your best to make a difference now, to balance the scale against what happened in that city."

Eric opened his mouth to reply, but suddenly Alastair was leaping to his feet. "Get up – *now!*"

"What?"

"Up, quickly, get your back to the fire. *Now!*" Alastair hissed.

Eric rose, spinning to face the surrounding darkness. He clenched his fist around the knife in his belt. The flames had robbed him of his night vision, but his eyes were quickly adjusting. His ears seemed to be playing tricks on him. Stones scattered away to their left. Then crunching footsteps from the right, or was that his imagination? His eyes flicked back and forth, but there was nothing to see. The only living things in sight were the horses, tied to a dead tree a few feet from the fire.

A roar erupted from the darkness, shattering the silence. Eric's body shook with fear; he had not imagined *that.* His nose caught the scent of rotting meat. He gagged and held a hand over his nose.

Alastair drew his sword and dropped into a crouch. Despite his wound, he looked strong and steady. The firelight flickered on his coat, catching the silver lines that threaded the fabric.

Elcano and Briar began to shriek and tug at their tethering. Their feet shifted on the hardened earth, ears flicking back against their skulls. Ripples ran through their muscles as they shivered, bodies taught and ready to flee. Eric wondered if they should be doing the same.

Eric stood with his back to the fire. The roar came again. Fingers trembling, he bent and picked up a burning branch with his spare hand. He shuddered, fear chewing at his mind. Whatever was out there sounded big – and fast. He did not know if Alastair could face it alone, especially with his wounded shoulder.

A chill wind swept through the camp. Eric felt it and fought to calm himself. *Was that me?*

Then the beast appeared. One moment there was nothing. The next the creature stood in the circle of light, ten feet tall on its hind legs. Corded muscle bulged from its limbs, its muscular tail stretching out behind it. Sleek, black scales flickered in the firelight, coating its body like armour. Scars crisscrossed its chest, pale streaks on the reptilian skin.

It took a step towards them. Gravel crunched beneath its feet. Arms longer than any man's reached for them, its claws like daggers. Blood red eyes locked on his, as the whisper of its husky breath began to race. Saliva dripped from its giant, gaping maw. Rows of razor sharp teeth grinned at them. The smell of rot was strong enough to taste. It roared and the horses screamed.

Eric hardly noticed the thunder of hooves as their mounts broke free and fled. All his energy went into keeping himself upright. All he could see was the monster not three steps from him, about to hurl itself at his feeble body. The impact would shatter every bone he had. He looked into the depths of its bloody eyes, frozen in its dreadful gaze.

The beast leapt. Eric flinched backwards a step, only to see the monster hurled sideways by an invisible force. Alastair rushed after it, sword in hand, the other waved high as he worked his magic. The creature smashed against an outcrop of rocks, shattering them on impact. Alastair lunged with his blade, but it was already on its feet. With a bound of its powerful legs, it cleared Alastair's head.

The old man spun, but not fast enough. The massive tail whipped out, crashing into his chest. Alastair cried as the blow sent him tumbling through the air.

Eric winced as his mentor vanished into the darkness.

He clenched his burning branch tighter and raised his knife. He crouched as the monster turned towards him. This time he was ready. Before it could charge, he hurled the flaming branch at the creature's eyes. Sparks erupted into the night air as it struck.

The creature reared back. Its high-pitched screech forced Eric to his knees, hands against his ears. It felt like shards of glass were driving deep into the recesses of his mind. He closed his eyes and endured.

When it ceased, he threw himself at the fire, gathering up another stick. He turned, slipping in his haste, and braced himself for the worst. His breath came in rapid gasps, adrenaline pumping through his veins.

A few feet away, Alastair and the beast circled each other warily. Alastair's face was cut and bruised, already beginning to swell. His coat was in tatters and all his weight was on his right leg.

The monster, on the other hand, looked ready to kill. Their attacks had done nothing to pierce its scaly armour. Eric shuddered again as he stared at the long, yellowed teeth, already imagining them tearing at his body. A low growl echoed from its throat, sending shivers down his spine.

Alastair's sword spun, orange firelight sparkling along the steel edge. It lanced out, tearing through the brute's forearm. The monster roared, its claws slicing at Alastair. The old man danced backwards and they cut thin air. His movements were steady despite his injured leg. The tendons in his neck strained and there was a tightness to his face. It was taking everything he had to stay in the fight. Just one mistake with this beast would be the end of them both.

Snarling, the creature bent its legs and threw itself at Alastair. A rock the size of a man's head flew from nowhere, smashing into the monster's jaw and knocking it to the ground. Alastair lowered his arm to release the magic and drove forward, sword striking at his foe.

This time the beast was waiting for him. The sword plunged into its arm, but the other was already moving, tearing into the calf of Alastair's good leg. Ligament and muscle tore from bone, and the metallic tang of human blood sprayed through the night.

Alastair screamed and fell. Somehow, he kept a hold of his sword, tearing it from the creature. Thick black blood ran down its arm, dripping to the ground to mix with Alastair's. The beast loomed over him, neck outstretched, jaws open to bite through his skull.

Eric could hesitate no longer. He let out a shriek that was half rage, half despair, and threw himself at the giant.

It twisted its head and watched him approach, waiting until he came within reach. With graceful ease it lashed out with its tail, knocking him to the ground and pinning him there. Eric strained to lift the muscled tail from his bruised body, but could not find the strength. Stars flicked across his eyes as it began to crush down. Suddenly he found himself unable to draw breath. The edges of his vision began to go black.

It turned back to Alastair.

"No!" the word was crushed from Eric's chest.

He felt the familiar power within him stir. For once he did not try to resist. It was their only hope now. He surrendered to it; let its power boil through his blood. Strength flooded his body and his vision cleared. Faint sounds whispered to him on the edge of his hearing.

Above the monster's growls, the wind whistled with a violent voice. Gales formed above, driving down towards them. They rushed around the campsite, picking up dust, sticks and stones. The firelight flickered, threatening to die.

The winds gathered around Eric, tearing at his clothes

and hair. He closed his eyes, trying to direct it, willing it to obey. He had no idea whether it would work, but it was all he could do. A surge of power rushed from him and the winds roared.

They struck the monster, hurling it from Alastair and pinning it to the ground.

Before the gale could dissipate, Alastair was somehow back on his feet. He bared his teeth, his face stretched tight. Blood dripped from his nose and soaked his leggings. He swayed, a groan escaping him.

It did not stop him. He stumbled to where his foe had fallen, where even now it was struggling to regain its feet. Alastair did not give it the chance. He drove his sword through its chest, straight into its black heart.

Screaming, the monster lurched up and smashed Alastair from his feet. It turned and reeled towards Eric, the sword still sticking from its chest. The creature's breathe came in a whistling wheeze. Claws reached for him.

Eric scrambled backwards, eyes wide, mouth open in horror. He could not believe it. How could this thing suffer such a mortal wound and survive.

The beast gave a horrible cry, a gurgle rattling from its chest. It cried again, fainter this time. It took another step towards him.

Then it fell, slowly toppling forward and crashing to the ground. A cloud of dust whooshed out around it, blinding him. When he looked again, the creature's glassy eyes stared up at him. But it breathed no more.

Eric sucked in a great, shuddering breath of air.

****

Gabriel stood at the edge of the desert. Night had fallen less than an hour ago and they could go no further. He stared out into the darkness, impatience gnawing at him. He did not want to stop, not when they were so close. *I won't let them slip through my fingers again!*

We must wait, the wolf's voice spoke in the sanctity of his mind.

"Why, beast? Why should we be afraid of the desert creatures?" Gabriel spoke aloud.

Because they will kill you, fool. My master's magic will not protect you from teeth or claw. It will be safer in the woods tonight. One less night spent wandering the cursed desert.

Gabriel gritted his teeth. "Very well," he snapped, storming into the trees.

He could see the wolf shadowing him as he looked for a place to camp. He had already grown to hate it; a constant reminder of the deal he had struck. Regret was never far from his thoughts. *What was I thinking?*

You needed help. You took it from the only option left to you, the wolf supplied.

"Stay out of my head! If I wanted your opinion, I'd ask for it"

The creature lifted its shaggy head and howled. The noise cut through the night, raising goose bumps on his neck. The hoot of an owl and the chirping of crickets vanished.

Gabriel glared at the wolf and drew his sword.

The howling ceased. The black beast lowered its head, teeth bared. Its growl sent a shiver down Gabriel's spine.

"Just keep quiet, mutt," he snapped, sheathing his sword.

Gabriel closed his eyes and put his head in his hands. How had his life crumbled so quickly? He tried to picture his parents, his fiancé. Their images floated through his mind and he felt his chest constrict with love and pain. Yet their faces were blurred and indistinct. Then flames burst within his mind, consuming his family once more.

He opened his eyes and smashed his fist into a tree. They had taken everything from him, even his memory, it seemed. He could no longer even grieve – the tears would not come. All he found was his hatred. He could not stand the thought of their freedom. They would be punished, he would see to that.

Perhaps then he would find peace.

NINE

Silence settled like a blanket over the night. The fire burned low, leaving nothing but mere embers to light the camp. The shadows it cast were long and haunting. The air reeked of blood, rot and ash. The stars stared down from above, uncaring witnesses to the slaughter of the night.

Sharp stones ground beneath Eric's knees, tearing into his pants, stabbing at his skin. He didn't care. He crouched beside Alastair, his trembling fingers searching frantically for a pulse. The old man's eyes were closed and he did not respond to Eric's touch. His body lay crumpled on the ground, his clothes soaked with blood.

"No, no, no, no!" Eric whispered.

He could not bring himself to believe the mighty Magicker who had spirited him out of Oaksville could lie dying. An iron fist wrapped around his heart and began to squeeze. His breath could not come fast enough. This couldn't be happening.

"Come on, Alastair. You can't do this, you can't die. You have to live!" he shook him. Tears ran down his face and dripped onto Alastair's.

It did not take a doctor to see the wounds were beyond

any mortal man's will to live. Alastair's right leg was a tangled mess; muscles torn from bone, threads of tendons dangling in the dirt. His left foot twisted at an awful angle. The final blow had shattered his ribcage, leaving a deep indentation in his chest. His face was torn and bruised, and a cold sweat beaded his brow. A thin red trickle ran from his mouth.

Eric finally found the vein in his neck and felt a weak pulse. It was already growing fainter as the life fled from his friend. He would not survive the next few hours, let alone until morning. Even if he did, they were still stranded in this cursed desert, miles from help.

He sat back on his haunches, defeated. "Please wake up," he begged.

"Don't cry, Eric," a voice spoke from the darkness.

Eric's heart skipped a beat. He leapt to his feet, swinging around to face the new threat. It was almost beyond him to care, but he was determined not to go down without a fight. pitiful as that might be. His body was shaking from pain and exhaustion. It would take little more than a child to defeat him.

"Don't be afraid, Eric," the voice was soft and feminine.

Eric was not about to let his guard down. "Who are you? How do you know my name?"

Stones rattled as a young girl stepped forward into the light. Her features were faint, as if glimpsed through a misty veil. All he could see of her face was the violet glow of her eyes. An elegant sky-blue dress wrapped about her slight figure, spotted by the blurred green images of what might have been flowers or leaves. A faint glow seeped from her pale skin. The scent of lilies and roses fluttered on the air, bringing with it images of a summer meadow. Her bare feet carried her closer.

"I am Antonia, Goddess of Plorsea," she said.

Eric gaped, eyes wide, his mouth unable to form a response. It was not possible. Antonia was a Goddess. This girl could not be older than twelve.

"Ho– how?" he stuttered. His mind was reeling. *This cannot be possible.*

"How did I come to be here? How could I be the Goddess? How, how, how…" Antonia's tone sounded amused, as though she were holding back laughter. Eric could not make out her expression, but he imagined she was smiling.

The Goddess came closer. "We can 'how' all night, Eric. First, though, I need to save the wily old man. Step aside."

Eric stood, speechless, as she moved past him. Her movements were smooth and graceful, as though she glided over the ground. Only the soft crunch of her footsteps gave her away. The night around them had suddenly lost its terror, touched by the gentle light of the Goddess. It was as though sunrise approached, banishing the evil of the wasteland back to the shadows.

His eyes followed Antonia as she crouched beside Alastair. His heart pounded like a galloping horse, his breath coming in rapid gasps. He still could not believe what his eyes were telling him.

Antonia looked up at him. "Would you stop *staring?*"

Eric's mouth opened and closed, but no sound emerged. His stomach clenched in knots.

"Honestly, you look as though you've seen a–," her eyes widened. She placed a hand over her mouth and groaned. "Oh damnit, I'm so sorry, Eric. Sometimes I forget!"

She snapped her fingers. The mist faded away and the radiance of her skin softened. Her features finally came into focus.

Curls of silky brown hair hung across her face and cascaded down her back. A button nose sat between her violet eyes and there was a faint sprinkling of freckles on her cheeks. Strands of hair caught above her left ear, until she shook her head to free it. The wisps of hair fell to the side of her face. Staring into her eyes, Eric was struck by their depth. They spoke of an ancient wisdom held only by the immortal. Her mouth twisted in a wry grin.

Antonia laughed, the sound bubbling like music. "You look more stunned than before. Not what you expected?"

Eric found himself grinning in spite of himself. The tightness in his chest relaxed and he found his voice again. "Not exactly," he paused, his chest swelling with hope. "Can you really help him?"

"Just watch and see," she turned away and placed her hands on Alastair's chest.

Antonia closed her eyes. A slight frown creased her forehead and a shadow passed across her face. She hunched her shoulders, her little fingers digging into the torn cloth of Alastair's shirt. Blue veins appeared against the creamy skin of her arms.

A faint green light bathed the two of them. Eric felt its warmth on his cheeks, as though he stood before a great fire. The light settled around Alastair, soaking into his skin and wounds.

Eric watched wide eyed, as the muscles of Alastair's leg reattached themselves to the bone. The angry red of the skin surrounding Alastair's wounds faded, while colour rapidly returned to his face.

All over Alastair's body cuts closed and bruises vanished. His broken limbs straightened with sharp cracks. Within minutes the only sign remaining of the battle Alastair had endured were his torn clothes and bloody sword.

Antonia gasped and sat back on her haunches. A trickle of sweat ran down her forehead. The invincible aura had vanished; now the Goddess looked tired and strained. Her hands shook when she stood.

She looked over to Eric. "He'll sleep for the rest of the night. That should give us some time to talk, Eric."

His head shot up when she spoke his name, his heart racing with sudden fear. Antonia was the Goddess of Plorsea; was she here to punish him for the disaster he had brought to one of her cities?

Antonia smiled, the weariness falling from her face. "I am not a vengeful person, Eric. But I know you desire redemption, and I would like to offer you that chance," she paused, her grin turning mischievous. "And I can answer a few of those burning questions dancing around your head."

"What do you mean by redemption?"

Antonia laughed. "Always so serious. Why don't we save that for later? Ask your other questions."

Eric sighed, frustrated. Then he smiled and asked the question that had burned since she first appeared. "Why do you appear as a child?"

Antonia giggled. "Blunt too, aren't you? Most people take a few hours to gather the courage to ask that."

"And do you answer them?" Eric felt unusually bold around the young Goddess, as though some spell had been cast to dismiss his usual caution. Her cheerful personality was catching, her smile infectious.

"Of course – people should know the history of those with power. Even their Gods," she paused, her voice taking on a serious tone. "Five hundred years ago, the three of us were just spirits. We were still the eternal embodiments of magic, but powerless. A few lonely priests recognised us in their rituals, but we were unable to touch the physical realm."

"There were just two nations then, Lonia and Trola, and they were constantly at war. Death besieged the land. The

Magickers cast horrible spells and entire armies were lost in the chaos. It seemed the two nations were destined to wipe one another from existence."

"Eventually the destruction became so great, the priests of Trola decided to embark on a great gambit – to summon the spirits of magic to physical form. Knowing us to be creatures of balance, they hoped we might bring peace. Joining their powers, they worked a grand magic – one unlike any that had been or has come after. The spell condensed our spirits, allowing us to assume the bodies we still wear today. It was then I chose this appearance."

"Did the plan work?"

Antonia smiled. "In a way. Darius, my oldest brother, remained in Trola, while Jurrien went east to Lonia. Together they returned the surviving soldiers to their homes. I gathered the refugees, those disillusioned with their home nations, and led them to the wastelands left behind by the war. Together we created Plorsea from the wreckage, to be a buffer between the two nations who had hated each other for so long. The people loved us, for we were gentle and kind where their rulers had always been hateful and selfish. And the new kings and queens we brought them were loved as well."

"Yet our summoning also inadvertently created Archon, and the seeds for a fresh conflict that almost destroyed all the good we had created."

A breeze carried the stench of the dead beast to where they sat. Eric wrinkled his nose, stomach roiling. Antonia must have smelt it too, as she stood and walked over to the corpse. Eric joined her.

"The two of you did well to slay it. Few survive the wrath of such a beast."

"What are they called? How can they survive in such a wasteland?"

"They are Raptors. And not by my will, I assure you," she raised a hand.

Light spilt from her hand to bathe the beast. Tendrils shot from the ground to wrap around the corpse, small, green and strong. They twisted and turned, growing tighter and thicker as leaves sprouted. The body shook as though it had returned to life, then shoots erupted from its flesh, weaving together with the others to engulf the corpse.

Within minutes, a bush stood where the body had lain. Pink flowers began to bloom. A beautiful azalea plant now stood amidst the stark desert plain.

"There, that's better."

Eric sat down, hard. He recognised the significance of what he had witnessed. Antonia had created the bush from nothing. He stared at her, seeing what his ancestors must have seen all that time ago when they followed her to Plorsea.

Yet he could also see the strain on her face. Her skin had paled and she was panting softly. A sheen of sweat beaded her forehead.

"Are you all right?" he asked in concern.

Antonia nodded. "It's hard to work my magic in this place. The curse that lies over the Wasteland is not one I can break alone. The land itself is ingrained with Archon's taint; it fights the magic of the Earth. Within a few days the bush will die, as does everything good in this desert."

"That is why you cannot restore the forest?"

"Alone, I do not have the strength. It is Archon's last mockery; that *my* nation be cursed with such a place of death," Antonia's voice was laced with bitterness.

Silence fell. It seemed war was the incurable blight of the Three Nations. Eric had only heard legends of the Great Wars from the time before the Gods, but all knew the details of Archon's war. It had been over a century since those dark times, yet mention of his name could still cast a shadow over the brightest of days.

Eric breathed in the sweet scent of the flowers, drawing strength from the plant's beauty amidst the wasteland surrounding them. His mind toyed with another question, one he felt Antonia might be able to answer.

"Who is Alastair? What is his purpose?" the words slipped from his mouth in a whisper.

Antonia turned the glow of her violet eyes on him. Her smile faded. "Ah, so we have come to the crux of the night."

Eric turned his head in confusion. "What?"

"Alastair is a complicated man and his purpose is one of great secrecy. Can you be trusted with such a secret, Eric?" she flicked a strand of hair away from her face.

Eric felt a rush of fear, but it fled before his rising excitement. He owed Alastair his life. The least he could offer in return was his aid in whatever undertaking had driven him through the Wasteland.

Eric stared into the Goddess' eyes. "I swear by… err, Antonia, that you can trust me," blood rushed to his head as he spoke. The purple of Antonia's irises seemed to swirl.

Then his vision cleared and he found the Goddess smiling. "Good, I'll hold you to it," she cleared her throat. "I'd better start at the beginning, although you will know parts of the story. Two hundred years ago, my brother Darius vanished. He abandoned Trola and the Three Nations, and no one has heard from him since. He did not care to tell even his siblings where he went, or what he was doing."

"I hope this isn't your big secret, because I hate to disappoint you – everyone knows that. And what does it have to do with Alastair?"

Antonia grimaced. "I said I'd start from the beginning,

Eric. So try not to interrupt. When Darius left, he at least had the foresight to leave behind a sword infused with his power over the element of Light."

"Which became the Sword of Light?"

"Yes. Now, is this my tale, or yours?" Antonia's eyes glittered dangerously.

Eric blushed and shut his mouth.

"Unfortunately, the sword was useless. Worse than useless, in fact – it was deadly to any mortal who touched it – or so it seemed. Even Jurrien and I were repelled when we tried to wield it. For a time, we allowed Magickers from across the Three Nations to test the Sword. It burned them all to ash. Eventually we had to stop; the price had grown too high."

"So for the next hundred years, Trola was Godless. Worse – without Darius' power over the Light to aid us, Jurrien and I were stretched thin. The land weakened and the dark things crept from the holes we had banished them to. The hearts of the people grew hard. Even in Plorsea and Lonia they suffered, for our power is infinitely weaker without the Three."

"Then there came a day when the dark things vanished. No one could explain it, but somehow there was peace again. The people began to speak of Darius' return, that the God of Light was in hiding and would soon reveal himself. Jurrien and I knew better; we would have sensed if our brother was near."

"At the end of that year, the dark things returned. Ghouls and Raptors and countless unnamed beasts flooded from the Northern Badlands, marching beneath the banner of Archon."

"That was the beginning of Archon's war, wasn't it?" Eric had never heard this part of the tale before – the legends spoke only of the war itself, not how it had begun.

He looked up when she did not continue. Fire burned in Antonia's eyes, but he found himself grinning. It seemed even the patience of the Gods was limited. Perhaps they were more human than he realised.

Eric managed to look contrite. "Sorry, won't happen again."

Antonia rolled her eyes and he ruined his act with a soft chuckle.

The Goddess smirked; a sly twist to her lips that spoke of drastic consequences if he disturbed her again. Eric's laughter died in his throat.

"Okay, where was I? Archon. He was a Trolan man once, one who fought against the appearance of the Gods. He wielded a powerful magic, but it was not enough for him. He gave himself to its dark side. With the power it gave him, he killed the Master of the priests who had summoned us. For that, they banished him to the badlands in the North."

"It wasn't until he reappeared leading his army that we realised our mistake. His mastery of the dark magic had given him immortal life, and he had spent the centuries building his powers. I have never seen a more potent human, nor one with so little humanity remaining to them. The darkness he wielded could not be matched."

"Even by you?" this had always confused him. How could Archon have wreaked so much havoc when two Gods still opposed him?

Antonia sighed. "With Jurrien at my side, we stood against Archon's madness. We attacked him with every ounce of the Earth and Sky we could muster. The darkness consumed it all and threw it back in our faces."

"The dark magic tore into us, ripped at our skin and stole into our very souls. For a second I thought it would consume us. I felt myself teeter on the brink of madness;

and then a blast of lightning shattered its grip. My senses returned and I threw up a wall of vegetation between Archon and ourselves. Before he could burn his way through, we fled. We barely escaped with our lives."

Antonia's tiny body shook and a glitter of tears were gathering in her eyes. Eric hesitated, and then reached out a hand. Antonia took it with a small smile. It seemed a futile gesture, considering who and what she was, but he made it all the same.

Antonia shifted so they sat side by side. "You're a sweet soul, Eric," she hugged him before continuing with her tale. "With our magic defeated, the Three Nations were left with no choice but battle. Archon was powerful, but his army still had to cross The Gap. So we mustered fighters from every town and city of the Three Nations and, for the first time in four hundred years, the people marched to war. Together the armies of Trola, Plorsea and Lonia manned Fort Fall and prepared to defend The Gap. It was the first time in history Trola and Lonia stood side by side against a common foe."

Eric was silent now. He had heard this part of the tale before, but the way Antonia told it was personal. She had been there, witnessed and mourned the deaths of her people. They were not just historical figures from an old book or legend to her. She had felt the fear that plagued the land, the hate that had taken seed in human hearts.

"We did not have to wait long. They came like hell itself unleashed – demons, beasts and men. A thousand Raptors like the one you fought tonight, and many creatures more horrible. The men who fought alongside them were the scum of society, those who had been banished to the north in punishment for their crimes."

"Against them stood the men and women of the Three Nations. Flames seared holes in our ranks and the earth opened to swallow men whole. The claws and swords of the enemy seemed endless. Yet whenever one brave soul fell, another stepped forward to take their place. And damn it, we were winning."

"Then Archon took his place on the battlefield. He flew overhead, morphed beyond all recognition, darkening the heavens with his magic. Clouds gathered around him and my heart clenched in terror. I felt Jurrien release his magic, trying one last time to tear the monster from the sky. It was only seconds before he collapsed to the ground coughing blood."

"But Archon did not care about our feeble attempts to stop him. Until then he had only toyed with us. I felt his whisper in my mind. *Feeble, powerless beings; can you do this?*"

"Then the sky opened up, and it was not rain or lightning that fell, but *fire*. Flames engulfed The Gap. Thousands upon thousands of our people fell in the minutes that followed, consumed by Archon's dark firestorm. Brave souls, all."

"I watched in horror, powerless to save them. My heart broke as I felt the lives of my people erased from existence, as those who had loved me were cast burning into the abyss."

Now tears spilt down Antonia's face and ran down her freckled cheeks. Eric hugged her again, unable to imagine the horror. All those people. Their bravery and strength meant nothing against Archon's magic. They had never stood a chance.

Antonia sniffed and in a half-choked voice, continued her story. "We fled with the shattered remnants of our armies. I used what feeble magic I could still summon to stall the dark host that chased us, but we lost many more as we retreated. Jurrien's defiance had cost him dearly, leaving me alone to stand against Archon's might."

"Only one king survived the catastrophe at The Gap. His name was Thomas, the king of Trola, and he led the retreat. At his side was his champion and bodyguard – Alastair."

Eric blinked. It took a full second to process what he had just heard. He broke away from Antonia, staring at her in shock. "That's not possible – that would make Alastair over a hundred years old!"

Antonia nodded. "Alastair has enjoyed an unusually long life. One in a thousand Magickers will age far slower than a normal human. Alastair is one of these lucky few."

Eric's mouth hung open.

Choosing to ignore Eric's disbelief, Antonia continued with her story. "Thomas and Alastair led the remnants of the army south as far as Chole, but there they were ensnared and forced to make a final stand. The enemy had spread out across the land, wreaking havoc as they went, until we were completely encircled."

Eric remembered what came next. "Isn't this where you give–"

"*Eric!*" Antonia shrieked.

He winced, glancing across at her meekly. "Sorry?"

Antonia shook her head. The sly grin returned and her eyes sparkled with humour. Eric had a feeling the laugh would be at his expense.

"Eric, you really are impossible. I think we'll try doing this a little differently."

She leaned across and placed her hands either side of his head. Her grip was light and her skin soft to the touch. The smell of roses grew sharper. Slowly, she began to apply pressure. Eric looked straight into her eyes, fascinated by the intense concentration on her youthful face.

"This won't hurt – much."

Pain exploded through his skull and everything went

black.

TEN

"These are Alastair's memories, enjoy," Antonia's voice was soft and distant.

Eric's vision returned, but he no longer sat by the fire in darkness, was no longer even himself.

****

Alastair looked out over the forest of campfires encircling the city like a giant claw. The specks of light stretched north as far as the eye could see; more enemies yet to reach the battlefield. The night tasted of ash and above the stars hid behind clouds of smoke.

Plorsea was burning, and Chole was all that remained to stand against the dark tide. It would not be long before they swept this city away as well. Archon's armies would attack before the dawn; he could feel it in his blood.

The walls of Chole stretched away to either side of him. Men and women packed the battlements. The light of the enemy campfires lit their faces, revealing their masks of courage. Alastair's chest swelled with pride. These were ordinary people: farmers and merchants, fishermen and foresters. Yet he knew they would not break. They would stand to the last against the hosts of evil, hopeless as it may be.

Alastair took a deep breath and moved back from the ramparts. They were sixty feet high and just over fifteen feet wide. No siege engine would breach them, but the massive forest surrounding Chole would supply plenty of wood for scaling -ladders.

Taking another breath, he began to stretch, loosening his muscles in preparation for the coming fight. His chainmail rattled with each movement. Its weight did not bother him, but he knew it would grow heavier as the battle stretched on.

He closed his eyes, allowing fear and thought to drift away. It would be a long night, and a longer day. He needed to focus.

The men stared as he moved through a sequence of blows and parries. He ignored them, concentrating on the host of ghostly soldiers surrounding him. His movements grew faster as his muscles warmed. His frosty gaze revealed nothing of his inner turmoil; There was no need to add his fears to their own.

Unsheathing his sword, he began a new string of attacks. His blade hissed as it sliced the air, each cut deflecting imaginary blades, each thrust piercing a phantom heart. The soldiers nearest backed away to give him space. He stepped up the tempo again, his sword becoming a blur, his feet stepping from stance to stance without hesitation.

There was a slight sheen of sweat on his forehead when he finished. Warmth flowed through his muscles and the steady beat of his heart told him he was ready. His worries had fallen away, replaced by a cool determination to survive.

A trumpet sounded from out on the plain. Alastair sighed. Soon real enemies would replace the phantoms, and chaos would embrace the night.

"Are we ready, Alastair?" Thomas made his way through the soldiers packing the fortifications.

Alastair nodded to the king. "We'll show them a thing or two, old friend."

Thomas gave a grim smile and took his place beside Alastair. He too sported chainmail armour, its strong steel links glowing in the light cast by their enemy's torches. He wore an open-faced war helm over his short auburn hair, but no gold or gems to mark him as king. His hazel eyes stared out over the battlefield, his mouth set in a stubborn frown.

Alastair reached out and gripped his friend's shoulder. "Smile, man. The men need to see our confidence. You'll terrify them with that scowl."

Thomas gave a toothy grin. "This better?"

Alastair laughed. "You look like a lunatic, but it'll do."

Beneath the great walls, the enemy began to form up. It was difficult to make out details in the dim light, but the glint of metal from below suggested human warriors would make up the first wave.

The thump of ten thousand marching feet echoed off the walls. Alastair glimpsed the massive ladders held at the ready. Soon they would come crashing down against the ramparts and a flood of men would rush up the walls towards them.

The enemy's horns sounded again. The men below surged forward, their battle cries washing over the defenders like a wave. Blades quivered in the hands of wide-eyed men – as fear sank deep into their hearts. Below the enemy rushed towards the walls, weapons raised, wooden shields held above their heads.

"Archers, ready!" Thomas' voice carried no fear. Others carried the call along the line.

The men nearest them straightened and held their weapons higher. Thomas' bravery was legend among the men, his deeds at The Gap almost gospel. His courage inspired them; they would follow him to the end.

Alastair watched their enemies charge across the open ground. He counted slowly, knowing they would be within range in seconds. *One, two, three…*

"*Fire!*" Thomas shouted.

A volley of arrows rose into the air, steel tips reaching for the dark sky. The shriek as they flew sounded through the night. Below the enemy charged on, ignorant to the death that hovered overhead.

High above, gravity took hold, and the host of missiles fell. The deadly rain smashed into the ranks below. The enemy's charge faltered, their war cries turning to shrieks of agony. Hundreds fell – Yet the men behind pressed on, trampling their dead and injured beneath iron shod feet. There was no mercy for the injured in Archon's army.

A second volley struck the enemy's ranks – and a third. Fewer fell now, and Alastair saw the following ranks were better armoured than those who had led the charge. Their progress slowed, but still the dark mass drew ever closer to the wall.

Then the enemy archers began to fire back. A flight of arrows flew over the defenders' heads. The men ducked for cover, but a swordsman nearby was too slow to react. He toppled backwards, an arrow jutting from his throat. He clawed at the black feathered shaft as blood spurted across the bricks.

The bang of wood on stone drew Alastair's attention back to the enemy. He looked across as another ladder rose out of the darkness to crash against the stone. Men were already racing to the ladders, struggling in vain to push them away. But the weight of the enemy had already pinned them to the wall.

Another ladder struck close to where they stood. Thomas leapt to meet the threat, Alastair close behind. They crouched beneath the stone battlements, weapons at the ready. Alastair licked his lips, tasting the salt of his sweat.

A man's face appeared above the battlements, dagger gripped between his teeth. Alastair's blade flicked out, crunching into the man's face. He fell away without a sound. Blood stained the tip of Alastair's sword.

The sound of battle engulfed the wall. Men and women, fears forgotten, launched themselves at their assailants. Countless enemy fell beneath the defenders' blades. Yet their deaths still came at a heavy price for the defenders, and they could not spare a single soldier. Not while the endless thousands of Archon's army stretched out around them.

Another man sprang to the ramparts. He came up fast, axe already swinging as he crested the stone battlements. Alastair ducked beneath the blade, while beside him Thomas' sword lanced into the axeman's chest.

Blood sprayed through the air and the man disappeared over the side. Another clambered to take his place. Alastair thanked the Gods they only faced humans. When the beasts came, they would have no need for ladders.

He could not have said how long they fought. At one point, a lunatic with a mace had exploded over the parapet, mace swinging about his head. A blow smashed Thomas from his feet, but Alastair had cut him down before he could gain a foothold. Thomas now sported a gash across his forehead and his helmet was lost to the night. Yet still the king fought like a man possessed.

Alastair's body ached with exertion, but adrenaline fed strength to his limbs and stole the worst of his pain. Blood soaked the sleeves of his coat, none of it his own. His exercises had served him well. So far he had not needed to exert his magic; he would need that for the beasts.

Finally the enemy horns sounded and their foes began to retreat. A ragged cheer went up from the defenders. Alastair smiled. They had earned their reprieve, brief as it might be. Fresh men would soon replace those of the enemy who had fallen. Or worse, Archon might send his beasts to sweep away all resistance.

Thomas sat heavily beside him. He had found his helmet, but the dent left by the mace left it unwearable.

"Not much use to me anymore," Thomas tossed it over the side. "Saved my life though. For a minute I thought the bastard had me."

Alastair smiled. Thomas was an inspirational fighter, but his recklessness was not a great trait for a king. It amazed Alastair that he was the last king standing in the Three Nations. It certainly made protecting him a difficult affair.

Silence fell. When Thomas finally spoke, it was in a whisper. "Where is she, Alastair?"

Alastair wiped sweat from his brow. His hands were sticky with blood and shaking from exertion. Exhaustion had settled in, and Antonia's continued absence was not helping.

"I don't know. Helping, I hope."

"Or I'm right here," Antonia's youthful voice was out of place amidst the carnage on the battlements.

Alastair spun. The girl enjoyed catching them by surprise. There was no amusement now though. Antonia looked beaten. Her leaf green dress was scorched black. In places the silky material had melted to her skin, while in others it still bubbled, as if it had come straight from the furnace. Her sooty hands were scratched and bleeding and her face was haggard. Dark shadows hung beneath her eyes, but power still shone from their violet depths. Her hair was dry and tangled. Tears ran down her face, carving through the dirt and soot.

Alastair stepped forward, wrapping the girl in his arms. When he pulled back, he whispered the question they had been dreading the answer too. "Is there a way out, a way to save our people?"

"No," Antonia's voice shook and he could see the grief in her eyes. The screams of her people burning haunted her still.

His shoulders slumped. Burying his face in his hands, Alastair turned away. Tears leaked from his eyes. He quickly wiped them away, furious with himself. They could not afford to show weakness in front of the soldiers. They relied on his strength – and Thomas's.

"I'm so sorry, Alastair," he felt the Goddess' hand on his shoulder.

His despair turned to anger. "Damn your sorries, Antonia. Where is your brother?"

Antonia's face darkened and a dangerous flicker appeared in her eyes. Her tiny fists clenched. Alastair thought he glimpsed a faint light seeping between her fingers. It was easy to forget how dangerous Antonia could be. He remembered it now.

"Leave my brother out of this, Alastair," she spoke each word in a carefully measured tone.

Thomas stepped between them. He attempted a smile, and failed. "Stop this, the two of you. It solves nothing," his voice was soft, but commanding.

Alastair drew a deep breath and allowed himself to relax. He nodded. "You're right," he turned to Antonia. "You must leave, Antonia, so you can live to defy Archon. Gather a new army. perhaps we can take enough of Archon's forces with us that you will be able to defeat them."

Antonia shook her head. "There is no hope there. Archon is too strong to be defeated by mortal powers. We've seen that. He has been toying with us. There is only one hope now, one path to salvation. The Way."

Alastair's stomach clenched in fear. "You cannot be serious?"

"It is the only choice we have."

"Then there is no choice at all. The curse is too strong. Far better men than I have tried to break it. None returned. The Way is certain death."

"Still, it is our only chance. I can collect Jurrien and wait for you in Kalgan. We cannot take you ourselves, but The Way can get you there. If you make it through, perhaps we will have a chance," the amethyst of her eyes stared straight into his.

Alastair's hands shook. He clasped them together, mind racing. Antonia was right. The Sword was in Kalgan. If they could get to it, there might be one last chance for victory. If they stayed, they faced certain defeat. He gave a sharp nod, lips tight with worry.

"I'll see you in Kalgan," she stepped close and hugged Alastair tight. "Thomas has the better chance," she whispered. "Protect him with your life."

With that, Antonia stepped back, already fading from sight. For a moment, the scent of flowers and the forest hung in the air. Alastair stood still for a long time, gathering himself. Her last words rang in his ears.

"Come, Thomas," he said at last, speaking quietly so the men would not hear. "We must go as well."

Thomas nodded. "One moment."

He signalled one of his officers over. Blood stained the man's uniform, but he seemed uninjured. Alastair could not recall his name.

"Captain, I need you to take over the command here. Antonia has a plan, but you need to hold out long enough for it to work. We'll be back soon, I promise you. Hold the wall for as long as you can. Should it fall, sound the retreat and regroup in the town keep. Good luck."

"You too, sir," the captain turned away, already shouting commands.

Alastair led the king from the wall. They raced down the stone steps, sheathed swords slapping at their sides. Their breath whispered in the cool night air. Above, Alastair glimpsed a star shoot across the night sky. He prayed it was a good omen.

He turned right as they reached the ground, following the base of the wall. Long grass grew from the packed earth, giving way beneath their booted feet. Alastair's eyes swept the granite blocks of the wall. It had been years since he'd contemplated the mystery of The Way and he did not want to miss the entrance. He trailed his fingers along the cool stone as he walked.

They moved faster, the buildings nearest pressing in. Each house was packed with families, refugees from the surrounding towns and villages. They had come here to escape Archon's roving armies; now they were trapped like rabbits. If the city fell, it would be a massacre.

A war horn sounded from above, followed by the muffled cries of enemy warriors. Alastair's keen ears picked up the twang of bowstrings as the defenders unleashed their first volley. Time was running short.

Alastair cursed as his hand caught on a thorny vine. Drawing to a halt, he held up his hand to inspect the damage. Blood dripped from his fingers. Rubbing it on his cloak, he stared up at the dark surface. Thick vines hung like snakes from above, swaying gently in the breeze. Their bright green leaves hid the stone beneath them. Tiny white flowers blossomed between the thorns, adding their rosy tint to the air.

Sword blades rung out overhead. The enemy had made it to the top of the ladders. The screams of dying men quickly followed.

"Hurry, Alastair, Chole does not have much time. The wall will not last the night if this continues."

Alastair nodded. "I know. It would fall within minutes if Archon unleashed his beasts. It's a good thing he enjoys toying with his food. But I am afraid we have arrived, and my knowledge cannot take us any further. Your magic is needed now. These vines are a part of an ancient magic the founders of Lonia put into the walls of Chole, before it became a part of Plorsea. Only those with power over the Earth can command them to reveal our path."

Thomas nodded. His magic gave him control over living things; he would have little trouble with the vines. They both knew the real test would come later.

The king stepped up to the wall and took hold of the nearest vine. His face revealed nothing as the thorns pierced his skin. Thomas closed his eyes, his breath softening. The vines began to ripple and a faint green glow lit the dark alley. Slowly they curled back on themselves, slivering upwards, retreating from Thomas' touch.

Beneath was not solid stone, but an empty abyss stretching away into oblivion. A strange light shone from within, bathing them in its power. Alastair felt the dark pull of the shadows in his soul. The world around them began to fade until only the abyss remained.

Beware, Alastair, he heard Antonia's voice in his mind. He shook himself and shouted a warning. "Beware, Thomas. The ancient magic is corrupted. Keep your soul closed or it will destroy you."

Thomas nodded grimly. "Where does it lead?"

"Follow and you will see," Alastair's voice was bleak. There was little chance they would see the other side of the portal.

Taking a deep breath, Alastair stepped forward into the abyss. His doubts did not matter now. All his energy must go to seeing Thomas safely to Kalgan. It was their last hope.

As he crossed the threshold a twisted rainbow streaked across his vision. The world spun and his mind burned. Gravity vanished and then suddenly pulled him skyward. He spun, a terrible screeching tearing at his ears. Blood ran from his nose and his stomach churned. Gritting his teeth, he endured.

Thunder clapped and all sensation vanished. An instant later, he struck the ground.

Alastair groaned, struggling to keep himself from throwing up. Slowly his senses returned. He opened his eyes, looking around for Thomas. His eyes returned only blurred images, before the world around him clicked into sharp clarity.

Around him lay the bones of long dead men and women. The empty eye sockets of human skulls stared at him, toothy grins fixed to their stark, white faces. No trace of flesh or cloth remained. Thomas sat nearby, his eyes wide with shock.

Alastair shook his head, pulling his wits together. A blood red sky stretched overhead, its infinite expanse unmarked by cloud, sun or stars. Sheer peaks rose all around, their bleached white cliffs hemming them in, in all but one direction. A path led through the piles of dead. The bones grew thinner as it wound its way down the hill. Obviously most did not survive their first step into this strange world. There was not a living thing in sight. The air was deathly still.

"What is this place?" Thomas' voice shook. Alastair glimpsed fear on his friend's face.

"The Way," he said, standing. "And we had better move quickly. Time passes differently here and there's none to waste."

Thomas stood, brushing off the dust of the dead. His hands trembled, but there was determination in his eyes.

"This way," Alastair waved at the path. "Stay alert, who knows what lurks in this realm."

Alastair began to pick his way amidst the bones, Thomas following close behind. His boots crunched on sharp gravel and shards of bones. The sound echoed off the surrounding cliffs.

"What happened here, Alastair?" Thomas' voice had regained its composure.

Alastair sighed. "The Way is ancient, predating the Gods themselves. It served as neutral ground for negotiations between Lonia and Trola when the two nations were at war. Only a few souls can enter at one time, so there was no way one nation could ambush the embassy of another. It was obviously a much safer place then."

"How-," Thomas broke off, staring around at the red waste. "How did it become like this?"

"It was cursed. At first, no one understood who would have the power to achieve such a feat, but we know now it was Archon. Dark magic has corrupted everything in this small land, sucking the life from it. Your magic is useless here; the raw energy of the Light is the only Element to still hold sway against the darkness."

Thomas loosened his sword. "Then we must rely on your powers – and our steel."

Alastair nodded. "Something waits out here. No one has passed this way in four hundred years and lived to talk about it."

Thomas fell silent. They plodded on, their passage witnessed only by the glares of long dead souls.

****

A granite arch stood guard at the end of the canyon. Flowers were etched across the stone, entwined one over another. A dull fog hung in the air beyond the arch, concealing what lay beyond. It could only be the exit.

Alastair's blood was cold. Beneath the archway stood the embodiment of the curse. It grinned at them across the short distance, yellowed teeth jutting from milky bone. Empty eye sockets glared at them from the naked skull, held aloft by a crooked spine. Bone rattled as skeletal arms drew a rusty scimitar. The blade grated as it slid from its sheath. The skeleton's bony toes gripped the rocky ground.

Alastair felt as though the canyon walls were closing in on him. He shivered, a cold darkness sweeping across his soul. A weight settled in his chest, freezing him in place. This creature had killed those hundreds who had come before him. Now it sought their lives and Alastair doubted there was much chance of survival.

"Whatever you do, stay behind me, Thomas," he whispered the words from the corner of his mouth. His eyes never left the undead skeleton.

Alastair walked forward, his short sword sliding into his hand. "Out of my way, damned hell spawn," his voice echoed back and forth off crumbling stone. Slowly the words died away, until it seemed they had been spoken by some feeble old man. Alastair felt his confidence wither.

The skeleton laughed, the soft whispering cackle of the

dead. It raised its blade in mock salute.

Alastair braced himself, fear gnawing at his courage. The creature would not die easy. *Best not to go charging in.*

Instead, he turned his mind inwards, seeking out his magic. It leapt at his touch, an old companion eager to aid him. power flowed through his veins, giving strength to weary limbs. Time passed slowly here and it seemed as though they had trudged for hours through this grim land.

The magic focused his mind. With it, he reached out to the land around him. Rocks groaned. Small stones rattled and rolled as man-sized boulders took to the air. Soon a host of boulders hovered around him.

Pressure throbbed in Alastair's head. He clenched his teeth and threw out his arm. The boulders leapt to obey, accelerating towards his dark foe.

The skull's grin widened. It too raised its hand. Alastair's projectiles hurtled onwards. Twenty feet, ten, five. Alastair grinned and gave one final push with his magic.

An earth-shattering crack ripped the air. The boulders exploded, turned suddenly to splinters that flew in all directions, burying themselves in the valley walls. The stench of burning stone filled the air.

Alastair staggered back, the aftershock of his failed magic tearing through him. His mind reeled from the force of the creature's counterattack. He started to fall. Strong arms reached out and caught him. Through the pain he could hear the creature's mocking laughter.

Alastair struggled to regain his feet. Footsteps crunched as the monster walked towards them. He cursed and pushed Thomas behind him. Bracing himself, he summoned his magic again. It came faster now. He screamed his anger, arms swinging out. The magic surged through his mind.

The skeleton rose ponderously into the air. Alastair gave

a violent gesture, hurling it into the canyon walls. Dust exploded outwards, the crash deafening in the narrow canyon. The skeleton vanished into the dust cloud.

When the air cleared, it was still coming.

Alastair gritted his teeth in frustration. His attacks had not even phased it. He saw now the hardened blood that coated the scimitar. Now he knew how his fellow Magickers had meet their end. He realised with dreadful certainty this creature would not be defeated.

He took a firmer grip of his short sword. "We cannot win here, Thomas. I do not have the power. I will keep it distracted. You must make a break for the gate."

Thomas frowned. He opened his mouth to speak, but Alastair cut him off. "It is our only chance. At least one of us must reach Kalgan."

Thomas scowled. He edged away to the right, and Alastair could only pray he had listened.

The skeleton halted a few steps away. "Yield, and your deaths shall be quick," its rusty voice grated like nails on a chalkboard.

Alastair answered with steel.

Their blades rang as they met, sparks flying in the dry air. Alastair jumped back as the scimitar reversed its cut. The tip tore through his shirt, narrowly missing skin. He swore and slashed out. The rusty blade spun to block. The shock of the collision rattled Alastair's sword arm.

The creature pressed forward, but Alastair dove to the side. Its blade whistled over his head. Rocks ground through his cloak as he rolled to his feet. His foe turned to follow him and Thomas darted past.

Alastair allowed himself a smile and almost lost an arm for it. Time disappeared, as he found himself locked in desperate battle with the monster, all thought driven from his mind. His sword became a blur, each movement made through sheer instinct. Even so, it was not enough. The scimitar came closer and closer, tearing shallow slices down his arm and chest.

Another attack slipped past his guard. The rusted blade flashed out. The blunt tip lanced into his side, tearing through chainmail and driving into flesh. The shock forced him back a step. Pain struck, forcing a scream from his lips that he quickly cut short.

The blade began to twist in his side, and this time he could not bite back his cry. The blade burned and the strength fled from his muscles. His sword fell from limp hands. He collapsed to the ground. The skeleton jerked back its bloodied sword and raised it over his head.

The rattle of gravel was all that gave Thomas away. With a hiss the skeleton spun, parrying Thomas' desperate attack. Its blade flashed out at Thomas once, twice, three times. On the third blow, Thomas' blade shattered. The creature was angry now. Its scimitar rose, aimed now at Thomas' head.

"*No!*" Alastair flung what little strength he had left at the skeleton. A last, desperate attack.

The magic swelled and rushed at his foe. It struck the skeleton, sweeping it backwards into the canyon wall. The blade slipped from its hand, tearing a gash down Thomas' cheek as it spun through the air.

Thomas ignored the wound. He rushed to Alastair's side and hauled him to his feet. With his spare hand he swept up Alastair's fallen sword. Alastair hung one arm over Thomas' shoulder and the two of them stumbled for the exit. The distance seemed to grow with each step; the skeleton would be on them at any moment.

Alastair felt Thomas' strength fading beneath his weight. "Leave me, you fool!"

Thomas took no notice, staggering on towards the great

archway.

From behind them came the grinding of bone on rock. Their deathly foe stepped back into the light. Air hissed between its teeth. Alastair closed his eyes and hobbled faster.

"*For that, your deaths will take an eon,*" the ground shook with the creature's rage.

Above, the rocks began to creak. Dust seeped into the air. Alastair glanced up and saw cracks racing along the weakened cliff face. The rattle of stones as they shook loose came from overhead.

For every step they took, the skeleton took two. The click of its bony joints echoed amid the sound of creaking rocks. Then, with a mighty roar, half the cliff face broke away. The cursed skeleton had only a second to turn and roar its defiance – before a tonne of rock smashed down on it. It disappeared beneath the rubble.

Thomas and Alastair stumbled for the exit, the landslide rumbling its way towards them. They passed beneath the arch and the mist rose up to meet them. At its soft touch, the sound behind vanished.

Safe, the word echoed through Alastair's mind.

Blazing light lit the world, banishing all sight. When it faded, the citadel of Kalgan had materialised before them.

Alastair looked around, taking in the great grass lawns within the walls of the keep. The night sky was clear overhead, revealing a full moon that lit the world beneath. The seamless granite walls of the inner citadel stood before them, the only entrance a pair of massive steel doors.

Somewhere in the darkness, an owl began to hoot. The chirping of crickets soon joined in. A cool sea breeze touched Alastair's face, bringing with it the tang of the ocean. The scent of freshly baked bread hung in the air, its source somewhere in the city outside the walls. They had returned to the real world; it was almost enough to wash away the debilitating pain of his wound.

Almost.

The citadel was dark, its doors barred shut. The building stood empty, the people long gone north to the battle for The Gap.

It did not matter. What mattered was the crystal case that stood centre stage of the lawn. Within, throbbing with a dull white glow, was The Sword of Light. It stood tip down, its three-foot blade silver in the moonlight. He knew that with the coming of dawn, the blade would turn the softest gold. Leather wrapped around a two -handed grip below the hilt, although the blade was lighter than any short sword. A smooth diamond decorated the pommel of the blade, shining like a tiny sun.

A shriek pierced the night's silence. "*You made it!*"

Antonia came sprinting across the lawn towards them. For a second it looked like she would make a running leap at the two men. He braced himself for the impact, angling himself to protect his wound.

At the last moment Antonia skidded to a stop. She eyed Alastair, concern replacing joy. "Are you okay?"

Alastair grunted, fighting to stay conscious. His legs buckled, but Thomas kept him upright.

The king answered for him. "He's been stabbed."

Antonia nodded and moved to stand with them. She laid a hand on Alastair's wound. Warmth flooded his side. He watched the concentration etched on the young girl's face and kept his eyes averted from his wound. The sight of his own flesh knitting itself back together tended to make him retch.

When Antonia finally removed her hand, Alastair allowed himself to look down. The jagged hole in his side was gone, and the pain had vanished. He sighed and took his weight off Thomas.

"Thank you, Antonia," he looked across at The Sword of Light. "What now?"

"Now..." the Goddess hesitated.

"Now Thomas must take up The Sword. If Darius meant anyone to use it, it would be the kings of Trola. I know your father tried, Thomas. But age had stripped him of his strength and I believe you are strong enough to succeed where he failed. If you can wield its power, together we will have the strength to stop Archon," a man's voice spoke.

Alastair glanced up as Jurrien strode into view. The Storm God had seen better days, but looked more alive than the last time they had met. Exhaustion still lined his face, but determination shone from his ice blue eyes. There was a spring to his step now and some black had returned to his greying hair. His clothes were blood stained, although he did not seem to notice. The musty scent of fresh rain clung to the air around him.

He drew up beside Antonia. "You must do it now, Thomas. The two of you have been gone for over an hour. Chole won't last much longer."

Thomas nodded, eyes locked on the Sword of Light. There was a determined set to his jaw. He knew the risks. If Jurrien was wrong, the Sword would burn the king to dust.

Alastair turned back to the Gods, his chest tight with fear for his friend. "Is there anything you can do to protect him?"

Antonia shook her head. There were tears in her eyes.

"It doesn't matter," Thomas walked towards the case. "If we cannot use the Sword, we all die."

Thomas carried Alastair's sword in a tight grip as he walked. A powerful spell had been cast on the crystal to protect the Sword of Light, but Alastair's blade was infused with spells of its own. Thomas lifted the weapon above his head and brought it down on the case. Light flashed, and then came the tinkling of a thousand tiny crystals falling to the ground.

Thomas let Alastair's sword fall as well. Slowly he reached out a hand. His fingers wrapped around the leather hilt of the Sword of Light. He lifted it from the case, hands shaking with reverence. He stood for a moment, eyes closed and brow furrowed as if he fought some great battle within his mind.

When his eyes finally opened, he wore a smile on his face.

The tension fled from Alastair's muscles. He grinned back at the young king.

Antonia broke the silence. "Okay, we must be quick," her voice was all business. "Thomas, all we need is for you to link the power of the Sword to ours. We will do the rest."

"How?"

"Spread out," Antonia and Jurrien stepped back, so that the three of them made a triangle. Alastair backed away.

"You should be able to call on the Sword's magic the same way you do your own, Thomas. When you feel the Sword's magic respond, focus it into the centre of the triangle. Like this."

Her face closed over, her lips drawn into a grimace. Alastair shivered, feeling the power emanating from her tiny body.

Antonia raised an arm and green light flowed into the centre of the triangle. The pure embodiment of the Earth flowed like water, rolling across the grass. As he stared into its depths, Alastair glimpsed images of great forests and rolling hills.

Jurrien did not bother raising an arm. Blue light seeped

from his body, joining with the Earth magic. It swirled between them, mixing, but never becoming one. The image of a stormy sky over a raging sea appeared in Alastair's mind.

He watched Thomas close his eyes, his breath slowing. For a long while there was nothing, though his face shone with sweat. Bathed in the glow of the God magic, Alastair held his breath and waited.

The glow from the Sword of Light flickered and grew brighter. Thomas opened his eyes. Arm shaking, he pointed the blade towards the centre of the triangle. The air crackled with energy and a beam of pure white light poured from the Sword. It joined the whirling tide of magic.

The conflagration flickered, colours changing now – white, then green, then blue. The magic began to bubble and steam, leaping and pushing against invisible barriers, seeking escape. It grew higher, towering above them, a column of pure, unimaginable energy.

"Now!" yelled Antonia.

The column burst. Light shot upwards. A thousand feet above there came another explosion, and a million colours flooded the sky. The magic spilled outwards in all directions, burying the stars.

In that instant, Alastair thought he glimpsed a shadow sliding towards the trio. He took a step towards them, but it vanished before the flickering glow of the magic above. Shaking his head, he dismissed it as a trick of the light. He looked up at the sky, feeling a weight lift from his shoulders. This was the end of Archon. With the Gods' power over the three elements restored, they were invincible. It was time to stop jumping at shadows.

The dream ended and Eric woke.

Antonia sat at his side. The fire had died, leaving the night in almost perfect darkness. "Did you see?"

Eric nodded. "I did. You saved us all. But how does that explain Alastair's purpose today?"

"Ask him. For now, you have seen what you needed to. Don't worry, the answers will come soon. Now sleep."

She stood. Eric made to follow, but his legs refused to obey. A great weariness settled over him and he fell from the log. His eyelids felt like lead.

"Good night, Eric," Antonia whispered.

Eric was already asleep as she vanished. This time, there were no dreams.

ELEVEN

Eric woke to a long wet tongue dragging across his
face. Choking in disgust, he rolled away from the
unknown assailant. Opening his eyes, he saw the
long snouts and friendly eyes of the two horses staring
down at him. They shook their heads and snorted, the
sound almost like laughter.

Eric found himself laughing as well, glad to see they had
returned in the night.

"Good morning, Eric," Alastair called. "How was your
night?"

Eric's smile widened when he spotted Alastair standing
over a fresh fire, a rack of sausages hanging over the flames.
Eric's mouth began to water as he smelt the cooking meat.
His stomach rumbled with hunger. The sun hung low on
the horizon behind him, colouring the sky bright orange.
The morning was still young, but he could already feel the
heat of the desert searing his skin.

Walking across to the old man, Eric drew him into an
embrace. His eyes stung, but he did not cry; There had been
enough tears the night before. Pulling away, he grinned at
Alastair.

Alastair smiled back. "Glad to see you too, Eric. I take it

we had an unexpected visitor last night?"

Eric nodded. "Unexpected doesn't begin to describe it. You didn't tell me you were on a first name basis with the Goddess of Plorsea!"

Alastair laughed. "We have a complicated past."

Eric stilled. "I know," he hesitated. "She showed me Archon's war. Who knew you were so *old*!"

Alastair scowled. "Old and a great deal wiser than you, boy. How much did she show you?"

"Until Thomas and the Gods cast the spell to banish Archon."

"I see. Did you see what happened after Archon had been banished?"

Eric shook his head.

"Typical Antonia, always forgetting the finer details. It was the clash between Archon and the God magic that created *those*," his hand swept out to encompass the trio of volcanoes marring the horizon. "The collision of magic tore the crust of the earth, releasing the pent up forces beneath. The three cursed peaks were what resulted."

Eric shivered, remembering the power the Gods had unleashed. "I see."

"Do you see the greater lesson there, though?" Alastair probed. A gust of wind toyed with his thin grey hair.

Confused, Eric shook his head.

"Even pure magic, cast with the best of intentions, can have disastrous results. Nature is an infinitely complex force, and magic is only a small part of that complexity. The smallest act can set in motion a chain of events not even the wisest of Magickers could predict."

"Was that how this desert formed?"

"That is a part of it. The peaks created a rain shadow over Chole, cutting it off from the moisture laden air blown from the ocean. But the severity of the desert was Archon's last curse. The God magic was enough to banish him and shatter his armies, but without complete control of the Light, it was not enough to remove all trace of his presence. Here was where his army made camp and where he cast his magic. Their evil still lingers here, cursing the land and everything in it. Maybe if Darius were to return it would be different. But without his true mastery of the Light, here it remains."

Eric shivered, glad the light of day had returned to the desert. His thoughts turned to the young king who had risked everything to wield the Sword of Light. "What happened to Thomas?"

"He lived a good life and then he died," Alastair said softly.

"But what about his life?" the tales spoke little about the king after the war had been won.

Alastair sighed. "He was a good king and a good friend. He travelled the Three Nations for many years, visiting the new kings and helping the lands to rebuild after the war. He led several hunting parties after the last of Archon's creatures. And he visited the wildlands of each nation, even Dragon country for a time."

Eric sat up at that. "Why?"

"With his Earth magic, Thomas could befriend most creatures."

"Was it the dragons who killed him?"

"No, though it was there that he died. I was not with him at the time, but I had left him well protected. Yet when his party reached Malevolent Cove, where they were to meet one of the great dragon tribes, something went wrong. When they did not return as expected, I set out at once. I found them there on the shoreline. Some had died by the blade, others had fallen without a mark on them. Thomas was not among them. I searched for weeks for a trace of my friend, but to no avail."

Eric swallowed. "And the Sword of Light?"

"It passed to his children, and grandchildren after that, and so on until today."

There was a sense of finality in Alastair's words. Eric fell silent, his mind conjuring images of events long since passed. At last he rose to his feet and wandered over to the horses. Reaching out to stroke Briar's long snout, he pondered again over the question he had asked the night before. Antonia's story had not given an answer.

Across the camp, Alastair began to pack the last of their food into the saddlebags.

Eric took a deep breath and asked the question before his courage deserted him. "What is your purpose, Alastair?"

Alastair grew still. His head turned slowly to lock Eric in his steely gaze. "Antonia did not tell you?"

Eric shook his head. "No."

For the briefest of seconds, confusion swept across Alastair's face, and Eric wondered if he would answer.

"I am looking for a family."

"Who? Why?"

"You don't need to know just yet. Now let's get moving. We still have one more night in this hellish desert, let's not make it two," he finished strapping the last of the saddlebags to Elcano and swung himself into the saddle.

Eric sighed. Scrambling onto Briar's back, he glared at Alastair. "Any idea when I *will* need to know?"

The old man laughed. "When you're ready. Now, let's ride!"

He gave his horse a quick kick. Elcano leapt forward in response, steel shoes slashing into the scorched earth. Splinters of rock flicked up behind him as he galloped away.

Briar pranced about in the dust cloud Elcano left behind. Eric coughed, hacking up the mouthful of dust he'd swallowed. He struggled to point Briar out of the dust cloud and then turned the horse to follow. Ahead Alastair had already checked his speed, and as Eric bounced in the saddle the distance between them quickly evaporated.

Eric groaned as his bruises began to throb. Resigning himself to another nightmarish ride, he locked his eyes on the volcanic peaks and prayed for them to grow.

****

Gabriel jogged across the barren plain, buoyed by a newfound energy. He carried his sword in one hand, his waterskin in the other. It was easier than having them slapping at his side and catching between his legs. The skin was already half empty, but the wolf had promised it could find more water.

The burning sun engulfed the horizon, stained only by the dark peaks far to the east. He squinted into the distance, although he knew his quarry was still at least a half day ahead. If only he had not lost his horse. The wolf loped effortlessly alongside him, tongue panting in the boiling air. It was never far from his side now.

They had started out an hour before sunrise, Gabriel's impatience eventually winning out over caution. The night had been a long one, his sleep racked by nightmares. Faces flew through his mind, the ghosts of people he had once known, spirits demanding revenge. One by one they had faded away, leaving only a burning hatred to fill his heart.

They came across the campsite around midday, but Gabriel could make little sense of what he saw there. Three distinct sets of footsteps were evident in the loose gravel. From the size of the third step, they could only come from by a bare footed child.

What was a child doing here, of all places?

Gabriel pondered the question a moment before casting it aside. There were more important things to consider.

There were also obvious signs the camp had come under attack during the night. Blood splattered the ground and congealed in a pool in one place. Gabriel wondered if anyone could lose so much blood and survive, but There was no sign of a body or grave.

Strangest of all was the bush that stood in the centre of the campsite. Pink flowers were sprinkled amidst the green leaves, glowing in the midday sun. Breathing in the sweet scent, Gabriel felt a fluttering in his chest. For a fleeting second the hate that gripped his heart melted away and he felt the pain of all he had lost seep through.

Beside him, the wolf began to growl. *They have already left, hours ago on horseback. We must move if we are to catch them.*

The tendrils of hate snapped closed. Gabriel nodded grimly, fingers running across the hilt of his sword.

They set off once more, picking their way through the rocky desert. The path threaded its way among the boulders and petrified trees, often splitting in two or disappearing altogether. The wolf led the way without hesitation, leaving Gabriel no choice but to follow in frustration.

The wolf whispered as they walked, always in his mind. *Yes, they came this way. Just a few hours ago now. Keep moving. We're close.*

Yet even Gabriel's newfound strength was fading beneath the heat of the sun. As the day wore on, he found himself slowing, his sword growing heavy. By mid-afternoon his legs burned and his calves were beginning to cramp, making every step an agony. Still he pushed on, determined to claim a few more miles before the sun set.

In his mind, an image flickered into life. He found

himself in a tiny room before a great fire, his arms up to their elbows in a pair of thick leather gloves. In his hands he clutched a heavy pair of tongs, a horseshoe glowing in their iron grip. A man larger than life stood beside him, his giant grin hidden beneath a woolly beard. The roar of the furnace rang in his ears and the smell of burning metal touched his nose. His chest swelled.

The image vanished. Gabriel groaned, finding himself on his knees, the wolf growling at his side.

He closed his eyes, searching for the picture, for whatever he had felt when it had come to life. *Was it a memory?*

They are escaping.

Gabriel swore, remembering his prey. He leapt to his feet, exhaustion forgotten. He still remembered one thing. He could see their faces with crystal clarity.

Kill the ones who hurt you!

****

Inken lay on the hard desert ground. The jagged rocks stabbed through her clothes and dug into her skin. The pounding in the back of her head was growing worse, leaving her thoughts jumbled and confused. Her mouth was as dry as the parched desert soil. A groan came rumbling from deep in her throat at the thought of water. Her muscles ached and her skin burned beneath the hot sun. She could no longer muster the strength to stand.

The shortcut across the desert had been a foolish move. No one came this way anymore, and certainly not alone. Yet the reward had been too tempting. Just three nights ago, the messenger pigeons had flown into Chole. Within hours the city's underground was alive with the news – of the reward offered for the head of the demon boy said to have burned Oaksville to the ground.

At first most had scoffed at the news. The letters must be a hoax; there was no demon, no boy, no attack on Oaksville. But other birds soon followed and the news spread that Oaksville had been attacked; first by magic, then by Baronian raiders. No one could say whether the city still stood, but the bounty stood regardless.

Inken had wasted a day dithering before she finally decided to pursue the bounty. Unfortunately, by then half the bounty hunters in the city were already out to find the 'demon boy,' leaving her far behind the pack.

She knew most would not dare the ride through the desert. The short cut would take at least a day off the ride, allowing her to comfortably overtake the other hunters. She scoffed at the superstitious fear which blinded the others, confident that with her longsword and bow she could fend off any trouble.

How arrogant she had been, how foolish. The childhood tales of the monsters that lurked in the desert should have warned her. The people of Chole made no secret of the dangers lurking outside their city walls.

It had not taken long for her to discover the truth behind those tales. She had never even seen the beast. The first she knew of the danger was when her gelding suddenly reared up on its hind legs, its steel-capped hooves flailing. With a terrified scream the horse bolted, leaving her clinging desperately to the saddle horn. Even then, the beast almost had them.

Just a few feet from the path, the beast exploded from the earth. It ran on all fours, short yellow fur bristling over its catlike body. Powerful muscles propelled it after them, its claws digging deep into the hard ground. On four legs, it was almost as large as her horse, with a mouth large enough to crush her skull. Giant teeth glinted as it roared, sending ripples of terror down her spine.

The chase seemed to last hours, with only inches separating the two beasts. Hungry jaws snapped at her gelding's tail. She spurred her horse on, although it hardly needed the encouragement.

Then, as quickly as it had appeared, the beast vanished.

Her horse ran on. Desperately she tugged at the reins, eager to slow their pace in the treacherous terrain. Here the ground was a perilous tapestry of rocks, scree and petrified trees. The gelding plunged onwards, oblivious to everything but its terror.

Suddenly, the horse collapsed beneath her and Inken was flying from the saddle. The earth rushed up to meet her. She raised her arms to protect herself, and then came the jarring thud of impact. She heard something go *crack*, followed by searing pain as rocks slashed and stabbed through the flesh of her stomach and chest. She tumbled head over heels, the rocky ground scraping skin from bone.

The horse screamed again, struggling to rise behind her. Inken shuddered with pain, a moan growing in her chest. She glimpsed the terrified animal from the corner of her eye. Its leg bent at a sickening angle.

Inken felt herself slipping away and gladly gave way to the abrupt relief of unconsciousness.

When she woke, the horse's screaming had ceased. She looked across to see its still body lying next to her, its glassy eyes staring into nothing.

Inken closed her eyes, willing strength into her shattered body. Summoning every ounce of her courage, she struggled to regain her feet. Agony lanced through her right arm and leg and she knew they were broken. The rest of her was a red and purple mess, as though the skin had been flayed from her body. Her nose throbbed and she reached up to twist it back into place. The cartilage gave a sickening crack, but the relief was almost immediate.

Somehow, she had pulled herself to her feet. Somehow, she had hobbled on her left leg back towards the road, evading the beasts for Gods only knew how long. Somehow, she had survived.

But now she was finished. She could no longer muster the strength to stand. The pain was unbearable, her energy long since melted away by the heat of the sun.

Her body still found the water for tears. *Fool,* she cursed herself. *How could you have been so arrogant?*

Lying helpless in the cooking sun, Inken waited for death. It didn't seem right for it to end like this. She had yet to reach her twentieth birthday. Of course, life was never fair. She knew that better than most. Fair would have been two loving parents, rather than a mother who abandoned her to an abusive father. The evil old man would be laughing now; he had always said she was nothing without him.

The clatter of hooves on rock came from off to her left. Her eyes shot open. She turned her head and squinted into the painful light. Two horses were riding past not five yards away, their riders talking softly in the dying light.

"Help!" Inken tried to shout, but her throat cracked and the word came out as a whisper. She swore silently to herself.

"Help me!" the call was louder this time. "Please!"

****

"Alastair, why did my magic only... awaken... when I

turned fifteen?" the question had plagued Eric for a while now.

"So late?" Alastair asked. He sat on a rock opposite Eric where they had stopped to rest the horses.

Eric nodded.

"Most develop earlier, but then that is in families with a long lineage of magic," he closed his eyes, his brow furrowed in thought. "Magic always awakens on the anniversary of our births, but which birthday depends on each individual and the environment they're exposed too. The more magic you come into contact with in your childhood, the faster your own will develop."

Eric shook his head, still coming to grasps with the intricacies of the mysterious force. "Okay."

Alastair stood, brushing crumbs from his cloak. "We're running short of water and supplies, but there is a spring ahead. If we make good time, we should be able to reach it by nightfall."

Eric rolled his shoulders and groaned. The riding was slowly growing easier, but his body still ached from the long hours in the saddle. "Alright then, well we're not getting any closer sitting here I guess."

They mounted up and rode on, pushing their horses to a fast trot. The rocky miles wore away beneath pounding hooves, as the sun slowly dropped towards the distant horizon. The land around them was silent and still. The burning sun stung their eyes, leaving them squinting into the distance in search of danger.

At last, the sun touched the horizon behind them, and Alastair slowed their pace to a walk. It would be easy in the lengthening shadows to make a mistake on the rough terrain.

"It won't be far now," Alastair reassured him.

Eric did not reply, drawing his horse to a stop. He

listened to the whisper of the wind through the rocks around them. He thought he had heard a cry. The leather reins scrunched in his hands. His eyes roamed the landscape, searching for movement. The creature's attack the night before was still fresh in his mind.

"Help me!" the call was so soft Eric would have missed it had he not stopped his horse.

"Help!" it came again.

He turned his head, trying to identify the source. Hairs prickled on the back of his neck as he considered the possibility of a trap. The voice was distinctly human though, *and female.* Yet he could see nothing amidst the tumbled rocks and petrified wood adjacent to the trail.

Eric shook his head, wondering if his mind was playing tricks. Then one of the rocks seemed to move and he realised he had been looking straight at her. The dull brown of her leather jacket and leggings blended in with the dirt and baked stone, camouflaging her into the desert.

"Alastair, wait!" he pulled on Briar's reins, sending the horse off the trail.

The young woman's hazel eyes followed him as he approached. Eric shuddered as he took in her injuries. He could not imagine the pain she must be suffering. Her bright red hair was thick with dirt and dried blood ran down her forehead and neck. Tears in her jacket revealed bloody wounds and purple bruises and her leg was twisted at a horrific angle. The relentless sun had burned the skin of her face bright red. Her eyes were swollen with exhaustion and her whole body shook as though she were outside on a winter's day.

Eric watched her struggle to sit up as he approached. He was shocked by the courage the feat must have taken. It was not enough though, and as Eric leapt from his horse she slid back to the ground. Her eyes closed as she slipped into unconsciousness.

Alastair dismounted behind him and the two crouched beside her. Alastair pulled his water skin from his belt and held it to her lips. Cradling her head, he trickled a small amount into her mouth.

After a few swallows she started to cough and Alastair pulled the skin back. "Don't speak, girl. Save your strength."

Eric pulled a blanket from his saddle and covered her, hoping it might help protect her from the sun. He wondered what horrific accident had befallen her. She carried no food or water and her only weapon was a knife strapped to her side.

Alastair gave her another gulp of water before capping the water skin. "That's enough for now. Anymore and you'll be sick."

"Thank you," somehow she managed a smile, her dried lips cracked and bleeding. "I'm Inken." Her eyes closed again.

"Eric, help me with her. We will have to be very careful, who knows what injuries she may have. I'll ride with her on my horse. We need to get her to the spring. She needs water and broth to replace the salts she's lost in the sun."

"Will she make it?"

"I don't know. Her best chance is if we can get her to the spring. It's not far now," they knelt either side of her and placed her arms over their shoulders. "Careful, this arm is broken. We'll need to do this very gently."

"What do you think happened to her?"

"We'll have to ask her when she wakes again. Now help me get her to Elcano."

Eric carefully took her weight on his shoulder. For a small woman she was heavy. He wondered again who she was, what she had been doing in the desert alone.

Together they managed to get her slung over Alastair's saddle. Alastair climbed up behind her, while Eric helped rearrange the limp woman so she would not fall. She did not stir throughout the ordeal.

Alastair took up his reins while Eric mounted Briar. He patted the horse's mane before they set off, knowing the horses needed the water as much as they did. They rode into the night, the horizon behind them stained red with the dying sun.

TWELVE

Eric poked restlessly at the fire with a stray piece of wood. Dust and sand had worked its way into every seam of his clothing and the rocky ground dug into his backside whichever way he sat. He was relieved to be free of Briar's bouncing saddle, but now he found himself on edge, his eyes constantly searching the darkness around them. He could only imagine what dread beasts might be staring back.

At least they had found the spring. A trickle of water ran down a nearby rock face and slowly gathered in a bowl of loose soil at its base. They had almost emptied the pool filling their water skins, and now Briar and Elcano stood patiently waiting for their turn to drink.

A rocky escarpment hemmed them in on three sides, hiding their campfire from prying eyes. The sun had set long ago, stealing away the world beyond the firelight. An eerie silence settled on the campsite, disturbed only by the crunching of their footsteps on the rocky ground. Eric's dread grew with each passing minute.

At least Alastair said they would arrive in Chole by noon the next day. He would not be sorry to see the last of the arid wasteland. Although the thought of entering the city was worrying in an entirely different way. Alastair had taught him the basics of magic, but he still knew nothing about controlling it.

The girl, Inken, lay opposite him, shivering by the fire. They had covered her with blankets and managed to feed her more water, but she had not stirred since they arrived. Her hair blazed red in the firelight, its glow intoxicating. The hard lines in her young face had softened with sleep.

They had cleaned the sand from the worst of her wounds and bound her broken limbs to branches they had scavenged from the long dead trees which scattered the desert. There was little more they could do until they reached Chole and found a healer.

Alastair sat stirring the pot of stew he had just taken from the fire. Earlier he had added the last of their food, a sprinkling of hard vegetables and salted pork. If Inken woke, she would need whatever they could get into her to restore what had been lost to the unforgiving sun.

Alastair placed the pot back over the fire. "It still needs some more time. I'm going to check our fire is properly hidden. I don't want any surprises this time; we might not get so lucky twice."

Eric chuckled softly. "Okay, I'll keep an eye on her. Be careful."

He watched Alastair disappear into the night and then returned his gaze to the young woman beside the fire. A thousand questions were bouncing around in his mind. What *was* she doing out here? While a few inches taller than him, she could not be much older than his own seventeen years. He looked closely at the burns marking her skin and shuddered. The only part of her left untouched was the fiery red hair, and even that was tangled and filthy.

With luck though, they would find a healer among Antonia's priests in Chole. The temples of the Earth were renowned for their healers; although whether the temple in Chole still survived was another matter. The Earth element held little sway in the Wasteland.

Eric added their last stick to the fire. Alastair had hacked the branches from one of the fallen trees. The heat and dust of the desert had turned the ancient logs the colour of rock, but beneath they were still wood, desiccated by time and heat into the perfect firewood.

"Who are you?"

Eric jumped, his reaction prompting a giggle from the pile of blankets. The laugh was rich and good-natured, but ended with a groan of pain. "Oh, I shouldn't have done that!"

Eric stood and walked around the fire to sit beside her. By the firelight, he saw one of the gashes on her face had split and was bleeding again. He offered her the water skin and then gently pressed a damp cloth to her face to stem the bleeding.

She grasped the skin and took a long swig. She sighed as she finished. "Water never tasted so good."

Eric removed the cloth as she took another mouthful. Then she handed it back, her eyes now sharp and alert. Eric could almost see the questions ticking over in her mind.

"Thank you, kind stranger," her big hazel eyes stared up at him. "May I ask who you are?"

Eric grinned. "My name is Eric and my old friend is Alastair. We're travelling to Chole. You're lucky we saw you as we passed."

Inken offered him her good hand, although it was still scratched and torn. Eric took it gently.

"Thank you, Eric. I owe you and Alastair my life. I'm Inken. I made a foolish mistake deciding to travel to Oaksville by the desert path. I was lucky my mare was able to outrun the beast that attacked us. Sadly, before I could stop her she tripped on the uneven ground, nearly killing the both of us."

Eric stilled at the mention of Oaksville. He scarcely heard the rest of the story, his heart sinking at the thought of breaking the news to her. He could already see the grief and tears on her face, and wondered who it was she had risked so much to visit.

Everything seemed to come back to that single, horrific mistake.

"I'm sorry, Inken. I don't know how to say this, but we came through Oaksville. There wasn't much left of the town," he spoke the words softly.

Inken nodded and her eyes closed tight with pain. "Argh, everything hurts. I know what happened to Oaksville. The town's Magistrate sent a letter. He offered a lot of gold for the head of the one who did it. I was planning on claiming it."

Eric's blood ran cold. He gaped, the muscles of his neck growing taught. He shivered, suddenly seeing Inken in another light. The lines of her face seemed to harden, a dark glint appearing in her eyes. He saw now the thick muscles of her arms and shoulders as those of a warrior, of a hunter.

His eyes flickered to the dagger at her side. Her fingers lingered near its hilt. He wished now they had disarmed her while she lay unconscious. An icy hand seized his heart. *What if she finds out who I am?*

He realised she was staring and that he had not said anything for some time. He gave himself a mental shake. "You are a brave woman. The wreckage that was left in Oaksville," he shook his head.

Inken chuckled. "I'm no longer sure if I was brave – or stupid. Trying to tackle the desert alone was certainly a bad move. I had given up hope when you appeared. I certainly don't have a chance in hell of claiming the reward now."

"Perhaps it's for the best. How could you have killed such a powerful demon?"

Inken absently flicked a strand of hair from her face. "Demon, Magicker, or mortal, an arrow from the shadows will kill most things."

Eric gulped, his voice deserting him.

Alastair's return saved him. He reappeared without warning, his footsteps somehow silent as he walked across the gravel. He sat down opposite them, letting a pile of firewood tumble to the ground.

"Hello, you must be Alastair," Inken greeted him.

Alastair smiled. "I am, and you are Inken."

She nodded. "So why are the two of you travelling to Chole?"

When Alastair did not answer, Eric spoke. "You'll have to weasel that out of Alastair, I'm just tagging along," he hesitated. "Perhaps you should get some sleep for now though," Eric no longer felt much like talking. Being around someone looking to kill him had robbed all the enjoyment from the conversation.

Moving away, he lay down on the hard ground and closed his eyes. The world seemed to rock beneath him. He struggled to ignore the queasy feeling in his stomach. Alastair had mentioned the motion of the horses could linger sometimes after a long ride. It would pass though – he only had to endure.

He heard Alastair move over to the fire and stir the pot of stew. The flames crackled as he added more wood to the fire. Eric licked his lips, stomach growling. He hoped the food would be ready soon.

His thoughts returned to the enigmatic Inken. Just thinking of her made his heart race. Beneath the burns and bruises, it was obvious she was a beautiful girl. And a very dangerous foe. Despite her seemingly agreeable nature, bounty hunters were notoriously ruthless. If she discovered who they really were, Eric had little doubt she would turn on them.

He found himself wondering whether they should just leave her in the desert. Then he shook his head, angry at the selfish thought. He could not leave an innocent girl to die, whether she wished to kill him or not. That would only make him as bad as the demon they thought him to be.

"It's ready," Alastair announced.

Eric opened his eyes and took the wooden bowl Alastair offered him. The thick stew gave off a rich aroma of meat and herbs, although there was little substance to it.

"Give it to Inken," he said.

Eric gave a reluctant nod and moved across to the injured woman. From the slow rise and fall of her chest she appeared to be asleep, but her eyes snapped open as he approached. She offered a smile when she saw him. "Ah, my hero returns. And with *fooa*. The two of you are resourceful, aren't you?"

Eric found his smile as he offered the bowl.

Inken reached out a hand to take it, then hesitated. Her cheeks flushed. "I'm not sure I can hold it," she opened her hands to show the raw flesh of her palms. She hesitated. "Do you… do you think you could help me?" her face turned crimson. This was a girl used to taking care of herself.

Eric felt his own face grow hot. Just sitting near the young woman made him nervous. Sweat trickled down his neck. A confusing string of emotions ran through his head. "I, I…" he stuttered.

"Please, Eric?"

Eric looked at her, lying there helpless, begging for his help. She had come so close to death in the desert and she was not out of the woods yet. Her broken arm lay limp at her side and he could see the muscles in her neck twitching with pain. The grazes on her hands were so deep you could almost see the bone.

He nodded at last, casting aside his doubts. "Okay."

Digging into the bowl, he offered her a spoonful of broth. It disappeared into her mouth. She closed her eyes and chewed, making even that simple task look to be an effort. However, it did not take long for her to finish, so he offered another mouthful.

Eric found himself smiling. The whole situation was surreal. Here he was, spoon-feeding a woman hired to kill him.

Her burns were almost invisible in the dim firelight. Eric studied her as she ate, finding himself torn. He searched for a hint of the killer in the glint of her eyes, or the sharp curve of her cheekbones. Yet all he could see was her injured beauty. He could not connect the girl before him with the image of a ruthless bounty hunter.

When she had finished the stew, Eric stood and returned to his own patch of gravel. Alastair offered him another bowl and Eric happily gulped it down. His stomach rumbled as he ate, grateful for the meal.

"Eat quickly, Eric. You'll need your strength. We have time for one more lesson before we reach Chole and I think we had better make good use of it."

"Ssh," Eric glimpsed at Inken to see if she had heard, but saw her eyes had closed.

Alastair waved a hand. "Don't worry about her. I waited a while outside the firelight and heard you talking. I slipped a pinch of sleeping herb into her bowl. She'll sleep through the night now."

Eric took a deep breath to calm his frayed nerves. "What do we do with her?"

Alastair shook his head. "Nothing. I don't believe she

has made any connection between us and her quarry. So long as we're careful, there shouldn't be any danger. Now finish that stew. We have some real magic to learn now."

Eric swallowed the last morsel and placed the bowl beside him. The meat had been tough and the vegetables tasteless, but even so he could feel the energy returning to his arms and legs. He hoped it would keep him going until they reached Chole.

Alastair walked from the firelight and into the night. Eric followed, eyes drawn to the deep shadows of the canyon. If any beasts were lurking, they had just moved into their territory.

Alastair stopped and faced him. "Okay. As you know, magic at its most basic level is controlled by the emotions. Fear, anger, love, hate; it will respond to each if not properly managed. To *harness* the power and bend it to our own will, you must discover how your magic and your emotions are linked. We achieve this through meditation."

"Meditation?"

"Meditation is a technique apprentices usually learn at a young age, which allows them to develop control of the mind and body. Eventually, it allows a Magicker to find the link between their emotions and magic, and summon their powers at will," he paused, his eyes growing unfocused. Around them pieces of gravel gently lifted into the air. "In other words, it will allow *you* to manipulate the weather, rather than your emotions."

"Right now I'd be happy just to stop myself losing control," Eric sighed.

Alastair smiled. "That will be a start. I hope with time you will be capable of far more than that. There are certain dangers to consider before then, but they are some way down the road. Now, let us begin. Sit down and cross your legs, laying your hands gently at your side," Alastair moved into the posture as he spoke.

Eric copied the old man, the hard desert gravel digging into his backside. Grimacing, he shifted until he felt more comfortable, then looked back to Alastair.

"Close your eyes and try to clear the thoughts from your mind. Take a deep breath and exhale slowly, until all the air has been emptied from your chest."

Eric closed his eyes and sucked in a mouthful of air. The muscles of his chest stretched and then compressed as he released the breath in a drawn out sigh. He repeated the exercise, smiling. This was easy. He wondered whether the old man was playing a joke.

"You're thinking, Eric," Alastair's voice broke across his thoughts.

Eric's eyes snapped open. "What?" he glared.

"Your eyes were flickering beneath your eyelids. Think of *nothing,* Eric. It's okay, most take a long time to master the practice. Try again."

Eric nodded, slightly shaken by Alastair's interruption.

Alastair stopped him again after another minute. "You're still thinking too much."

Eric sighed. His mind kept flickering from one thought to the next, unable to turn off. So much had happened in the last few days; it was all too much for him to simply set it aside.

"It can help to repeat a word each time you exhale."

"Like what?"

"Well, when I was an apprentice we were told to breath out 'ing'."

"I don't think that's even a word, Alastair."

The old man scowled. "Just try it. By focusing on something benign, you will find it easier to allow your other thoughts to fall away."

Eric grimaced. "Okay, I'll give it a go."

He closed his eyes again and breathed out, whispering 'ing' as he did so. In, out. In, out. In, out. His heart slowed and the tension began to fade from his shoulders. The word vibrated through his consciousness, his worries fading away before it. All sensation seemed to be drifting away on a sea of black.

I'm doing it, he exulted.

The thought shattered his concentration. He opened his eyes and grinned at Alastair. "I think I had it for a second there."

Alastair grinned and stood. "Good, keep practising then," he stretched his arms. "Call me if you need a hand, I won't be far away. I'm going to go keep watch."

The old man disappeared. Eric sat back and started again, convinced there would be no more surprise attacks. Alastair looked stronger than ever now, his injuries from both the city guards and the beast fully healed. Antonia's magic had done wonders.

Gradually he sank again into the calm centre of his mind, beyond the distractions of the world outside. It came faster this time. Now even the slow thump of his heart and stretch of his chest was disappearing into the vast ocean. He was left alone, cut off from sensation, from all sense of time. He drifted, separate from himself, a ghost within his own mind.

After a time, a memory surfaced once more. It was here amidst the tranquillity of his inner mind that he would find his magic. The thought infused him with purpose and he turned his inner eyes to the search.

A speck of blue light appeared in the distance. The radiance drew him towards it, slowly at first and then growing faster, until he became a blazing arrow. The speck grew to a lake of blue, stretching out before him, immense and overwhelming.

Instantly, he knew what it was. This was the source of his magic.

Its glow washed over him, its warmth intoxicating. Thin threads of light rose from the waters and drifted towards him. Tentative tendrils stroked his consciousness, gently wrapping about him. Eric felt a surge of power at each new connection. He could hear it calling to him, hungry. He sensed its need and felt his own desire flooding him. This force, this power, it could give him whatever he desired. He had only to use it.

He floated closer, the threads weaving around him, tiny hooks burying themselves in his mind. He no longer noticed, swallowed by the magic's call.

He toppled towards the lake below.

The light rose up to meet him, changing, becoming not a lake but the jaws of a great wolf. Teeth crashed shut as it swallowed him and the blue light crawled inside.

A rush of fear rose in Eric. Drowning, panicking, he tried to wake. Instead, the tendrils of magic wrapped more tightly about him, drawing him deeper into recesses of his mind.

Freed of its prison, the wolf blazed brighter, teeth glittering, hair bristling. It grew, even as Eric shrank in terror. He could feel it merging with him, its hunger eating away his resistance until they became one.

Eric opened his body's eyes, but they were no longer his own to control. The force within was master now, flowing through his veins and muscles, flooding them with power. His body tensed and he lifted to his feet.

His body looked around. Invisible wisps of magic stretched out around him, searching, seeking out power, seeking the storm. Over the rainforests to the west, they found it.

The storm clouds had been building through the day,

growing strong off the moist air. Their energy grew with each minute, water and air and dust smashing to create friction, igniting the lightning within. It waited to be unleashed.

The magic tore great chunks from the clouds, drawing it across the miles to where his body waited. It arrived with a crash of thunder and blast of light, as the lightning struck the ground. It rushed towards Eric, the crackling electricity scorching wherever it touched. Roaring, it gathered around him. Thunder boomed again and again, new bolts tumbling from the sky to join the conflagration.

Eric lifted his fists in exaltation, while deep within his mind a voice screamed. But the magic, the *power*, was everything now. Exhilarating, intoxicating, indestructible.

"Eric, stop!" a voice shouted over the thunder.

Eric raised an arm towards the speaker. No enemy would rob him of this power now. Blue lightning crawled along his arm, tingling where it touched. As it reached his fingertips, it leapt. A bolt of lightning shrieked through the night. He watched the shadowy figure dive from its path. Light flashed as it struck the cliff behind him, leaving only molten rock.

"Eric, listen to me. I am Alastair, your teacher!"

The name was familiar, but he shook his head. He needed no teacher now.

Another bolt chased Alastair into the darkness. The world was burning again, but now Eric breathed it in with relish, revelling in the smell. Yet still the man escaped him.

"Die!" he screamed into the night. Flashes of lightning shot from him, leaving tracks in his vision long after they passed.

"Eric, you must stop this. The magic will destroy you. Remember Oaksville!"

Eric broke off his attack. The word reverberated in his

mind, cutting a track right to his soul. Some small, forgotten part of him grabbed for it like a lifeline in the open sea. Sanity clawed its way back from the deepest recesses of his mind. Horror struck him as he took in the world around him. Bile rose in his throat.

Oaksville, Oaksville, Oaksville. The word rung out again and again, drawing him back.

Yet the magic rose again, burning away thought and reason. Eric gritted his teeth, determined to force it down, guilt eating away at fear. He would not let it consume him – he must tame this monster inside him.

The lightning around him flickered, but he could not let it go. Its heat radiated on his skin, stinging now where it touched, as his magic receded. If he released it now, it would destroy everything around him. Alastair and Inken would be helpless before it.

Eric sucked in a breath and with it drew the lightning to him. It danced over his skin, closer and closer, until it seemed his flesh itself was alive with electricity. Then, to his astonishment, it began to sink beneath. He did not stop to think.

He could not afford to hesitate, or the lightning might escape. Within he could still feel the lightning's sting. He gripped it and forced it deeper. He sank again into his inner mind, determined this time not to lose control and drew the lightning and magic with him. The power fought against him, the electric blue lightning merging with the magic. He drove them deeper, driven by instinct.

The lake appeared again. He directed the writhing ball of energy towards it and hurled it into the depths. Not a ripple broke as it disappeared beneath the calm surface.

Eric opened his eyes and collapsed. Footsteps crunched on gravel. He fought to move but found his muscles locked in paralysis. Not even his eyes would obey his weary mind.

He stared up at the stars in terror.

Alastair stood over him, his face grim. "Too close," he shook his head. "I am sorry, Eric. That was my fault. I have never seen anyone go so far, so fast. Magic is both friend and foe. Most do not discover this for years. But tonight you met the beast that lives within you and survived. Next time it will be easier. Rest now," reaching down, he closed Eric's eyes with a gentle hand.

THIRTEEN

Inken squinted into the noonday sun, blinded by its light, the heat searing into her burnt skin. Her face was the worst, the gashes and sunburn still fresh from exposure to the desert. Her cheeks throbbed, the ache of her broken bones dull by comparison. Sweat ran down her back. The air was suffocating.

A granite bridge stretched out before them, half a mile long. The old brick pavement was wide enough for five horses to ride abreast. Stone railings in the form of vines stood either side, worn smooth by the passage of time. Wind whistled between the bars.

Beneath the bridge stretched a crater almost two hundred feet deep and half a mile long. Around the edges, landslides had taken bites from the smooth crater walls. The bridge had stood strong through the years, but each year it cost more and more to maintain the old structure. The crater was all that remained of the great Lake Chole.

Inken glanced across at Eric and Alastair. Alastair had walked for the entire day, leading their horses across the perilous countryside seemingly without fear. He still looked fresh, almost excited, as they stood now so close to the city. For that she was thankful – neither herself nor Eric were well enough to walk. Between her injuries and Eric's sickness, they had been lucky to have the two horses.

They stopped at the foot of the bridge. No one spoke; in fact, no one had spoken all morning. The tension was unsettling – but she was not eager to break the silence. She had woken to a throbbing headache, her vision coming in and out of focus. Her thoughts had been sluggish, but she knew enough to realise she had been drugged. It took almost an hour for the symptoms to wear off.

Then there were the signs she had noticed around the campsite. The air reeked of smoke – and not from the regular campfire. Conspicuous scorch marks dotted the cliffs around the camp, even turning the rock molten in places. Something had happened during the night and she would put gold on it having something to do with Eric's illness.

The young man had barely stirred all morning. Alastair had not bothered to wake him as he packed up the camp or as he helped lift Inken into his saddle. Eric's eyes flickered as Alastair lifted him onto the other horse, but he had hardly made a noise. Inken had rarely seen such exhaustion, but a chilling suspicion had taken root. She'd heard Magickers sometimes experienced extreme exhaustion after performing great works of magic.

She almost dismissed the thought out of hand. The young man had been so kind, so innocent. Yet *something* had happened while she slept – and the signs around their campsite seemed all too similar to the description given of Oaksville. Their story did not add up and Inken could not ignore the signs.

Was Eric the boy she hunted, the demon of Oaksville?

Yet he had been the one who'd seen her in the desert, the one who had helped her, *saved her.*

Inken thrust the thoughts to the back of her mind,

focusing on the present. No longer able to stand the silence, she spoke. "This bridge is a reminder of our folly."

Eric stirred, twisting in the saddle to look at her. He seemed more alert now. "What do you mean?"

"The original bridge was destroyed when Archon laid siege to Chole. Afterwards, it took years for Chole to recover enough to rebuild. Almost a decade had passed before construction started. By then the rains had retreated behind the volcanoes and the lake had started to shrink."

"And they still built it?"

Inken nodded. "The change was so gradual; people were convinced it would be temporary. So they built the bridge, and here it stands traversing barren rock, testament to their ignorance."

The silence resumed and Inken looked away. She already missed the easy conversation of the night before. *Something* had changed.

Alastair tugged on the reins and led them out onto the bridge. Inken snuck a glance at Eric as they drew side by side. He sat straighter in his saddle now, although there were dark rings circling his eyes.

"What will you do in Chole, Eric?" she asked.

Eric was staring over the rails, at what by now would be at least a hundred foot drop. He shivered and looked away from the edge. "I'm not sure. I guess we'll take you to the temple first. Hopefully there are still healers there who can help you. That and find some food. I'm starving."

Inken's stomach growled in agreement. She could feel her injured strength shrinking with hunger. She prayed to Antonia that those at the temple would be able to heal her injuries. The two of them had done their best patching her up, but without a healer it would take months to recover. Even then, she would be marked by horrible scars for the rest of her life. She trembled at the thought. She had never been vain, but even so…

"What about you, Inken?" Eric ventured a question. "What will you do?"

What will *I do?* She asked herself. *Claim the bounty?* Aloud, she said. "When I am healed there are some friends I must visit, to let them know I am back and alive. I expect they will all enjoy a good laugh when they hear about my folly. At least it will make a good story."

Eric chuckled. "I'm sure they will be happy to see you."

Inken nodded. "Perhaps. How long will you be staying in the city?"

Eric glanced at Alastair. "I'm not sure. Alastair hasn't said."

Inken had quickly realised it was the old man who made the decisions but was surprised at how little Eric knew. *Perhaps Eric is his unwitting pawn*, she thought. *Or perhaps they are just two weary travellers*, she argued with herself.

"What are the people here like, Inken?" Eric ventured.

"They mostly keep to themselves. The desert has made them hard; they do not tolerate any weakness from their own. But they do like outsiders – the city would not survive without them. The only resource we have are a few gold and sulphur deposits in the hot springs around the mountains; everything else we buy from the trade caravans that come through every month."

The city walls loomed above them as they reached the end of the bridge. The wind had worn the stones smooth and cracks riddled the mortar holding them in place. Elsewhere the rocks had worked their way free, leaving pitted holes across the smooth surface.

The bridge finished at a gaping abyss in the wall where the gates had once stood. Now the tunnel stood open, the great wooden doors long gone. No one had cared to replace them. Timber was expensive here and the desert protected

Chole now.

A man stood within the shadow of the tunnel, garbed in the blue and black of the city guard. Despite the shade, he was sweating through his chainmail and half helm. He held a spear loosely in one hand, an iron shield in the other. A sword was strapped to his waist.

The steel rings of his mail chimed as he moved to bar their way. He held his spear defensively before him. "Stop. what is your business in Chole?" he did not seem too interested in the answer.

Inken grimaced. As much as they tried, that was the way of things in Chole. Order was slowly evaporating in the Dying City. As the population shrank, more and more turned to crime to make a living. Meanwhile, the city guard dwindled. The city's underworld no longer had much to fear from the Magistrate.

"My name is Alastair, and this is Eric. We found this woman, Inken, in the desert. She's been badly injured, so we're taking her to Antonia's temple to be healed."

The guard glanced at Inken. She didn't recognise him, thankfully. It would be bad enough telling the tale herself without word of her folly spreading ahead of her.

One look at her face was enough to convince the guard. He waved them through without another glance.

Inken sighed as the shadow slid across her face. The relief from the sun was instant, soothing her burning skin. Unfortunately the stifling heat remained.

On the other side of the wall the tunnel opened out into a short street. Buildings hemmed them in on all sides, each in a state of disrepair. Those who lived closest to the walls were generally the poorest and here the houses were little better than flea ridden hovels. Open sewers ran along the roadway, carrying with them the stench of human waste. Garbage littered the streets. A pack of dogs looked up from a pile as they approached, then retreated down the street. The rats ignored them.

They rode deeper into the impoverished city, seeing little of its human inhabitants. The few they did glimpse moved about their business quickly, ignoring the strangers. Others sat hopeless against the grimy walls, their hands stretched out in silent entreat.

As they passed a homeless man who had lost both of his arms, Inken caught a glimpse of Eric's face. His eyes were wet with tears, his gaze lingering on the desperate man as they passed. His mouth opened, but no words emerged.

His reaction only added to her confusion.

They moved on, leaving the poorest districts behind. Dried out fountains appeared, although Inken had never seen them run. They stood as another silent reminder of Chole's past. The muddy road turned to brick, but even here the passage of time and people had worn deep grooves into the ground. The piles of garbage shrank. Unfortunately, the stench remained.

Alastair led them confidently through the maze of streets. Inken watched him closely. It was clear he had been here before, probably many times. Chole's streets were a rabbit warren at best and few other than locals could find their way confidently. Landmarks were rare – one dead garden looked much the same as another.

The city seemed empty and they made good time. Inken was thankful it did not take them long to reach the temple of Antonia. Here at last was a building that had resisted the erosion of time. Marble columns as thick as the giant redwoods to the west towered over them, bordering the stone steps which lead up to an outdoor patio. Overhead stone eaves rested atop the pillars.

Priests garbed in light green robes sat in quiet meditation in the shade of the courtyard, while behind them the pillars gave way to the walls of the inner temple. The quiet chanting of a hymn drifted on the breeze. A priest waved to them from his seat at the bottom of the stairs and said he would take care of their horses.

Inken stared up the steps, heart sinking. They were only two dozen in number, but even so, they were well beyond her strength. It took a shoulder from Alastair and her own grim determination to make the climb.

Her heart warmed a little when she noticed Eric following them up. It made her feel slightly better to see he also needed a hand from a monk to reach the top. She had enjoyed his quiet company, whoever he really was.

They made their way through the meditating monks, drawing the eyes of a few curious watchers. Inken's shoulders were tense with anticipation. If there was no healer here, she would have to make do with the services of a doctor. One would probably be among the priests, but she knew which option she preferred.

Another monk stood waiting for them in the doorway to the inner temple. His robes were edged with gold, with white bands adorning the sleeves and collar. A purple diamond patch on his right breast marked him as a doctor. He offered a friendly smile as they approached, wrinkles appearing around his amber eyes. His hair was jet black streaked with grey.

His smile faded as they reached him, a concerned frown taking its place. "Welcome, travellers. My name is Michael. Please, come this way," he spoke in a warm voice. His eyes lingered on Inken before he added, "Quickly."

They followed him through the doorway. Inside was dark, lit only by a scattering of candles, and the air was thick with incense. The scent carried the whisperings of fruit and flowers, a rare offering in the desert city. The floor was covered by a worn green carpet, which led to a simple wooden alter at the end of the room. Citizens and priests knelt on the ground around the room, offering their silent prayers to the Goddess Antonia. In the far corner a young man played the piano, the gentle music welcoming them into the sanctuary.

Michael led them to a small door beside the alter and through into a corridor. Doors lined the hallway on the left, while on the right windows opened up onto a central courtyard. Inken shrugged off Alastair's hand and hobbled across. She peered through the panes in astonishment.

The building encompassed a courtyard at its centre. In the courtyard was a garden, filled with the green of life. Plants grew from soft, moist earth, defying the fierce heat of the sun. They thrived amidst the brick walls, trees and vines thrusting from the earth, ignorant to the desert without.

Inken stared, feeling a new respect for the priests who lived here. To be able to grow anything in Chole was an accomplishment, and they had achieved far more than that.

Michael coughed, drawing her attention away from the miracle beyond the glass. They continued along the corridor, Inken snatching glimpses of the garden as they moved. She wished she had visited this place earlier. She had never paid much attention to the religions of the Three Nations, but perhaps she needed to reconsider.

She was thankful it did not take long for Michael to find the room he sought. He pulled open a plain door and beckoned them inside.

Within was a simple room without any decoration or furniture. A man sat alone on the tiled ground, watching them with pure white eyes. Skin hung in folds from his face and long locks of grey hair tumbled down his back. A narrow scar stretched across his face. His arms were frail and marked by old battles. He wore robes similar to

Michael's, except where a pink diamond had replaced the purple.

Inken sighed in relief, recognising the mark of a healer.

"Welcome, Alastair. It has been a long time," the healer's voice rasped like gravel.

Alastair grinned. "So it has, Elynbrigge. I fear my time has been rather occupied lately. *She* has had me dancing to the old tunes."

"Ay, and without luck I have heard."

Alastair nodded. "But I hear you might help me with that."

Elynbrigge smiled. "Ay, I can."

Inken looked from one old man to the other, a dozen questions jostling for her attention. *How ao these two know each other?*

Michael was clearly just as confused. His frown had grown as the two greeted one another like old friends, and it took him a moment to regain his composure. "Elynbrigge has only been here a few weeks, but he is a great healer. You are very lucky, young lady. Our temple is not usually so fortunate to host someone of Elynbrigge's talents."

"Nor will it for much longer, I am afraid," Elynbrigge added.

Michael nodded, an edge of sadness in his eyes. Inken could understand his disappointment. It was clear the priests were dedicated to preserving the Goddess' temple. It must sting their pride to lack anyone with healing magic.

"Now, Alastair, I am afraid you will have to wait just a while longer. First, I shall attend to this young lady. I can feel her pain from here. Please, miss, sit down."

Michael helped Inken to sit before the ancient man. Her broken leg made even this simple act a struggle. She tried to sit with her good leg beneath her in support and the broken one stretched out in front of her. She used her good arm to hold herself straight, cradling the other close to her body.

Elynbrigge laughed. "Michael, her discomfort is screaming in my ears. Please, young lady, you may lie down. The others can clear out if there is not enough room."

Inken sighed in relief, stretching out on the cool tiles. "Thank you. My name is Inken," she added.

"My pleasure, Inken," Elynbrigge replied. "Now, to business. Your injuries are quite severe, but they are within my ability to heal. It will be painful, however, and time consuming. You will need to be brave, and patient."

"It's okay, I can take it," she glanced over at Eric and Alastair. "Thank you for saving me. I owe both of you my life. If you ever need my help, you need only ask."

She closed her eyes then, wondering where the words had come from and unable to look them in the face. Yet she had meant them. Whoever they were, they *had* saved her life, and one should always pay their debts.

"It was our pleasure, Inken. Perhaps we will see each other again. We shall leave you to your healing," Alastair turned to Elynbrigge. "We will talk soon, old friend. I will return after we have made ourselves comfortable."

Elynbrigge nodded in return.

Alastair waved goodbye and left the room. Eric moved to follow but turned back at the doorway. "I hope we do meet again, Inken. In better times though. Take care," he flashed a gentle smile as he slipped out the door.

Then he was gone and Inken felt suddenly, unexpectedly alone.

"Brace yourself, Inken. We begin."

****

Eric stared up at the pale ceiling, wondering at the feel of a bed beneath him. He could not remember how long it had been since he had slept in a real bed. It wasn't a very soft bed, but compared to hay, hammocks and the rocky ground, it felt like heaven. He closed his eyes, wanting the peace of sleep but knowing it would not come. A restlessness had come over him as they left the temple, one he could not shake.

Outside the sun was setting on the Dying City. There was no mystery as to where that nickname had come from. Their second storey room looked out over empty streets. Most merchants had already packed away their wares, surrendering the city to the unscrupulous night. A scattering of guards still patrolled, but Eric suspected they could do little to control the city's denizens once darkness descended.

He hoped the inn would prove a safe haven, standing proud as it did amidst the abandoned buildings and hovels. The bar downstairs was well lit and decorated with old wooden chairs and tables, giving it a homey feel. The keeper had unlocked the door cautiously, but welcomed them with a smile when he recognised Alastair. He offered them their pick of the rooms, with Alastair finally settling on one that suited him.

The room held two single beds and a small table and chairs, which sat before the large double window. The tiled floor offered some cool relief from the heat outside. The room smelt of dust and old cloth, but the thick wooden door ensured little noise could be heard from downstairs. They had draped their saddlebags over the foot of their beds, leaving the horses to the inn's stable hand.

Eric's thoughts turned to Inken. He had been unable to shake her from his head since they left the temple. Images flashed through his head: the moonlight reflecting off her soft curves, her gentle smile as she looked at him, the cool glint of the killer in her eyes. He pictured her slipping through the night, bringing the soft kiss of death to her foes.

He groaned, hands running through his hair. None of this mattered any longer. Despite its poverty, the city was huge and Alastair had not told her where they would be staying. And she still did not know who he was. At least, he hoped she didn't.

The noise from downstairs was gradually growing louder as the dining room and bar filled. His stomach rumbled and he guessed it was probably almost time for dinner. Alastair would be waiting for him.

He rolled off the bed and pulled himself to his feet. Stretching, he fought down a groan. His exhaustion that morning had shocked him. His muscles felt as though he had run ten miles, gotten to the end, then turned around and ran it again. The ache had begun to fade, but Alastair still had not told him what had happened. The old man was reluctant to give answers where others could overhear.

He pulled open the heavy door and turned left down the hallway, searching for the stairs. Their room was the last in the corridor and he did not appreciate the extra distance. No doubt Alastair had his reasons. He grabbed the railings as he descended, staggering his way down to the first landing. Each step sent a jolt up his shaking legs, his knees threatening to give way.

At the bottom he pushed through the double doors into the diner. The room was already half full and the last of the tables were going quickly. Waitresses threaded their way between the tables, balancing plates of food and great mugs of beer in outstretched hands. The floor was old oak, worn smooth by the passing of patrons and scratched by moving chairs. Behind the bar, three men stood serving those customers looking to quench their thirst after a long day's work. The rich aroma of stewed meat and spilled ale filled the air.

The roar of voices throbbed in his ears, but the prospect of food drew him deeper into the crowd. He moved among the tables, his gaze sweeping the room for Alastair. He had promised to meet him here for dinner. Eric found the old man near the back, sitting at a small table by the windows. Eric sank into the opposite chair with a sigh of relief.

Alastair grinned across at him. "About time you showed up. I was afraid I'd have to eat yours for you," he gestured at the large bowls of stew sitting on the table. Eric glimpsed chunks of beef and potato mixed with carrots and green vegetables of some sort. His stomach growled again.

He licked his lips, not needing any further encouragement. He took a spoon and started gulping down the hot food. It had been a long time since they'd enjoyed a proper meal. The spices in the stew were unfamiliar and after a few mouthfuls his tongue began to burn. He stopped to swallow some water, his eyes watering. By the time he'd emptied the bowl he was sweating heavily. Eric glared across the table as the old man chuckled in amusement.

Eventually a waitress came to clear the table and Alastair slid a few silvers across in payment. Eric swallowed hard when he saw the price. Apparently, food did not come cheap in the Dying City.

Together they stood and made their way back up the stairs. When they reached their room Alastair unlocked the door, then stood aside as Eric stumbled inside and collapsed onto his bed.

Eric gathered his strength and asked the question that had been eating at him all day. "Okay, I think I've waited long enough. What the hell happened last night?"

Alastair stood still, staring out the window. "You tell me."

Eric sighed, thinking again of the insanity in the desert. "It was as though my magic was alive, like some whole other consciousness. Its power was… irresistible."

Alastair sat down on the opposite bed, nodding. "What you achieved last night usually takes months. I seriously underestimated you," he paused. "Perhaps the way you've tapped into it in the past helped. Either way, it is a dangerous thing, a Magicker's first conscious contact with their magic. I am sorry, I should have warned you."

Eric shivered, remembering the icy grip of the magic encasing his consciousness, of something *else* taking control of his body. He recalled the *power*, the terrible craving to unleash it.

"What makes it so dangerous?" it did not seem fair, that he finally had a way to control the curse within, yet still it sought to destroy him.

"Magic is not an inert force. It lives to escape, desperate to break free from its prison and take control of its host. Last night you touched it, unprotected, and it struck back. Without the right preparation, you never stood a chance."

"I could have killed you," the thought terrified him.

Alastair nodded. "That was my fault."

Eric looked up to see the old man smiling. "*How do I control it?*"

"You master your fear. That is its only weapon against you. If you do not fear it, your magic cannot harm you."

Eric stared. He had never experienced such terror as when the wolf appeared. It was as though his fear had turned to pure energy, fed by his magic. How could he conquer such a beast?

"Eric," Alastair interrupted his thoughts. "Do you know what you did there, at the end?"

He shook his head.

"You drew the lightning into yourself," Alastair

whispered.

Eric shrugged. "I didn't know what else to do. If I released it, it would have killed you."

"Such an ability is incredibly rare. I have only heard tales of those who could draw aspects of their element into themselves. Many believe it to be only legend. It is an extraordinary ability. You should be able to summon that lightning from within, whenever you might need it."

Eric allowed himself a smile. He doubted he would ever find such a skill useful, but Alastair's enthusiasm was amusing. The room fell into a comfortable silence. He closed his eyes, feeling the gentle pull of sleep. A final thought came to him. "Alastair, what would have happened, if I hadn't come back?"

"Your magic would have sucked your life force dry. Your powers are limited and your magic was converting massive amounts of energy into magic. That is why you could barely move afterwards. A few minutes more and you would have died – or at least your soul would have. Your body would have lived on, controlled by your magic. That is how true demons are made, Eric."

Eric drew a deep, shuddering breath. He tried to control the quivering of his body and failed. His heart hammered in his chest and his stomach clenched tight as iron. Horror rippled through him.

Alastair lay down on his own bed. "Good night, Eric."

It was a long time before Eric slept.

FOURTEEN

The room was sweltering. Eric threw off his sheets and looked around, spying the telltale glow of daylight seeping beneath the curtains. Through fuzzy eyes he saw Alastair's bed was empty. He groaned, his body still stiff and sore. But if Alastair was gone, the morning must be growing late.

He crawled out of the bed and stumbled across to the window. Sunlight flooded into the room as he threw open the curtains. He groaned again, his sleepy eyes blinded by the light. The sun was high in the sky, almost noon. Eric was not surprised. He'd lain awake half the night, willing himself to sleep. And when he finally had, blue flames and demons stalked his dreams.

At least he felt better than the morning before. His arms still felt like lead weights, but the sting in his muscles was fading. Cramp threatened his legs as he stood, but receded after a few moments.

Stretching his arms, he pulled on a fresh shirt. His stomach grumbled. Looking around he saw a handful of silver coins on his bedside table. Presuming Alastair had left them for him, he swept them up and headed for the door. It still took an effort to reach the bottom of the stairs, but he made it safely through the big wooden doors at the bottom and into the diner.

Lunch was still an hour away, but the aroma of roasting meat filled the inn. The scent set his stomach rumbling. The few other occupants ignored Eric as he made his way to the bar. He hoped he would be able to get an early meal, before the place became too crowded.

Seating himself on one of the barstools, he waved to the bartender. As the man approached he realised it was the inn's owner. He smiled when he saw Eric, showing his yellowed teeth.

"You look like you're feeling better today, young man," he observed.

Eric smiled back. "A little. I'll feel better still with a bit of food though," he slid the coins onto the counter. Alastair had not mentioned the price of the dinner last night, but Eric guessed lunch would be no cheaper.

The innkeeper laughed. "No doubt. I'll see if I can find you some lunch then," he took two of the coins and handed the others back. He disappeared into the back room.

Eric slumped against the counter as he waited. Through the windows he could see the street outside, baked dry by the harsh sun. The reflection off the pale bricks was so bright it hurt his eyes. The air was still, heat radiating through the air like a sickness. A trickle of sweat ran down Eric's back, leaving his clothes sticking to his skin.

A few minutes later a waitress placed a plate of hot food in front of him. Eric picked up his fork and knife and attacked the tender steak. Gravy ran off the meat into the mashed potatoes and boiled vegetables. Eric shovelled his way through the food, eager to ease the ache in his stomach. He felt a pang of disappointment when he scraped the last crumbs from his plate.

Eric licked his lips, thoughts drifting over the last few

days. He was surprised to find himself smiling. The guilt of Oaksville still weighed on him, but despite the twists and danger, there had actually been good moments. The old man might be quiet company, but it was better than the exile Eric had suffered for so long. Then there was the enigma of Inken and the confusion which swept over him whenever he thought of her.

His life was changing so quickly he could scarcely believe it. In less than a week he had gone from fugitive to apprentice Magicker. He had met a man over a hundred years old, a bounty hunter hired to kill him, and the Goddess Antonia herself.

Yet Alastair's purpose remained a mystery. Where was the old man now?

I should be helping him, the thought leapt into his head. Alastair had saved him, lifted him up instead of leaving him for dead. He had put a name to his curse, taught him about magic. Eric owed him his life. He just hoped he could find some way to repay him.

The noise at the bar was beginning to grow as people filled the room for lunch. Deciding it was time to leave, Eric rose from his seat and left through the oaken doors.

Upstairs he quickly found himself with nothing to do but wait for Alastair's return. Outside the air shimmered with heat and only a trickle of human traffic still flowed through the streets. Eric fanned himself with his hand, wondering how the people here could cope with such temperatures. Why did they stay, knowing their city was coming apart at the seams. Eric felt a deep respect for their courage, to toil on against such adversity.

He thought again about his magic. Goosebumps shivered down his neck as he remembered the night in the desert. It had left a terror in him, one that lurked just beneath the surface. He could not ignore it.

Alastair had promised his magic would be a gift. The old man had lied. Every day it appeared more and more the curse he had always believed it to be. Magic it might be, but it was no less perilous for the name. His dread grew as he imagined what could have happened if he had not regained control, if it had swallowed him.

He remembered the ruins of Oaksville. Shuddering, he closed his eyes as the guilt came rushing back. The dead still came to him when he slept, their eyes accusing, demanding vengeance. He must redeem himself – must take the opportunity Antonia offered. Yet how could he help anyone, unless he could master his magic.

A tremor ran through his body. The notion would not go away. He could not change the past, but he might still change his future. Without magic, he could spend an eternity righting wrongs and it would never be enough. With it, he might just be able to make a difference. If only he could overcome his fear.

A memory leapt unbidden from the depths of his mind. He had been swimming in the river near his house when a strong current dragged him under. It took all of his energy to pull himself back to the surface. The undercurrent threatened to drag him back down and with water filling his mouth he had made one final lunge for the bank. His hand had found an overhanging root. With the last of his strength he had pulled himself onto the bank.

When he finally made it home he had found his father and sobbed the story to him.

"I was so scared, dad. I'll never go swimming in the river again," he had finished.

"Why, Eric? You have always loved the water. Why let one bad experience ruin that? Next time, you'll be more careful."

Eric remembered the terror then, sapping away his

courage. "I can't dad, I'm afraid."

His father had sensed his shame at his admission. He crouched down and took him by the shoulders. "There is no shame in fear, Eric. Fear is natural. We are all afraid at times. But you must not run from fear. If you do, it becomes a beast that will devour you. Real men take their fear and learn from it. Do not feed the beast, Eric, instead you must make it your own," he stood. "Come."

"Where?"

"To the river."

Eric smiled at the memory. He had swum again that day, and many times since. The fear had still been there, but each time it grew less. His father would tell him to face it now too, not run from it. He knew what he had to do. Today would be his first step towards redemption. He only hoped he was strong enough for the task.

Closing his eyes, he sat back and began to meditate. It took a long time for the chaos within to clear. He persisted, determined to put the last few days behind him, for a while at least. One by one, the worries he had brooded over fell away as his thoughts flowed inwards. The darkness of his inner consciousness rose all around him.

He flinched as the first tendrils of magic touched him. Its voice whispered in his mind, its lure sinking into the recesses of his conscious. Terror rose in his throat, but he crushed it down. Eric summoned his courage.

Light flooded his consciousness. The pool of magic filled his vision, banishing the dark. Yet here he did not fear the darkness – the light was far more treacherous. When he touched it, the wolf would come. Could he tame it?

Eric gritted his teeth. He had come too far for second thoughts. He had to do this. If he ran now, he might never stop. He braced himself, then stepped off the ledge into the pool.

For the longest time, nothing happened. Then, slowly, the light began to shimmer and change, drawing in upon itself. Legs clawed their way into existence, lightning rippling along each limb. Gradually the wolf took shape. The beast snarled, teeth snapping, its monstrous image filling his mind.

Eric shivered. The wolf took a step forward, towering over him. His courage began to crack, his fear shining through. His defences were crumbling. Eric tensed, preparing to flee.

You must not run from fear, Eric, his father's words echoed in his mind. They shot through him and his heart surged in response. He relaxed and looked back at the wolf, his fear slipping away like water between his fingers.

The wolf growled, yet as Eric watched it seemed to shrink. His soul swelled, feeling its power fall away. He approached it, seeing through the wolf to the magic at its heart. *His* magic. The magic he needed to save Chole.

He towered over the wolf now. It nipped at his heels, no more threatening than a fly to a giant. He smiled to himself and reached down to catch it.

Power flooded him, but this time it rose at *his* command. He was master now. Gone was the lust, replaced by his determination to use it for good.

If only he knew how. Sensing the magic building within him, he thought back to when his magic had taken control. It had reached *outside* of him to summon the storm. Could he do the same?

Eric looked to the sky, imagining himself amidst the cloudless heavens. His mind spun and he felt the weight of his body vanish. He opened his eyes and watched the rooftops of Chole fall away beneath him. His soul soared upwards, the magic branching out around him in search of his Element.

For a while he drifted, his purpose forgotten. He had never felt anything like this, never seen the world in such a way. All physical sensation was left behind – hunger, pain, and exhaustion were gone, left below with his body.

Eric felt the arid air blowing around him, its heat sucking life from the land. It sapped at his strength as well. Death lingered with its touch. It was time to put an end to it.

Gathering up his magic, he raced east, sensing the gathering of storm clouds in the distance. Their power called to him, guiding him over desert and volcanic peaks. A ripple passed through him as he flew across the last of the mountains and the sickness vanished from the air. He pushed on.

The ocean was close now, the storm clouds waiting. They raged over the dark waters, wind driving great waves to batter the rocky coast. Trees bent beneath its onslaught, the air filled with torn branches and flying leaves. Precious rain fell on salty seas.

Again Eric drew on his memory of the night in the desert. His magic had formed hooks to draw the storm to him. He would do the same.

The clouds beneath him glowed blue with his magic. Claws formed, sinking into the hurricane, while lines wrapped their way around the dark clouds. Wisps of cloud slipped from his grasp and seeped away, and the storm railed against him. Eric tightened his grip, determined.

With a surge of energy, he started to pull. The storm began to move, slowly at first, then picking up speed. Leaving behind the ocean that had born it, Eric drove it across the forests and rivers. He had no sense of time, but felt his strength beginning to fade.

Finally, the storm reached the mountains. There they stalled and he felt an invisible barrier pushing back against him. The rain would go no further.

Eric would not give in. Gritting his teeth, he drew on more magic. Power poured through his spirit and into the storm. He pulled harder, the air crackling with pure energy, the magic giving him strength.

The air screeched, sparks flying within the clouds. Lightning flashed through the barrier. The storm shot forwards, wheeling across the volcanoes of Chole. Eric heard a faint tinkling of glass, as if something had shattered, but there was no more time to pause. The storm had passed the mountains and was rushing now towards Chole. Rain was on its way.

Back in his room, Eric's soul crashed back into his body. He opened his eyes. Agony lanced through his head. He lay back on the bed, embracing the pain, as a grin spread across his face. He had faced the beast and conquered his fear. Nothing was beyond him now.

Sleep beckoned. This time, there were no dreams.

****

The door slammed. "Thank Gods," a voice shouted.

Eric jerked awake. He looked around wildly as Alastair stalked into the room. The old man towered over him, his face dark with anger. Veins popped in his neck and his eye twitched. He reached down and grasped Eric by the front of his shirt, hauling him from the bed.

"What were you *thinking?*"

Eric gasped for words, fighting for breath as his collar bit into his neck. His mind was still foggy with sleep and he struggled to understand Alastair. "Wh… What?"

"What? *What? You damn well know what!* You summoned

your magic!" he added an expletive at the end.

A strange calm descended on Eric. He had no idea how the old Magicker had found him out, but it did not matter now. He had cast the dice and, against all odds, had succeeded. "I had to do it, Alastair. Otherwise, the fear would have only grown. How did you even know?"

Alastair shook his head, his expression unreadable. Gently, he set Eric back on the bed. "Every Magicker in the city would have felt such a massive expenditure of power. When I felt it, I thought... I thought the worst had happened."

Eric looked up at the old man, seeing the red in his eyes and the dark rings beneath them. His mouth was a tight line and the lines of his face had deepened. Alastair was exhausted, and the fright Eric had given him had only added to his burden.

Neither spoke. Eric glanced out the window, surprised to see night had fallen. Then, to his pleasure, he noticed a trickle of water running down the glass and heard for the first time the pattering of raindrops on the roof. Light from the inn reflected off falling raindrops.

Eric smiled in satisfaction, taking heart from the sight. It was raining in Chole and he had faced his fear. That was well worth the fresh pain sweeping through his body.

"You need to understand, Eric, just how dangerous magic is when used recklessly. You have no idea the destruction you could have caused were things to go wrong."

Eric turned to meet Alastair's gaze. "You're wrong, Alastair. I know the risks better than anyone. I have lived with them for years."

"Then why did you do it?"

"Because I had too. My fear had mastered me, unmanned me. If I allowed it to fester, it would have destroyed me. And I knew I could make a difference here, if only I had the courage. And I did, just look!" he pointed out the window.

Alastair closed his eyes and sighed. Eric waited for him to argue. The old man shook his head and then smiled. "Yes, you did. Chole will celebrate this day for many years to come. I hope that it lasts. Jurrien tried and failed to do the same a century ago. Perhaps Archon's curse has weakened over time."

"Perhaps. I felt something break when I drew the storm over the mountains."

"I am glad you proved to yourself you could be master to your magic, Eric. But this isn't the end to your learning. Your magic can still be treacherous, even when you intend to use it for good. Please, *please*, refrain from using it when I am not around. And I would leave it for the next few days too," he waved at the rain falling outside. "Such a feat will have emptied your pool of magic and anything more will be drawing on your own life force."

Eric laughed. "Deal," he paused. "But I want you to take me with you tomorrow."

Alastair frowned. "Why?"

"Whoever you're looking for, I want to help you."

Alastair fell silent and for a moment Eric thought he would refuse. "Okay. But you will need your strength. Let's get something to eat," he stood and pulled Eric to his feet.

Eric stumbled, his legs refusing to take his weight. He grasped Alastair's arm to keep from falling. "I don't suppose you could bring a plate back here for me?" hungry as he was, he knew how painful the trip downstairs would be.

Alastair laughed. "Not a chance. You did something foolish and now you have to pay for it. Besides, there's a party downstairs, and after the fright you gave me I could use a glass of ale."

The trip from the room to the bar downstairs seemed to take an age. For Eric, every movement was an agony. The ground no longer seemed a solid object, but one that shook and shifted with each step. By the time they pushed open the doors to the dining room, Eric almost wished he'd gone hungry.

Noise washed over them as they entered. A band played in the far corner, its two guitars, cello and drums setting the bar alive. Someone had pushed the tables into the corners, making room for the city's revellers. People packed the room, dancing and hugging and laughing while water dripped from shirts and coats. There was not a sober soul present.

The few tables still standing had been abandoned by the merry townsfolk. Eric slid onto the seat of a spare table, then watched as Alastair vanished into the throng. He prayed he'd gone for food. Sitting back, he tried to comprehend the chaos. Men and woman danced in open joy, bodies pressed close with hardly the space to breathe, their voices raised above the music, arms over their heads.

Eric grinned at the sight.

It took quarter of an hour for Alastair to return, a plate of steaming food in each hand. He placed them on the table and disappeared again, returning with two flagons of ale. The room was too loud for speech, so together they dug into the food. Roast pork and potatoes vanished in minutes, golden liquor washing down each mouthful.

When his plate was empty, Eric sat back and belched. "Thank you, Alastair, I needed that," he shouted over the din.

Alastair chuckled, wiping gravy from his beard. "My pleasure."

The double doors to the street opened with a bang. Rain

spilled into the room, whipping about the revellers on the swirling wind. People stumbled away from the door, although many were laughing.

Lightning thundered outside, silhouetting the two men standing in the doorway. They stepped inside and swung the doors shut behind them. Each wore a sword at their hip and a steely glare, suggesting they were not here for the celebration. Their eyes swept the crowd, falling on the table at which they sat. They moved across the room, parting the crowd before them.

The two said nothing as they pulled up chairs and sat down opposite Eric and Alastair. The four of them sat in silence, staring at each other across the thick slab of wood. Despite the revelry around them, Eric felt a sinking feeling in his gut. Had the bounty hunters found them?

"Was it you, Alastair?" the older of the two asked.

He wore a purple robe pulled tight around him. Eric glimpsed chainmail beneath the faded fabric. His bald head shone in the firelight and a wiry moustache hung beneath his long nose. He regarded Alastair with a cool stare, his eyes seemingly unaware of Eric's presence.

Alastair returned the frosty glare. "Who are you?"

The speaker turned out his hands. "Forgive me. My name is Balistor. I am a Magicker of the Plorsean army. I have seen you once before, though I doubt you would remember me."

Alastair turned to the other man. "And you?"

The man straightened his shoulders. He too wore chainmail, its links clearly visible beneath his scarlet tunic. He was not a large man, but his arms were finely muscled and he had moved with the subtle confidence of a fighter. There was the faintest trace of stubble on his chin and his hazel hair was soaked with rain.

"Sergeant Caelin, at your service. It's an honour to meet

you, sir," he offered his hand to Alastair.

Eric was impressed. Unlike some of the higher ranks to which young nobles were appointed, sergeants worked their way up from the infantry on the back of their accomplishments. Caelin could not be much older than twenty. He must be very skilled to have advanced so quickly.

His tawny green eyes flickered towards Eric. He held out his hand. "And who are you?"

Eric blinked, taken by surprise. He reached out and took Caelin's hand. "I'm Eric, Alastair's apprentice."

"It's nice to meet you."

"So, was it you, Alastair?" Balistor interrupted.

Eric turned his attention back to the Magicker. The man's eyes sparked, his forehead creased with impatience. Eric wondered what two members of the Plorsean army wanted with Alastair.

"The rain, you mean?" Alastair smiled. "No, that was Eric."

Both men turned their heads to stare at him. Eric felt his cheeks turning red. Dropping his eyes, he studied the tabletop in embarrassment.

Alastair saved him from answering their questioning looks. "How can I help the two of you?"

"Why, it is us that would like to help you, Alastair," Balistor replied.

"What makes you think I need your help?"

"King Fraser himself sent us," Caelin spoke over Balistor. "He told me who you are searching for, and why. I was sent to offer whatever aid I could. Balistor caught up with me on the road, with the same instructions. When Balistor sensed the release of magic earlier, we guessed it might be you. It took a while to find the right place…" Caelin trailed off as he noticed the look on Alastair's face.

There was fire in the old Magicker's eyes. His fists tightened around his cutlery. Eric watched the steel knife slowly begin to bend. "How, pray, did the king of Plorsea find out about my purpose?"

Caelin swallowed. "A… a dream, sir. He said Antonia came to him in a dream."

Alastair cursed. "That girl needs to learn when to keep her nose out of my business. So why do I need the two of you?"

Eric glanced from Alastair to the two soldiers, his confusion mounting. What was so important about the family Alastair was searching for?

Caelin bowed his head. "All I can offer you is my sword. I was chosen because I won the king's Tourney of the Blades last year."

Balistor snorted. "Of course, that counts for little when you are surrounded by Magickers. The king chose me for my magic. I am a master of fire and I am at your service, Alastair," his tone was rich with pride, bordering on arrogance.

Eric wondered how much truth there was in their tale. He found it strange the king would send only two men to help Alastair, if his quest was so important. But then, Eric still had little idea about what was going on. He closed his eyes, swallowing his irritation. It seemed everyone but himself knew Alastair's purpose. He was tired of being kept in the dark.

The conversation between the three men continued for some time. Eric laid his head on the table, too tired to care. He had heard their story. Alastair would judge the truth of it. After all, he was the one with all the answers.

Finally, Alastair seemed to accept their tale. He sent them away to restock their supplies. Eric was surprised. It was a menial task to give a Sergeant and Magicker of the

Plorsean army.

They watched the two leave and then headed for their rooms. Eric fell onto his bed before the door had even closed. His eyes were already drooping, his mind close to sleep. He rolled over, glancing out the window. Outside the rain poured down, flooding Chole's parched soils. Lightning flashed across the sky, but it was far from the city and no danger to anyone.

Eric closed his eyes and slept, a smile on his lips.

****

Gabriel stared at the ancient walls. Rain poured down around him. It ran down his face and into his teary eyes. His clothes were soaked to the skin. He held out his hands, watched the water wash the blood from his fingers.

He looked down at the body again. The guard lay sprawled across the ground, Gabriel's dagger embedded in his throat. His blood still pumped from the wound, staining the ground red.

The guard had stopped struggling. His eyes were open, but there was no longer anyone behind them. He was just a corpse now. His soul had fled.

Why did I do that?

He was in your way, came the voice of the wolf.

Gabriel shivered. *In my way?* The man was only doing his job.

He looked at his hands again. The blood was gone, but the guilt could not be washed away so easily. He was a murderer.

What have I become?

What you must. Now come, before anyone sees us, the wolf

padded through the gates. Gabriel walked after the beast, the guard forgotten. His purpose came crashing back. *They must die. They must suffer for... for...*

He paused midstride. "What did they do?" he whispered into the night.

It doesn't matter. The old man must die.

Gabriel nodded. His wolf was right. *The old man must die.*

He followed it into the dark city.

FIFTEEN

Outside the rain poured down. It gushed in torrents from the rooftops, pooling in the streets below. Eric and Alastair strode through the puddles, water filling their boots. Everything was wet. In any other city such weather would have driven everyone inside. Not for Chole, however. Revellers filled the streets. The night's party refused to cease with the new day, though the sun had yet to appear from behind the heavy clouds.

Eric shivered, glad for the cloak Alastair had given him. The rain had banished the desert's heat and the chill of autumn was closing in. The city folk could not get enough of the rain and cool air, but Eric preferred his clothes dry. Of course, that did not stop him from smiling at the childlike antics of the people dancing in the morning rain.

Alastair strode confidently through the flooded streets, casting occasional glances back over his shoulder. At first Eric thought the old man was checking he was keeping up, but he soon realised there was more to it. Alastair was searching for anyone who might be following. The thought gave Eric the chills.

Alastair had not mentioned where they were going – in fact he had ignored all of Eric's questions. Eventually he had given up. Now silence stretched between them. But he could sense Alastair's tension. Wherever they were going, it was important.

It took half an hour to reach the house. Rain ran down its white washed walls, bubbling over the cracks in the bricks. With its solid tile roof it looked like any other house they had passed in the central city, although in better condition than most.

Alastair walked past the old picket fence and through the empty garden. The ground was muddy with rain and churned up by the recent passage of heavy boots. Looking at the footprints, Eric guessed the owners to be large men.

They stood together beneath the slight overhang of the roof and knocked on the heavy wooden door. Eric huddled closer, making the most of the poor shelter. The rain had already started to seep through his thick outer cloak to his clothes beneath. The wind sent gusts of rain swirling against the door. Eric shuddered, hunkering down against the cold.

No sound came from within. Eric glanced through the windows beside the door. It was dark inside; all he could make out was the empty entranceway. There was no movement.

Alastair knocked again.

"Maybe they're out?" Eric ventured.

Alastair shook his head. He squinted through the windows. Eric waited, unsure what to say or do. The old man stepped back into the rain, ushering Eric out with him.

Eric groaned, already dreading the long wet walk back to the inn. As he moved away from the door, Alastair flicked out his hand. Wood cracked behind him. Eric spun in time to see the door cave inwards. Splinters exploded through the air, leaving a gaping hole where the door had stood.

His mentor strode through the wreckage, sword drawn. Eric stood, gaping. The wind tore away his hood and the rain ran down his face. Water soaked his hair, but he was too shocked to care.

A crash from inside snapped him from the trance. He glanced around, realising how exposed he was out there in the open, and moved quickly after Alastair. He stepped over the remains of the door, leaving the rain behind him. Fear tightened his chest. Inside, there was no sign of movement. He walked further into the house, head twisting in search of danger. His hands clenched into fists.

Another crash came from down the hallway, from the far room. It took all his courage to move towards it. *It's just Alastair,* he repeated to himself.

Eric moved through the doorway, eyes taking in the room with a single sweep. A large woven mat covered the wooden floors and a table and chairs were set in one corner. The cutlery and food were set on the table, untouched. A cactus sat in a pot on the windowsill, tangled with the sun-bleached curtains. Flecks of blood stained the white washed wall.

His stomach churned. He tasted bile in the back of his throat and struggled to keep it down. Blood had soaked the mat, surrounding the bodies of the man and woman who were sprawled in the centre of the room. They lay face down on the rug. Their clothes were slashed and tattered, exposing the hideous wounds beneath. The tang of blood carried to his nose.

Eric shuddered when he saw their hands. Their fingers were missing and long shallow slices ran down their arms. Theirs had not been an easy death.

He dropped to his knees and lost the fight with his stomach. His breakfast came hurling up. Tears stung his eyes as he sucked for breath. He scrunched them shut, blotting out the gruesome sight. He could not believe what he was seeing. Who could have done such a thing?

Footsteps echoed on the wooden floors. He jumped to his feet, heart racing, and spun. Fear clogged his throat, but it was only Alastair. His face was grim and he seemed to have aged a decade. Tears ran from his bloodshot eyes. He held his blade in shaking hands, veins standing out along his wrist. There was blood on his hands, but Eric had not heard any sound of fighting.

"Who's blood is that?" he demanded. "What happened to them? What are we doing here? Why... why, why, why?" he scrambled to find the right question.

Alastair sheathed his sword and walked past Eric. He knelt beside the woman. "The blood is theirs. I had to check... to check to see if they were still alive," his voice was cracking.

"Who were they? Who did this to them?" Eric could not breathe. He had seen death before, but never like this.

"They were the family I was looking for. How did they find them? *How?*" his fists clawed at the rug.

"Who?"

"Archon's minions. Vile, scheming men willing to sell their souls for a little reward," Alastair's voice was acid.

The blood in Eric's veins froze at Alastair's words. He blinked, opened his mouth, but no sound came out. A shadow fell across the room, one no flame could cast off. *What do you mean?* Eric screamed in his head.

A crash came from the back of the house. Eric gaped, feet frozen in place. Alastair's sword whispered from its scabbard. The hairs on Eric's neck stood up.

Voices echoed through the house. "Spread out. We had better find the little one, or there'll be hell to pay. Who knows where she's hiding."

Alastair raised a finger to his lips. His sword hand ceased to shake. He gestured Eric to stay and moved for the doorway. The grief had vanished, replaced by a burning rage, tightly controlled.

Eric felt his own anger stir. Who were these people, who could commit such terrors on an innocent family? He glanced at the fallen couple and felt a red-hot rage twist in his chest. Turning, he moved to follow Alastair.

Just as Alastair reached the open door, a man appeared in front of him. The man's eyes widened in shock at the sight of the two strangers. He held a crossbow in his hand and a sword at his waist, but in his confusion did not raise either. Blood covered his pants and tunic.

He opened his mouth to yell. Alastair's sword crunched into his face and he fell without a word. Blood sprayed the air. He crumpled backwards into the corridor with a thump. The voices from deeper in the house fell silent.

Alastair strode across to the man and yanked the sword free from where his magic had buried it. He walked over the corpse and disappeared through the door.

Eric followed, orders forgotten. He stared at the fallen killer as he passed, anger mounting. He felt his magic stirring within, but it was weak and drained. He prayed Alastair knew what he was doing. They raced down the corridor, bursting through into the next room.

Crossbows bristled and pointed in their direction. A dozen men stood in the tiny space, each armed with the deadly bows. They wore the blue uniform of the city guard, though the clothing was old and tattered. The reek of their unwashed bodies was overpowering. Eric wondered how Chole's city guard had fallen so low.

He swallowed hard, glancing at Alastair. The old man dropped his sword and raised his hands. Eric raised his own, his rage evaporating before his fear.

A bulky, black bearded man stepped forward. His uniform was newer than those around him, although it sported a hole in one shoulder. A scar ran from his right eye to chin, turning the iris blood red.

"Where's the girl?" he asked in a cold voice.

"Which girl?" Alastair replied smoothly.

"Enala, the daughter of the two in there," the man growled, face to face with Alastair. Spittle landed on the old man's cheek.

"Yeah! Where is she!" another of the men shouted, brandishing his weapon.

Eric's heart stopped in terror. The man held his bow in trembling fingers, tight around the trigger. He could not tear his eyes away.

"Where is she?" the first speaker repeated.

Eric took a shaky step backwards and tripped on an unseen stool. The chair toppled to the ground and crashed on the wooden floor.

Every bow in the room turned on Eric. He dived to the floor, instinct guiding him. Air exploded from his lungs, as crossbow bolts shrieked over his head. They smashed into the wall behind him, slashing it to pieces.

Above them, the roof groaned. Eric looked up in time to see Alastair's arms come sweeping down. The room exploded. Wood and bricks flew from the ceiling, dust filling the air. The men crumbled beneath the falling timber, disappearing beneath the rubble.

Coughing dirt from his lungs, Eric sat up and began patting himself down. Somehow he had come out unharmed, and through the dust he saw Alastair still stood. No one else remained. No movement came from the pile of debris that lay where the men had been. Rain began to fall through the hole in the ceiling.

"What the hell is going on?" Eric shrieked.

Alastair bent and picked up his sword. He turned to look at Eric, his face grim. "Those were the men who murdered that couple. There is someone in this city working against me, someone who wants to ruin everything and usher in a new age for Archon. The girl they talked about, Enala; she is our last hope now," he turned to leave.

"Whose last hope?"

Alastair glanced back. "Everyone's."

****

Gabriel stood in the middle of the road and watched the house. People walked past, giving him a wide berth when they saw the beast at his side. He ignored them – Let them stare. He no longer cared. Not about the rain, nor the mud, nor the cold wind.

"They went in there?" he asked.

Yes, its voice was inseparable from his own thoughts now.

"Are they still there?"

The wolf lifted its rain soaked muzzle. *No, but they have not been gone long. You must see inside.*

Gabriel nodded and crossed the street. Approaching the house, he could see something had gone wrong inside. The door was in ruins. Rain swept through the jagged hole where it had stood, pooling on the floor inside. He walked over the splintered remains and moved into the house.

It did not take long to find what he needed to see. They lay in a pool of their own blood, faces to the ground. He felt a pang of grief. A picture flashed through his mind – a house in ruins and three familiar faces lying dead amidst the rubble.

They did this, he realised.

There is something else, the wolf raced around the room, nose to the ground. *Someone else.*

The beast bared its teeth, sniffing at the edges of the rug. It sank its great fangs into the fabric and dragged it sideways. The bodies came with it, leaving a smear of blood on the wooden floorboards. He walked over as the floor beneath appeared. The blood had soaked through the rug and congealed in the gaps between the wooden boards.

Gabriel crouched down and inspected the floor. The blood made it difficult to make out the trapdoor the rug had hidden. It was well fitted and tightly shut, but his fingers quickly found the groove with which to prise it loose. The hinges groaned as it opened, revealing a ladder leading into the darkness.

"Stay here," he told the wolf.

He levered himself over the hole and began his descent. The ladder went down less than ten feet before he reached solid ground. The only light came from the hatch above and the cracks between the floorboards.

Something shrieked from the dark. Gabriel hardly had time to look around before a body hurtled from the shadows. A fist struck him across the face, knocking him backwards. He scrambled for purchase, but unseen objects littered the ground. His feet slipped from under him and he fell.

The creature landed on top of him, crying like a banshee. Tiny fists pummelled his chest and face. Nails scratched at his skin, aiming for his eyes. Gabriel lifted his hands in time to stop them being clawed from his face. He rolled, sending his assailant toppling.

"*Die!*" the girl screamed. The sound echoed in the tiny space, so loud Gabriel had to cover his ears.

She lunged forward, sinking her teeth into his shoulder.

Gabriel, still on the ground, cried out and threw her off. She fell heavily, rolled, and came at him again. "*Die, die, die!*" she bawled.

This time he was halfway to his feet when she launched herself into his stomach. The wind exploded from his lungs, but he managed to keep his feet. "Stop," he coughed. "It wasn't me. Please, let me help you!"

To his surprise, she obeyed. Sobs began to rack her body. She slid to the ground and buried her face in her arms. The light caught on the golden locks of her hair.

"Go on. Just kill me," she sobbed.

Gabriel crouched down and wrapped his arms around the girl. They sat in the darkness for a long while. He breathed in the musty scent of her hair. Memories flickered to life in his mind, of another woman he had once held and comforted. *My fiancé*, he remembered. Tears of his own sprang from his eyes. *I couldn't save her!* He wept.

After a few minutes, the tears began to slow. He realised the girl had stopped crying. He looked over to see her staring at him, eyes wide in shock. Gabriel shrugged. "Come on, we'd best get out of here."

The girl nodded, silent now, and followed him up the ladder. When they reached the top, Gabriel helped her over the lip of the trapdoor. In the daylight, he realised she was not as young as he had first thought.

She stood silent and still, sapphire eyes brimming with tears. The sunlight played across her hair, the blond curls hanging down to her shoulders. A single copper lock hung across her face, standing out like black sheep in a herd of white. She blew it from her eyes, thin lips tight with grief. She stood as high as his shoulders, her plain clothes torn and tattered. Despite her small frame, she displayed the curves and figure of a young woman. Gabriel guessed she might be sixteen or seventeen.

A growl came from across the room. He spun, remembering the wolf. It padded forward, teeth bared. The hair bristled along its back. The reek of wet fur overpowered the bloody stench of the room. It crouched, muscles tensed to spring. Snarling, it slunk closer.

Gabriel held out a hand. "Easy, it's okay."

She must die!

Gabriel drew his sword. The wolf was right. The girl had to die. He turned to face her – and fell into her sapphire eyes. They had gone wide with shock, tears spilling over to wash down her dirty face. Yet there was no fear in them. Instead, she tensed, prepared to fight.

He lowered his blade. His fiancé was dead. He clung to his one, irrevocable memory. He blinked and looked around. *What am I doing?* How could he consider murdering a helpless girl?

The wolf, he realised.

He turned again, holding his sword point out at the beast. The demon had tricked him, stolen away his humanity in return for… for what? Gabriel could not even remember now.

An image of the guard at the city gates flashed through his memory. Guilt ate at him. He had given in to evil, he realised. He had become a monster. It was time to put an end to it.

"No more, demon spawn. Our deal is done."

So be it. You will soon wish otherwise, the wolf whispered in his mind, and leapt.

Gabriel had no time to bring up his sword. The wolf struck him in the chest, flinging him from his feet. Its teeth snapped inches from his face before its momentum carried it past. The girl flung herself out of the way as it hurtled at her. Its claws screeched, digging grooves into the wood. It turned to charge him again.

He hauled himself to his feet and moved to stand between wolf and girl. From the corner of his eye, he saw her grab a chair. She held it out before her, ready for the next attack.

The wolf howled and began to circle. Its bright yellow eyes studied him, searching for a way past. He kept his sword low, pointed at its throat. It would not knock him down so easily a second time.

Gabriel lunged forward with his blade. The beast dodged backwards, but its claws could not find purchase on the hard floor and it moved slowly. His first sweep missed before he wrenched the tip around and brought it down on the wolf's head.

The blade bit deep, scraping against bone. He gagged as a rotten stench ran from the wound. The wolf yelped and retreated further. Gabriel let it go. If he followed, it might slip around him and attack the girl. Black blood dripped from his sword tip. The beast only had eyes for him now. When it rushed him, Gabriel was ready.

He crouched low, sword point out before him. At the last moment, he lunged forward, meeting the charge with his sword. The wolf ran right onto the blade, the tip tearing through its hide to sink to the hilt. There it lodged, ripping from his grip. The beast's weight carried it forward, driving him backwards. Gabriel fell. The wolf growled, stumbling forward. He struggled to climb to his feet. It leapt.

Air exploded from Gabriel's lungs as the sharp claws landed on his chest. He collapsed back to the ground, pinned beneath the weight of the wolf. It towered over him. Bloody saliva dripped from its jaws. The sword still stuck from its chest, close to where its heart should be. Not close enough, it seemed.

Goodbye, Gabriel, its voice whispered in his mind. Its mouth opened to rip out his throat.

Neither of them saw the girl. The chair lashed out, smashing the wolf from Gabriel. She bounded over him, weapon in hand and heartbroken fury on her face.

The wolf thrashed about, fighting to reclaim its feet. The chair crashed down on its back. The girl lifted it and swung again, screaming with each blow. Gabriel saw one smash its head, another its chest, a third the sword. Again and again she struck, long after the creature had ceased to move.

Gabriel pulled himself to his feet. His chest ached where the wolf had landed. Bloody patches marked his jerkin where its claws had torn skin. They were nothing to the suffering of this girl. The couple could only have been her parents. To have them murdered while she hid helpless below…

He shook his head and moved to her side. He reached for the chair, though there was not much left of it now. She threw herself into his arms when he took it. "They're gone," she sobbed.

Gabriel suddenly felt old. What could he say to this girl? He was lost, but the words slipped out before he could think. "I know. I'll look after you."

She stopped crying and pulled away from him. "We should go," her voice was steady. "There are people out there, looking for me," she closed her eyes. "I wish I knew why."

Gabriel nodded. He reached down and pulled his blade from the wolf. Wiping the blood away on the beast's coat, he made a silent vow to himself. Never again would it be used for evil.

He moved towards the door and paused. Turning back, he asked. "What is your name?"

"Enala," she said.

"I'm Gabriel."

They walked out the front door and disappeared into the heavy rain.

SIXTEEN

Three days had passed. Three long, endless days of searching, questions, and danger. Yet still there was no sign of the missing girl, not even a whisper. Instead, they found themselves leaping at shadows, worn down by the ever-present threat of Archon's hunters.

Eric sat at the table in their room, staring into his hands. His clothes were still damp from the search. The endless rain hampered their efforts and now another night was closing in. Another day was over and still Enala remained an enigma. Alastair sat across from him, exhausted. Each day sucked a little more life from the man. His eyes were downcast and ringed by shadows.

The rain lashed at the misty glass of their window. Balistor and Caelin would return soon. They had enlisted the men in the search, although Eric was unsure whether Alastair now trusted them, or was just desperate. Either way, even with the four, the task had proven impossible. They didn't even know what Enala looked like, and there were hundreds of empty buildings in which she could hide. It was like searching blindfolded for a needle in a burning haystack.

Eric glared at the old man, his irritation growing. He had

kept his silence until now, sure that Alastair would finally tell him why the girl was so important. It was galling, knowing the two strangers knew, while he searched in ignorance. Tired and hungry, he now found his anger bubbling just below the surface.

"Where are they?" frustration strained Alastair's voice. "We need a new plan. The longer she is out there, the more likely the other hunters will find her first."

Eric's anger finally snapped. "Who is she, Alastair? Why is she so important?" he all but shouted.

Alastair sat back in his chair, fixing Eric with a cool stare. There was no anger in his eyes, just a look of resignation. Then the old man leaned forward, resting his palms on the table. "Very well, Eric. You have been patient. But you should know, if I tell you the truth, you may never be safe again."

Eric sucked in a breath of air and exhaled. "So be it. At least I won't be blind to it."

Alastair leaned closer. "Do you recall, Eric, the memories Antonia showed you?"

"Of course."

"Good," Alastair responded. "Think back to the end, when the Gods and Thomas summoned their magic. Did you notice anything?"

Eric frowned, thinking back to the scene. As the magic erupted into the sky he had seen a shadow in the grass, but dismissed it as nothing. "The shadow?"

"Yes, the shadow. I saw it at the time, but Thomas was surrounded by power, protected by the Gods of Earth and Sky. And it vanished so quickly, I thought I had imagined it."

"What was it?"

"A fail safe cast by Archon. It was triggered as the God magic took hold and cast him from the Three Nations. It was aimed at the ones who wielded the God magic."

Eric stared, a cold dread seeping into his heart. He remembered the shadow clearly now, creeping across the green lawns of the Trolan palace, drawing closer to the unsuspecting king. "But they were fine. Thomas was fine. You told me he lived for decades after that, long enough to have children to carry the Sword after him. They were the only ones who could wield it."

Alastair nodded. "You're right. Archon's spell was not strong enough to touch Antonia or Jurrien over such a distance, so instead it sought out the weak link in the circle. The wielder of the Sword of Light – Thomas."

"But Thomas survived."

"Yes, but it was never meant to kill him. Archon knew it would take something more subtle to escape our notice."

"Then what did the shadow do?"

Outside thunder crashed. "The curse was a slow sickness, one targeted at Thomas' own magic rather than the Sword's. By the time it took hold, its roots were too deep for even Antonia to heal. Worse, it did not stop there. The curse affected his children and every descendent since, slowly weakening the powers of the Sword wielders. A decade ago, it was all but gone. Now the Trolan King has lost the last of his magic and the bloodline is at an end. There is no one left to hold the Sword of Light. Archon is already mustering his forces."

Eric's mouth went dry. Fear clawed at his throat. He remembered Antonia's terror when she spoke of Archon. He swallowed, struggling to suck in a breath. If even the Gods feared Archon, what chance did they have?

"Calm yourself, Eric. There is still hope."

"What?" Eric croaked.

"Thomas's line has ended, but he had a sister. A sweet girl called Aria. Aria had Thomas' blood, but the curse did not affect her. When we discovered what had happened, I took Aria into hiding. Only her descendants have the power to wield the Sword now."

"The family?"

Alastair nodded. "Antonia came to me a long time ago and asked me to track them down. But her descendants had vanished and everywhere I looked they had died out or moved on," he took a deep breath. "I failed. If it were not for Elynbrigge, I would never have found them. That couple and their daughter are the last of Aria's line. Enala is now the only person left who can wield the Sword of Light. If she is lost, so are the Three Nations."

Eric stared, speechless. How could this have happened? How could the Gods have let the lives of every man, woman, and child in the Three Nations come down to the life of one girl. And Archon was already one step ahead of them, his hunters ready to murder the girl on sight.

I know you desire redemption, and I would like to offer you that chance, Antonia had said. He knew what she meant now, the secret the Goddess had emitted. This was his quest. Help Alastair save this girl and maybe, just maybe, he could put his ghosts to rest.

Can I do it? Eric asked himself, and then shook his head. It didn't matter. He could not run from this. If they failed, everyone died.

The door to their room burst open. Eric looked up in shock. Lightning flashed outside, showing Caelin standing in the doorway. He took a step inside, the door swinging shut behind him. Thunder roared, whisking away his words. Eric heard the five that mattered.

"I think I've found her."

****

Inken sipped at her ale. The cool drink ran down her throat. The alcohol slowed her thoughts, but did nothing for her worries. The tavern was alive with the laughter of her fellow bounty hunters. It was a sight to see the grizzled men and battle-hardened women dancing as if they were children again.

Her friend Kaiden sat beside her, one hand on a jug of ale, the other grasping a greasy haunch of lamb. Words ran from his mouth, something about the rain and the water import market, but Inken's thoughts were elsewhere. Her spirits were low, weighed down by debt.

She had spent much of the last week resupplying, but even with the fresh rain, equipment in Chole was expensive. She had gone through several lenders to garner the funds she needed and it would take years to pay back the loans.

Maybe her spirits would be higher if it weren't for the horse. That particular decision irritated her beyond measure. The gelding was a nice animal and the only decent horse she could afford. But the colour! What was she going to do with a white horse? A bounty hunter had to remain inconspicuous and even the thickest criminal would soon hear about a warrior on a white horse riding into town.

The rest of her equipment was sound, if expensive. The sabre she wore was light and well balanced, and would be useful in a fight on horseback. It would serve well, as would the short recurve bow she had leaned against the bar. The maker had carved the black stained bow with great care and the oak would give extra distance to her arrows.

A man brushed passed Inken as he made his way through the tavern. She smelt a wisp of ash as he passed. He wore a black cloak with the hood pulled up, casting a shadow across his face. All she could see was the glow of his eyes. He wore a sword at his side, but that was common in this bar. Even so, something about him made her gaze linger. She watched as he walked up to one of the larger tables.

Several men looked up as he stopped before their table. Their conversation broke off as they stared at the man in confusion. Suddenly, he leapt. His feet easily cleared the table's top and his muddy boots slammed down on the wood. Plates crashed and food went flying. The men cursed as ale spilt in their laps and glasses smashed on the floor.

The room fell silent. Even Kaiden was staring, open mouthed. The stranger spun, sweeping the room with his dark gaze. His cloak swept out behind him, but the hood remained, hiding his face.

"Bounty hunters!" his voice boomed to the stunned room. "I have a message for you. Some days ago, a letter came from the Magistrate of Oaksville, offering a lifetime's gold in reward for the death of a demon. Some of your companions rode to claim it."

Inken saw that many of her fellow hunters were glaring in anger at the stranger. The men he'd knocked from their chairs scrambled to their feet.

"They failed!" the man's announcement halted any pending violence. "The demon is here, in this proud city, and Oaksville's Magistrate is slain. His word no longer counts for dust."

There were angry mutters from around the room. Inken's eyes widened. Her pulse quickened at his words. Had she been right? *No, he must be wrong.*

"However, my word is gold," he spoke over his audience. The man reached into his cloak and drew out a cloth bag. He tossed it to the ground where it split. Gold coins spilled across the floor, the chime they made silencing the tavern. "And I will reward a bag just like that to each and every bounty hunter who comes with me, *now*. We will bring this demon, and all his accomplices, to justice. Who's with me?"

The room erupted around Inken. She stood to join in, although her heart was sinking. She stared at the gold, thoughts racing. The reward would more than cover her debt. And if the hunt was for a demon, why should she hesitate?

Yet what if it was Eric?

Inken shivered. The man had leapt from the table and was leading the crowd out the doors and into the rain.

Inken rose, picking up her bow. She toyed with the carved wood, staring at the smooth workmanship.

"Are you coming?" Kaiden stood beside her, open greed in his eyes.

She pictured the gold coins spilling across the ground. This was too great an opportunity to pass up.

It can't be Eric. The boy is no demon, she told herself.

Inken smiled. "Of course. Let's go."

****

The man in the black cloak strode down the street. He did not look back. The fools would follow, they always did.

His anger flared. It had been a mistake to underestimate Alastair and now he was paying for it. These hunters were only loyal to gold. They were no replacement for the followers he had lost. They had known what they fought for and were dedicated to the cause. They truly wished to be free.

He cursed to himself. He should not have waited so long to set his plan into action, but it had been worth the risk. If Alastair had found the girl for him, the battle would have been won. But after three days, time was up. The plan would still work. They would finally be rid of the vexatious old Magicker. It would be a heavy blow to the cursed Goddess.

They strode through the muddy streets, the inn looming ahead. He reached out with his mind, searching for the aftertaste of magic. It clung to the boy like mud, seeping from his pores. Such power, misplaced in one so young and naïve. But it was missing now. They were not in the inn.

He left his hunters outside and went in to investigate. The innkeeper told him they had left an hour before, heading towards the eastern wall.

Outside again, he signalled for several of the men to follow. The rest he left to take up stations around the inn. He would take no chances this time. If Alastair and the others returned by a different path, they would not escape his net.

He moved down the street with his followers. They came to a crossroads. He stationed them there, ready to ambush the fools when they returned. In the meantime, there was one more thing to do this night, one last chess piece to eliminate. He allowed himself a smile. The game was at an end. The timer was almost empty and there would be no escape.

Alastair would finally die tonight.

****

Eric took another step up the worn stone staircase. He heard the footsteps of Caelin and Alastair from above, but he dared not look anywhere but his feet. To his left, the staircase ended in an abrupt thirty-foot drop to the city below. Silently, he willed himself on. The top of the wall could not be far now.

The wind grew stronger as they ascended, tearing through their rain soaked clothes and threatening to hurl them to the cobbles below. Eric shivered, wishing for the cloak he had left behind. They'd left with such haste he had not thought to grab it from his chair.

The crunching of footsteps above him ceased and Eric froze, gaze still locked to the steps. He blinked the rain from his eyes, cursing his fear. He could feel his weakened magic stirring and up on the city walls that could prove fatal. He took a deep breath to calm himself.

Laughter came from above. "What are you doing, Eric?" Caelin called down

"Why have we stopped?" Eric shouted back.

Alastair answered with a humour in his voice he had not heard for days. "We've reached the top. You're just a few steps away."

Eric's cheeks grew warm. He walked up the last few steps and scowled at the two men. Then, ignoring them, he walked out onto the battlements. The path along the top of the wall was neatly bricked and slick with rain. The ramparts stood up past his waist on either side, providing scant shelter from the wind.

Caelin moved past, leading the way along the parapet. Eric followed, looking back out over the ramparts. To the west, the city spread out beneath them, fires burning to ward off the chill of the coming night. He found himself longing for the warm embrace of the inn's fireplace. Gritting his teeth, he looked to the east where the three peaks of Chole towered over them. The slope of the nearest volcano stretched right to the base of the wall.

Lightning flashed above, a long way up. Thunder rung out and the wind howled. The air smelt of rain and wood smoke. The storm had continued nonstop for three days now. Eric could feel its energies whipping about him, charging the atmosphere with its power. It taunted him, daring him to reach out with his magic. He resisted. Turning his thoughts to the missing Enala, he followed Caelin's broad back through the hissing rain.

The night closed around them, until it seemed they were the only ones left in the world. Nevertheless, someone else was up here. A guard who claimed to have seen a young girl leaving the city. Caelin had gotten that much from him, but he was sure there was more to his story.

A figure loomed through the gloom. He wore a heavy trench coat pulled tight around him and his back was hunched against the rain. Neither looked to be doing him much good. The rain blew almost horizontal in the strong winds atop the wall.

A spark of lightning lit the mountainside behind him. Eric squinted and thought he saw movement on the slopes. Before he could make anything out, the rain closed in again.

Caelin moved towards the guard. Words passed between them, shouted over the storm's rage. Caelin nodded and moved back. "He won't talk," he ran his hands through his soaking hair. "This is the man I spoke to though."

Alastair scowled and elbowed past. As he approached the guard, he slipped one hand into his pocket. The guard flinched backwards, reaching for his sword. Alastair drew a small bag from his cloak and tossed it to him. The surprised guard fumbled the parcel and Eric heard the chink of coins from within.

The man's eyes widened when he looked inside. "Thank you, sir. I remember now. There was a girl. She left by the north gate a few hours ago. Pretty little thing. I was on gate duty then. Shouldn'ta been complaining. Commander put me up here when he heard."

Alastair nodded impatiently. "Yes, things can always get worse, can't they? Now, the girl. What did she look like? Did she follow the road?"

"Afraid I can't tell you much. Rain's great an' all, but makes keeping watch a right chore. Her hair was soaked and hooded, but it was blond I guess. Small face, small nose, small girl. Her cloak hid everything else. They kept north, as far as I could tell."

"They?" Alastair interrupted.

"Yeah. She was with some guy. Didn't get a good look at him either. He had a sword though. Can't have been much older than her I'd say. Strange business, two young folk venturing out in this."

"Yes, quite. Well, thank you, sir. I'd appreciate it even more if you told no one else about the girl."

The man clutched his money to his chest and grinned. "Don't think I need to, sir. A good day to you."

Alastair led them a few steps down the wall. They huddled close to hear his whispers. "This girl may or may not be Enala; the rogues at the house said nothing about a boy. But it's the only lead we have. Eric and I will go after them. Caelin, you find Balistor and head back to the inn. Bring the horses and catch up with us. Eric, are you listening?"

Eric was not. He stared into the distance, eyes searching the darkness. The movement had come again with the last flash of lightning. It was closer now and seemed to be moving faster. He sucked in a breath. *There's nothing there. It's not what you think. It can't be.*

Lightning tore across the sky. Its glow fell across the mountain slopes, revealing stark rock and stone. And mud – mud rushing down the slope towards them. A wall of earth snapped free from the mountain. As he watched, its dim rumble finally struck them.

"*Landslide!*" he screamed.

They all turned. The sky lit up with his voice and they all saw it. Tumbling earth, an entire mountainside rushing towards them. The wall shook beneath their feet.

"Run for your lives!" the guard sprinted past them.

"*Gods,*" Caelin cursed. "It'll bury half the city."

No, no, no! Not again! Eric sank to his knees, hands tearing at his hair. He watched the destruction approach, all his hopes disintegrating. He felt no fear or anger, only resignation. A sick sense of inevitability gripped him. "It's over," he whispered.

Alastair stepped up to the ramparts. The wind ripped around him, trying to cast him to the rocks below. He stood against the storm's fury, watching the landslide come with cool eyes. With slow determination, he raised his arms over his head.

"What are you doing?" Eric shouted above the roaring earth.

"What I must," Alastair faced the mountain.

Eric's head pounded. The rush as Alastair unleashed his power was like nothing he had felt before. Red burned across his vision, blinding him for a moment. The earth shook harder, knocking him from his feet. On hands and knees, he crawled to the ramparts and looked out on a nightmare.

The mudslide rushed on, but now the ground before the wall was rising into the air. Boulders and stones and soil and water hovered before them. The air shimmered with magic.

Alastair's arms began to shake, the tendons on his neck strained to breaking point. His lips drew back in a manic grin, his teeth grinding as though he held the city on his shoulders. The tremors quickly spread to the rest of the old man's body. Alastair dropped to one knee, arms still stretched out before him. His fingers bent to claws. Still more debris rose to join the conflagration before them. The landslide drew ever closer.

Eric closed his eyes, still on his knees. This task must be beyond even Alastair's power. He could not imagine how the old man could draw on such energy. Surely he had spent his strength by now, yet still the air burned with magic. The old Magicker would never give up. He would die first.

Alastair's back bent, the pressure forcing him down. It could not be long now. The old man's lips moved. His teeth glinted in the storm's light. If Alastair spoke, Eric did not hear.

Then Alastair threw down his hands. Eric felt another surge of energy and suddenly there was a second landslide, racing uphill to meet the first.

Mud sprayed forty feet in the air as the two mammoths of earth met. A high pitch screech split the air. Rock exploded on rock as boulders clashed with the force of galloping horses. Eric and Caelin ducked for cover while rock rained down around them. The grumbling of moving earth echoed off the walls. Mud swirled on the plain before the wall and began to settle.

Alastair crumpled to the ramparts. Eric crawled to where he lay. The old man's face was deathly pale. His eyes were closed and he did not respond when Eric shook him. He felt his wrist for a pulse and found the faintest beat. Cold sweat beaded Alastair's pale skin.

"Is he alive?" Caelin whispered.

"Barely," Eric responded.

Caelin shook his head. "I don't believe it. He did it."

Eric nodded, looking out at the mess below them. He couldn't believe it either.

SEVENTEEN

Elynbrigge opened his eyes. A cool breeze blew through the open window. Every breath was an effort now, each exhalation leaving him gasping. The blood flowed sluggishly through his veins and his chest ached with the pain of his labouring heart. With each beat, he drew closer to death.

Summoning his strength, he called out. "Michael! Michael, I need you."

It did not take long for the priest to appear. He frowned when he saw Elynbrigge and knelt beside him. "Are you okay? You're pale as a ghost."

Guilt bored a hole in Elynbrigge's chest. What he was about to ask would change the doctor forever. He closed his eyes and thought of the sacrifices he had made over the centuries. Now he must ask another soul to take his place.

"I am old, Michael, that is all. But my health is not your concern now. There are others who need your help."

Michael frowned. He rocked back on his haunches, studying the old priest. "Why do they need me? I'm only a doctor – surely you would serve them better."

"Perhaps, but I am weak and cannot travel. These folk will not be coming here. You must go to them."

He described the path Michael must take to the inn. As he spoke the doctor watched him with his amber eyes. Behind them Elynbrigge could sense the courage Michael had hid beneath the years of prayer and study. This man would not falter when he looked into the face of evil. His old friend would need such a man.

"Why do these people need me? Who are they?"

Your doom, Elynbrigge thought. He could not say it though. But he could at least offer a choice. "They are the ones who brought the girl to us. They will need a doctor before the night is done, and they will not be staying in Chole much longer. If you go to them, you must leave with them."

"Why?"

"If you return here their enemies will seek you out. They will take you and torture you until they break you. And they will burn this temple to the ground."

Michael's expression did not change, but Elynbrigge could taste his anger on the air. He had offered an impossible choice. To follow his calling and aid those in need, he would have to give up everything he knew and loved.

Time was trickling away though and death was fast approaching. He gave Michael a final push. "You should know, these people are servants of Antonia. And I believe if you go to them, you will meet her."

Michael exhaled sharply. "The Goddess herself?"

Elynbrigge almost wished he could take back the words. Who would turn up the opportunity to meet the Goddess, face to face? Instead, he only nodded.

Michael smiled. Elynbrigge felt the joy flooding Michael's soul. It made him sick to his stomach. "I would give my life to serve the Goddess. I will go to them."

You might yet, Elynbrigge thought. "Then go to them,

there is no time to spare. Good luck, my friend. May Antonia watch over you."

Michael fled the room. The old priest gathered his thoughts and sent a prayer for Michael's soul. If he survived this quest, he would be a priest no longer. The darkness would change him forever. He was strong though and the challenge would only make him stronger.

It did not take long for his second visitor to arrive. The dark cloaked man stepped into the room, sword in hand. Elynbrigge sat up, preparing himself for this final confrontation.

"Elynbrigge, it is a pleasure to finally meet you," the voice was soft, mocking. "I've heard so much about you, though I am afraid you don't seem to live up to the stories. Age does not become you."

"Time claims all of us."

The man laughed. "Not me, nor my master. The dark arts offer all manner of riches. When he comes, I will live forever."

"And yet you do not live at all. What is left of the man you once were? Where is your soul? What is immortality without joy?" Elynbrigge's voice was touched with sadness.

"It is immortality. I would not expect *you* to understand," he waved a hand. "Now, do you have any final words? I have other matters to attend to."

Elynbrigge sighed. "There is no need to kill me. I will play no part in this fight. I am an old man, my days of power long past. My only desire now is to spend my final years healing the sick. Will you not give me that?"

His visitor cackled. "You are the only mortal left who remembers the birth of the Gods. That alone is a death sentence. And I will take no chances in this game. The last shackles of the past fall tonight and neither you nor Alastair will be here to see the dawn of the new age."

"Alastair will not die so easily," at this moment he knew how false those words were. His old friend had nothing left to give. "And I would rather die than see your new age."

"Death I can grant you," the man raised his hands.

Elynbrigge stared into the man's dead eyes and let the void claim him.

****

Alastair's breathing was growing more shallow with each gasp. Rain had soaked through his clothes and he was starting to shake. He needed shelter, and help, fast.

Eric looked up at Caelin. "We need to get him back to the inn, now."

Caelin crouched opposite him. "I'll carry him," he wrapped his arms around Alastair and lifted him from the muddy stone. The old man seemed to have shrunk, as though the magic had drained away muscle and bone, leaving only a skeletal husk in his place. Caelin hauled him over his shoulders and marched for the stairs.

Eric ducked past him and took the lead. He glanced back, checking to see how the young sergeant was coping with his burden, but Caelin showed no signs of weakness. His stride was firm and confident, as though he carried nothing but air. They reached the staircase and started down. This time Eric scarcely noticed the height, his mind preoccupied on Alastair's fate.

The rain had begun to clear. Wind gusted around them, but it grew weaker as they walked. The flashes of lightning now came from far away, the thunder a distant rumble. The storm was finally ending, leaving silence in its wake. Loose stones clattered on the staircase, dislodged by their passage.

Eric continued down, Caelin a step behind him.

Eric did not hesitate when they reached the ground. There was no time to waste. Alastair's head bounced with each step Caelin took, his wispy grey hair hanging across his pale face.

The rain had ceased, but its smell lingered in the air. The shadows cast by the buildings closed in around them. The clouds still hid the moon and stars, leaving only a sparse scattering of street lanterns to light the way. Eric let Caelin take the lead. Even in daylight he could not have navigated the jumbled streets.

The young soldier led them through the night. Eric glanced into the shadows, breath coming in short gasps. He had not forgotten Archon's men, nor the underworld who ruled the night here in Chole. The image of the murdered couple was fresh in his head. The stench of blood came with it, so convincing he paused to search for its source. But it was just a memory, a nightmare. He moved on.

His eyes slid through the dark surrounding them. Anything could be hiding in the gloom. He searched for movement, strained to catch the faintest sound. He shivered. There was nothing. He hurried after Caelin.

Finally, they came to a crossroads Eric recognised. A single lantern hung on the corner, a frail beacon lighting the way. They were close, only a few blocks from the inn. Thankfully, as Caelin was lagging now beneath his burden. His breath came in ragged bursts, steaming in the cool night air. He would not make it much further.

Eric's ears caught the slight rustle of clothing from behind them. He spun, glimpsing the sheen of light on steel. A blade hurtled at him from the shadows. He dived aside, but not fast enough. The dagger tore through his clothes and plunged into his side. He struck the ground, white fire dancing across his vision.

Caelin dropped Alastair and leapt across Eric. His sword hissed from its sheath, a dagger appearing in his other hand. The soldier placed himself between the shadows and his fallen comrades, crouched in anticipation. His movements were smooth and practiced, his face unreadable.

Eric groaned, agony lancing from his side. He glanced down and saw the dagger's hilt still buried in his flesh. Hot blood ran down his leg. He tried to move and winced as the cool steel cut further. Lying back, he saw three men emerging into the light. Their dark clothing clung to the shadows at their back. Big, muscular men, they held greatswords at the ready. They towered over Caelin. Eric prayed his ally's skill was enough to take them.

The men spread out as they approached, attempting to encircle their prey. They moved quickly, eager to end the last opposition standing between them and their reward. Once surrounded, Caelin would have no way of defending against all three. The fight would be over before it began.

But Caelin was no fool. He didn't wait for the snare to close. He sprang at the man to his left, sword snaking out. His enemy made a clumsy jab to turn aside the blow, surprise written on his meaty face. Caelin drew back his blade and attacked again. The man blocked, but there was no avoiding the dagger. Caelin buried it in his stomach and tore it loose.

Caelin bounded backwards, bringing his sword to the ready. The wounded man staggered a few paces after him and pitched face first to the ground. He groaned, fingers clawing at the hole in his stomach. A dark puddle began to form around him.

Caelin grinned at the remaining thugs, beckoning them forward. They drew closer together; approaching warily now, fear making them hesitate. Caelin stood frozen in place, sword raised high in his right hand, bloody dagger low in his left. He stood like a statue, daring his opponents to break him.

The night rang with the clash of steel. These men were no novices and the death of their comrade did not move them. Their swords buzzed like wasps, stingers seeking out flesh. It was not enough. Wherever they struck, Caelin's blades were there to meet them.

For a while the young soldier seemed untouchable. Then Caelin grunted and staggered backwards, and Eric saw a trail of blood streaming from a cut across his forehead, dripping in his eyes. His foes closed on him, swords poised to strike.

The first man drew ahead, crossing the other's path. His sword lanced for Caelin's throat. Caelin straightened to brush the blow aside. The man came on, intent on the kill. He grasped his greatsword in both hands and swung it at his Caelin's head.

Sparks flew as their blades met. Caelin stepped back, bending beneath the force of the two handed blow. The thug swung again and again, forcing him back. He gasped for air, fighting for the strength to brave the onslaught. The second man struggled to join the fight, but Caelin was retreating too fast.

Suddenly, the two-handed attacker froze, sword raised above his head. Then he toppled backwards, his comrade leaping from his path. Eric's eyes widened as he saw Caelin's dagger buried in the man's throat.

Caelin strode over the corpse, his face grim. He held only his sword, its tip streaked with blood. The final man backed away, dropping his blade in surrender. Caelin continued towards him until the man fled.

He turned to Eric, exhaustion washing across his face. He smiled anyway. "Are you telling me I have to carry *both* of you now?"

Eric would have laughed, if it weren't for the pain. He felt dizzy and could not seem to get enough air. His stomach roiled. They were lucky the inn was not far. Gritting his teeth, he reached down to grasp the hilt of the dagger.

"I'd leave that, if I were you. You'll do more damage if you pull it out. And you'd likely bleed to death before we got two blocks. Best leave it for a professional."

"What do we do?"

"We get to the inn. When we're safe, I'll send for someone. Then we go after the girl."

****

The cloaked man watched from the shadows. The men's failure angered him, but he was not surprised at the outcome. They were a probe, a test of their strength before he revealed his hand. Now two were wounded, the third exhausted. He could hardly contain his glee. He crept closer. These three he could finish himself. He imagined the pleasure it would bring to drive his blade through Alastair's damned heart.

"Then we go after the girl," the soldier said.

He froze. What had they discovered? Had Enala emerged from hiding? If so, it would not take long to track her down himself. Yet, his master would not be forgiving if she slipped through his fingers a second time.

He retreated into the shadows and slunk away. If he beat them back to the inn, he could delay the ambush for an hour. He needed time to listen for what they knew about the girl.

Then he would wipe the board clean.

****

Eric groaned as Caelin kicked his way through the inn's double doors. A wave of warm air spilled over them and every eye in the dining room turned to stare. Caelin stumbled inside, Eric slung over one shoulder, Alastair the other. His body shook beneath their weight, overwhelmed by the cold and exhaustion.

A voice called from the back of the busy room. "Are you okay?"

"A doctor," Caelin croaked, sinking to the floor.

"Here!" a man shouted, threading his way through the crowd.

Eric looked up at the voice. "That's *Michael*, the priest from the temple. What is he doing here?"

Michael overheard. "Elynbrigge sent me. What's happened?"

"Explanations will have to wait," Caelin snapped. "Michael, take Alastair for God's sake, before I drop him."

Michael bent and took Alastair over his shoulder. The old man was still unconscious and Eric doubted the doctor would get very far beneath the burden. He was not a heavily built man and his hair was already streaked with grey.

"I'll take him," Balistor appeared beside the doctor.

"Where have you been?" Caelin grunted. Michael handed Alastair's limp body over to the Magicker.

"Looking for the girl. What the hell happened to you three? No one was here when I returned," he turned as he spoke, leading them towards the stairwell.

Eric looked around through a haze of pain. People were staring. It was not safe. Their enemies were closing in and word of their entrance would spread quickly. They needed to get out of the city and after Enala, if she still lived. He tried to speak, but each footstep sent a fresh wave of agony from his side. He had to bite his lip to stop from crying out. Blood ran down his leg, his strength slowly trickling away. Tears in his eyes, he fought to stay conscious.

People moved aside as they pushed their way through the room. They made their way into the corridor and climbed the stairs. Eric focused on the thud of Caelin's heavy boots, the sound anchoring him in reality. At the top, Balistor led them to their room and unlocked the door with Alastair's key. Caelin and Michael followed him inside.

Balistor laid Alastair on one of the beds as Caelin did the same for Eric. He sank back onto the soft cushion, the feeling unreal, as though he were floating on a cloud. His head spun as he stared at the ceiling. He closed his eyes, willing it to stop.

"What happened?" Balistor asked grimly.

The bed sank beneath Eric's feet as Caelin sat on the end. The soldier put his face in his hands, exhausted. Michael leant over Alastair, prodding his face and chest with steel instruments.

"We were attacked," Caelin offered. "Ambushed on our way back to the inn. I stopped them, just."

Balistor nodded, his face clouded. His eyes slid from the dagger in Eric's side to Alastair's pale face. Michael rummaged in his shoulder bag, glass clinking from inside. His hand finally emerged holding a small vial filled with a bright green liquid.

He glanced at Caelin. "This is a restorative potion. It's the strongest I have, but looking at his condition, it will not be strong enough. It might give him a few more hours, but ultimately, he is dying."

"No!" Eric struggled to sit up.

Caelin placed a firm hand on his chest, holding him down. "Stay calm, you need to save your strength. I'll take care of this," he turned to the doctor. "Is there anything else you can do?"

Michael shook his head. "I'm only a doctor, and he's too far gone for that. There may be something else, but I will tend to the young man first. He at least I can help."

Eric could almost feel himself shrink as Michael moved to his side. His eyes were grim and, though not unkind, they sent a chill down his spine. His heartbeat fluttered and a new fear gripped him. *Am I going to die?* He dared not voice the question.

Michael lent to examine the wound, his frown deepening. Eric struggled to calm himself, while the doctor reached down and gave the skin around the dagger a tender push.

Eric shrieked as fire ripped through his side. He swore, flinching away from the doctor's touch. His hand snaked out, grabbing Michael by his tunic, fury swamping him. He bared his teeth, a silent threat in his lightning blue eyes.

Michael tisked, brushing off Eric's hand. He dived into his bag again, coming up with a bottle of clear liquid. He removed the cap, releasing the harsh scent of alcohol. The hairs on Eric's neck stood up.

"Hold him down. This is going to hurt," Michael said.

Eric tensed as Caelin and Balistor took a hold of him but did not fight. The alcohol would burn away any infection in the wound, but it would also burn like nothing else. A cold sweat dripped from his brow.

Michael took a cloth and soaked it in the alcohol. Leaning over him he grasped the dagger's handle. Slowly, he began to draw the blade from his side.

Eric screamed, back arching against the pain. The wound was fire, the agony of a red-hot poker jabbed into his skin. Waves of shock ran through his body. His mind whirled. The bitter taste of bile rose in his throat as the world spun. Tears coursed down his face. He fought against his comrades, fought to free himself from their iron grip. Words tumbled from his mouth – senseless, nonsensical profanities that shattered on the walls of the room.

At last the darkness rose up to claim him, the pain falling away into oblivion.

****

Eric awoke to chaos. Distant screams came from the open door, where Michael stood staring into the corridor. Alastair lay in the bed opposite, unmoved, but Caelin and Balistor had vanished.

His hand went to his side, fingers finding the jagged edges of his wound. Stitches held together the angry red flaps of skin. It was painful to the touch, but his head seemed clearer now.

Michael looked back and saw he was awake. He moved to his side. "I washed it out as best I could and then stitched you up. I gave you a small concoction to help with the pain. You were lucky – I don't believe the blade hit any major organs. We'll put a poultice on it later, if there's time."

"Thank you. What's happening out there?"

"I am not sure. Your friends have gone to investigate."

At that moment Caelin strode back into the room. "We have to go," a scream from below emphasised his statement.

Caelin moved to the window and levered it open. The cold night air swept into the room. He leaned out to see what was below. "There are men downstairs – hunters, I think. They're looking for us. Balistor is holding them at the stairs. You three are going out the window."

"I don't think that's a good idea," Michael ventured.

"What about you, Caelin?" Eric demanded.

"Balistor and I will provide a rear guard. Pick up Alastair, doctor."

Michael hesitated. Caelin took a step towards him and the doctor raised his hands in surrender. He looped his bag over one shoulder, then reach down and picked up Alastair in both hands. Arms straining beneath the weight, he moved to the window. The frame was wide, allowing him to balance on the sill without difficulty.

"You don't expect me to jump, do you?" Michael asked, head hanging out the window.

Caelin gave him a kick to the back. Michael and Alastair vanished through the opening.

Eric gasped, turning on Caelin. "What did you do that for?"

Caelin smiled. "Alastair chose your room well. There's a big bale of hay beneath the window. They'll be fine, and it's your turn. Careful with the landing, you're probably going to burst a few stitches," he lifted Eric as he spoke.

"Wait!" Eric resisted.

Caelin didn't bother to stop. He stepped across and dropped him out the window.

Panic flooded Eric's foggy mind. His limbs flailed in every direction, scrambling for a hold that was not there. The stitches at his side pulled tight. Below, the haystack rushed up to meet him. He closed his eyes, hands out to break his fall. The air whistled through his hair. Eric surrendered to his terror. His magic leapt in response.

Eric stopped falling, so suddenly he gasped in pain. He opened his eyes and found himself hovering several feet above the haystack. Wind flowed around his body in massive gusts, holding him aloft. Straws of hay flew with it, dancing through the maelstrom of air.

Eric stared in shocked bemusement, the terror fleeing him. The winds went with it, dumping him into the damp hay.

Shouts came from overhead. Eric looked up in time to see Caelin tumbling through the air, angling his body away from him. The soldier yelled in defiance and disappeared into the haystack.

Balistor appeared in the window above. Fire leapt from his hands, burning up the window frame. Then the Magicker went stiff, his eyes widening in shock. His hands slid from the windowsill and he toppled awkwardly through the window. The fire in his hands died. An arrow protruded from his back. Flames engulfed the room behind him.

Then Michael was hauling Eric up. They stumbled from the haystack, Caelin a step behind them, Balistor leaning on his shoulder. *He'll have carried all of us by the end of the night*, Eric thought to himself.

They stopped in the alleyway, their breath steaming in the icy air. The doctor had already dragged Alastair clear, but there was no way Caelin and Michael could carry them all to safety. Eric looked around, searching for the rear door to the stables. His heart soared as he spotted it nearby.

The unmistakable whisper of steel on leather came from the shadows. Men began to emerge into the moonlight – five, ten, a dozen. Weapons held at the ready, they spread out to encircle the five companions.

Eric swallowed. Backs to the wall, surrounded by enemies, there was no escape.

Caelin stepped forward, sword sliding from its scabbard. "Come on then, who dies first?"

EIGHTEEN

The wet roofing tiles slipped beneath Inken's feet. She swore and took a quick step back. Too late – a tile broke free and tumbled down, shattering on the street below. The crash echoed in the empty alleyway. She winced, imagining the angry glares of the hunters below. Shaking her head in silent apology, she sat back at a safer angle and eyed the inn's dark windows.

The trap was a good one. The man with the gold had a dozen men set to storm the building when the conspirers returned. He'd also set men in the alleyway out back, in case anyone escaped that way. Inken had volunteered to scale the building out back, intuition telling her their prey would allude the frontal assault. There would be extra gold for each kill and she intended to collect it.

A shout pierced the night. Inken strung her bow and nocked an arrow, eyes narrowed in search of movement. It would not be long now. She doubted their prey had the numbers to withstand the hunters attacking from the front. Their only option would be retreat.

Two people hurtled from a second storey window. Inken gasped, expecting them to smash to the bricks below. *What the –?* Then the duo disappeared into a haystack. She smiled at their ingenuity. Another fell, but this one did not reach the ground. His plunge halted a few feet from the hay, gusts of straw whirling around him.

"Magic," Inken whispered to herself. She drew back her bowstring and took aim down the black shafted arrow.

Her target was completely exposed, without so much as a feather of shelter to protect him. Inken drew a deep breath, preparing to loose on the exhale. Then the figure spun in the air and Inken caught a glimpse of his pained face, the unkempt black hair and shocking blue eyes. Her jaw dropped, heartbeat fluttering. *Eric.*

Inken hesitated. Her arm began to tremble with the force of her bowstring, but she could not release. Then the forces suspending Eric in the air disappeared and he vanished into the haystack. She eased her bowstring back, struggling for breath. What could she do?

Footsteps clattered in the alleyway. The bounty hunters closed in, swords drawn. They would be on them in seconds. Two more tumbled from the window, taking Eric's group to a party of five.

They piled out of the haystack. Inken squinted, noticing a green robed man carry Eric free. Worry touched her heart. *Has he been injured?* She frowned at the thought, burying her compassion at the back of her mind. It was her job to put an end to these men, before someone else claimed the reward.

She nocked her arrow again. The hunters below had arrived now, spreading out to surround their quarry. The group had been backed against the alley wall. She imagined their despair. There would be no escaping this trap.

A shiver ran through her body. She took sight, drawing in a breath to steady her aim. Her heart was racing.

Can I do it? Inken asked herself.

The hunter exhaled, and loosed her arrow.

****

The largest of the men raised his sword and grinned. Michael stepped back, arms shaking. Eric struggled to summon his magic, but felt it slip from his grasp. Caelin braced himself, sheltering his defenceless comrades. The hulking hunter stepped towards them.

A black fletched arrow sprouted from the man's head, halting him midstride. His sword slipped from limp fingers, clattering on the bricked road. He slumped to his knees, then crumpled to the ground.

The others whipped around, scanning the skyline for the hidden archer. A couple turned and fled, but one leapt at them with a snarl. A second arrow took him in the shoulder, spinning him to the ground. Pandemonium broke out amongst the hunters as the black shafted missiles rained down amongst them.

Caelin did not hesitate to press the advantage. He charged into their foes, screaming with fury, his sword cutting a jagged hole through their ranks. Before the ferocity of his attack the last vestiges of the hunters' courage dissolved. They turned and fled down the narrow alley.

Caelin dared not chase after them. He turned back to his companions, sword still at the ready. His eyes squinted against the dark skyline, searching the rooftops for their hidden ally. They waited, frozen beneath the burning window. Time ticked away, each second giving the hunters more time to regroup.

Horse hooves clattered on bricks. Caelin spun, sword raised.

"Put that away," Inken ordered as she rode from the shadows. "And get your horses. We're going to need them."

Eric inhaled sharply as he recognised her. She rode up on a silver horse, aglow by the light of the fire. The curls of her scarlet hair tumbled down across her sun kissed face. The marks of the desert had vanished, revealing the smooth curves of her cheekbones and soft red lips. She wore a tight fitting leather jerkin and pants that hugged the curves of her body. She sat tall in her saddle, injuries forgotten and sabre at the ready.

Inken smiled in his direction. "It's good to see you again, Eric. I couldn't help but notice you were in a bit of trouble."

Michael's grip on Eric slipped, forcing him to take his own weight. He groaned, his head swimming with pain.

Inken dismounted and moved to his side, concern etched on her face. He attempted a grin. "You're a welcome sight. Although sadly we seem to have switched roles now."

Inken gave a quick nod and a wink in reply, then turned to Caelin. "The horses, quickly. They won't take long to regroup. And I don't know what's happened to the others in the inn."

"Fire," Balistor groaned.

Eric glanced up and saw Balistor was right. Half the inn was ablaze. A crash came from deep inside the building and a blast of hot air swept from the lower windows. He felt a pang of sadness. The little inn was the closest thing to a home he'd had for a long time.

Caelin ran into the stables, Inken close at his heels. Eric leaned on Michael, watching the alleyway for their enemies, tensed in expectation. For once, luck went their way and no one appeared.

A few minutes later the two emerged leading the horses. Michael had a light brown mare of his own, although she was blind in one eye. He boosted Eric into his saddle and then helped to strap Alastair and Balistor to theirs. Both were unconscious now. Inken mounted up and took the lead.

Eric urged Briar alongside her, fighting to ignore the pain of his wound. It felt good to have the horse beneath him again. The others trotted behind, the echoes of horseshoes on stone loud in the tight space.

They emerged from the network of alleyways several blocks from the inn. Inken said nothing and Eric did not press her. Her rescue still shocked him. She was a bounty hunter, after all. Those had been her comrades back there. He could not imagine what had driven her to make such a decision.

Caelin rode up beside them. "We need to take the north or south gate. The east is blocked," he ventured.

"We'd better move quickly then. There's a man spending gold like its nothing to stop you. Half the city could be looking for you by now. They won't be far behind."

"I'll take the rear then," Caelin turned his horse and dropped back.

"What happened to you?" Inken asked, urging her horse round a sharp turn.

Eric shook his head to clear his thoughts. Whatever Michael had given him had left his mind lethargic and his thoughts were distracted by the sight of Inken. "It's a long story," he hesitated. "But I was stabbed. I'll tell you the rest when we're clear of the city."

"You have magic," Inken pressed. "I saw it. Does that mean...?" she couldn't finish.

Eric closed his eyes, knowing the question and unwilling to answer. If he did, would she turn on him? But he knew he could not hold back the truth. Not now.

"Yes, it was me. It was there Alastair found me, and saved me. He's a Magicker as well. I'm his student. He is teaching me to control my magic. So... so no one else dies," he finished with a whisper.

He risked a glance at Inken. There were tears in her eyes, sparkling in the moonlight. Her expression was unreadable. Eric looked up. The clouds had disappeared, leaving a thousand stars to light the night's sky.

"Did you bring the rain?" Inken asked softly.

Eric nodded, though he shuddered at what that deed had almost caused.

"Thank you," Inken's voice was barely a whisper.

Michael drew alongside them, rummaging in his bag. "The medicine for your pain will fade soon. Take this before it becomes too much."

Eric accepted the small vial and removed the cap. A sour scent came from the purple liquid, but he threw back his head and downed it in one gulp. His eyes watered as the potion burned its way down his throat. Making a face, he handed the vial back to Michael.

Inken was smiling at him again. Eric fought to suppress a smile of his own, wiping his eyes with the back of his sleeve. His clothes were slowly drying out from the rain.

It was not long before the northern gates appeared. Inken turned to him. "Are you up for a race?"

Eric winced, but he could see what she meant. A guard was waiting by the gates, arms crossed as he watched them. Their passage this late at night with so many injured was bound to draw attention. Even the laziest guard would insist they wait for the sergeant to question them. They could not afford to be delayed so long.

He nodded, though a gallop was sure to burst his stitches. Inken whispered a hurried instruction to the others and then rode towards the guard. They followed close behind her, legs tensed in their stirrups. The guard stepped out to block the way as they approached.

A few feet from the gate, Inken shouted and kicked her horse hard in the sides. The gelding leapt in response, bowling the guard from his feet. Eric dashed after her, Briar pounding beneath him, his side shrieking with each stride. They raced beneath the wall, filling the tunnel with the clattering of hooves. They rode through the darkness, drawn on by the light at the end.

Then they were free, racing onto the plains outside the city. The road stretched out in front of them, straight and smooth beneath their horses' pounding feet. This was the main road to Chole, where most of the traffic into and out of the city passed. Further north the desert gave way to fields of grass and eventually the farmlands of Lonia.

The companions did not slow until they were well away from the city. Finally, Inken drew rein, looked around to check they were all still with her and then pushed on at an easier pace.

Eric took a deep, shuddering breath. His side was sticky with blood. He lifted his shirt to check his wound. Most of the stitches had burst, the flaps of skin pulled apart by the wild ride. It made him dizzy just to look at it, but the potion had taken hold and he felt almost no pain.

Michael rode alongside him, drawing Alastair's horse with him. Eric's eyes slid to his mentor's face. The slight flutter of his eyelids was the only hint of life.

"He doesn't have long, Eric," Michael spoke gently.

Eric shook his head. "He can't die, we need him," he hesitated. "What was the something else you mentioned before?"

Michael slapped his arm, chasing an insect of the night. "I'm afraid I don't know much about magic, Eric. However, I have heard tales of Magickers transferring energies between themselves. Alastair has expended too much of his own life force to recover naturally, but a jolt of energy may just bring him back from the brink," he glanced at the unconscious Balistor. "But it seems we are running short of those with power."

Eric took a deep breath. "I'm a Magicker."

The doctor gave him a long look before he replied. "No. You're injured as well. We would risk losing the both of you."

"I can't just watch him die, Michael. I have to try it."

Michael sighed. "I can't stop you, Eric. But we don't even know how such a feat is accomplished."

"I know."

Eric closed his eyes and shut out the world. He sank into the trance, physical sensation falling away easily with the aid of Michael's medicine. The magic rose in response, setting alight the darkness of his inner mind with its soft glow. It seemed weaker now, already spent and drained away with his life's blood. He hoped there was enough.

He reached out, summoning the fickle energies to the surface. Opening his eyes, he looked at Alastair's still form. He hesitated, the hairs on his arms prickling with power. What did he do now? How could he give this strength to Alastair?

Eric swallowed. He would not be here if not for Alastair. The old man had risked everything to throw him a lifeline. Now he was dying because of a mistake Eric had made. Whatever the danger, he had to find a way.

Taking hold of his magic, Eric let his soul take flight. The aches of his body fled behind him as the heavens drew him skyward. Opening his spirit eyes, he looked around. His conscious shivered. His comrades rode on, oblivious to his ghostly presence. Each glowed with an inner light, their auras lighting the night around them.

Their life force, Eric wondered, *or magic?* He thought as he looked at the bright beacon within Balistor.

He stole a glance at Inken. Her fiery red aura matched the ember glow of her hair, though there was no menace to the light.

Bracing himself, Eric left thoughts of her behind and turned to Alastair. The old man's aura was all but gone, reduced to a wan grey spark deep within his chest; A mere candle against the darkness.

Eric drifted closer, worry clouding his thoughts. His magic began to slip. Grimly he forced his emotion down and turned his mind to the problem. He grasped his magic in ethereal fingers. Slowly, it began to spin, thinning and stretching into a long cord. It stretched out into the night, a thin blue tendril reaching for Alastair. Eric concentrated, forcing it on towards his mentor. The thread leapt forward, sinking into Alastair and wrapping about the dying grey spark.

As they met, a flash of light erupted across Eric's vision. With a violent jerk, his soul hurtled back into the physical realm. He whimpered as the pain returned and exhaustion swept through his body. A dull ache began in his head.

Beside him, Alastair sat up on his horse. Michael jumped in shock and almost fell from his saddle. He recovered on the brink of tumbling to the ground. He opened his mouth but could not find the words to speak.

Alastair gave him a curious look. "What are you doing here, priest?" he asked in a gravelly voice.

"I... I... Elynbrigge sent me," Michael stammered.

Alastair nodded, eyes sweeping their other companions. "Inken, happy to see you have recovered. Did my old friend send you as well?"

Inken stared at him. She brushed a strand of scarlet hair from her face before answering. "No, I'm not sure why I am here. Maybe I will leave you in the morning," she looked at Eric. "Maybe not."

Alastair nodded. "Good enough," he drew back on Elcano's reins and dropped back beside Eric.

Eric smiled in greeting, warmth flooding his chest. Alastair looked like living death, his skin grey and eyes bloodshot, but the spark of life had returned.

"Thank you, Eric, for saving my life," his face darkened. He leaned across his saddle. His hand struck out and slapped Eric hard across the face.

Eric lurched back and toppled from his horse. Agony lanced through his side as he struck the ground. He screamed, looking up at Alastair through blurry eyes, mind reeling.

"Why?" He yelled from the dusty ground.

"*Never* do that again, Eric," his voice shook with fear. "What you just did is forbidden to all but the greatest adepts. A little more energy and you would have burnt me to a crisp. Or worse, you could have spent too much of your own power and died yourself."

Eric gaped, speechless. His head ached and not even Michael's medicine could stop the pain from his wound. *I was just trying to help!* He wanted to say, but the words would not come.

Alastair closed his eyes. "I am sorry I hit you," he turned his horse and rode past their stunned companions. "We'll make camp here. Morning's not far off and we must be gone by the time the sun rises. Michael, it looks like Balistor needs your attention."

The others dismounted and began to set up camp. Eric remained where he had fallen, too shocked to move. The blow had robbed him of his senses. He closed his eyes, fighting off tears.

Stones crunched as Inken sat down next to him. She

carried a bag from which she drew a needle and thread. Eric's sluggish mind quickly realised what it was for.

"I think your wound needs attention, Eric," Inken offered in a kind voice. "I'm sorry about the gallop, it couldn't have been easy."

By the moonlight, Eric saw his shirt was damp with blood. He wondered what Inken was thinking, whether she was laughing at his embarrassment. Gritting his teeth, he pushed the thought down. "Michael's potions must be strong; I didn't even feel them tear."

"Then I guess you won't mind this," Inken teased, lifting up his shirt to look at his side.

Eric scowled, not wanting to watch the procedure but drawn by a morbid curiosity. Inken's hands moved with practiced ease, taking a gentle grip of the inflamed skin. The thread trailed over her wrist, keeping it from the dirt. Carefully she pushed the needle through.

Eric blinked, realising he felt no pain. He watched as Inken weaved the needle through his skin, drawing the black thread tight with each stitch. Yet he felt nothing. It was the strangest sensation.

"He shouldn't have hit you," Inken ventured as she worked. "You were only trying to help him. And it worked, too."

Eric did not offer a reply. He didn't want to think about it.

It was another ten minutes before Inken finished the last of the stitches. She looked up, offering Eric a smile. "All done," she whispered.

Eric smiled back, noticing now how close her lips were. Strands of her hair stirred as he exhaled sharply. The scent of her filled his nostrils. Her eyes caught his stare, trapping him in their hazel depths. He was suddenly very aware of the hard pounding in his chest, the surge of excitement in his blood. It was intoxicating, though he could no longer tell whether that was the potion or the closeness of her body.

"Why did you save us, Inken?" he whispered, so close his lips grazed her cheek.

"For you, Eric."

And she kissed him.

NINETEEN

E nala crouched in the damp grass, staring into the shadows of the forest. The first rays of the morning sun peeked above the treetops, casting the undergrowth in green silhouettes. Puffs of steam rose from the rain soaked earth. The stark slopes of the volcanic peaks towered above, the treeline beginning where the earth began to flatten out.

A shiver ran through Enala – not of cold, but exhaustion. They had walked for two nights and a day, putting as many miles as they could between themselves and Chole. They had crossed the mountains last night, the desert turning to forest as they marched in darkness. Her legs burned from the effort and her shoulders ached from the heavy pack. Gabriel had filled their bags with enough supplies for a week's travel. If all went well, it would be all they needed.

She took a swig from her water skin, glad they had made it into the forest before sunrise. With the sun shining, the mountain walk would have become unbearably hot. They had crossed the northern slopes during the night; That had been hard enough.

Enala breathed in the crisp mountain air, savouring the

scent. It had been years since her parents last brought her this way, though it had once been an annual trip. The trail was nearly indiscernible now, but she remembered it well. It was a treacherous path, edging along cliffs and loose boulders. She hoped it would prove fatal to any who followed them.

The way would be slightly easier now they had reached the trees. They were thin here at the base of the mountains, but would soon change to dense rainforest on the floodplains of the Onyx River. She doubted anyone would follow them once they crossed the river. It didn't matter how determined they were, few had the courage to brave Dragon Country.

A shadow fell across her heart when she thought of the monsters who chased her. Shaking her head, Enala turned her attention to Gabriel. They had said little in the three days spent hidden in the abandoned house. They had listened to the pounding rain, occasionally making clumsy attempts at conversation.

Enala had slowly risen from her chasm of grief – enough to think again, enough to plan. Yet a terrible distance still stood between the two of them, one she could not bring herself to cross. The wounds were too raw, the pain so strong her eyes watered.

His presence was welcome though. Better than being alone, when her thoughts would turn inwards, drawn down by an unending cycle of self-interrogation and blame. The darkness of the basement clung to her still and at night she would wake screaming and thrashing, desperate to escape her sweat soaked blanket. Faceless men stalked her dreams, until she was terrified to close her eyes.

She flicked the copper lock from her eyes, forcing the black thoughts away. Gabriel was an enigma. He had appeared from nowhere – with a *wolf* – and plucked her from the darkness. Then he had saved her from his own beast. And she still had no idea who he was. That alone unnerved her.

"How are your legs?" Gabriel asked, breaking across her trail of thought.

"Fine," she replied.

An awkward silence followed. Enala frowned, unable to find the words. Thoughts of Gabriel inevitably summoned pictures of the wolf, or the blank horror of her parents' faces.

"Enala, it's been five days. I've had enough of silence. Listen, I know what you've gone through –"

"You know *nothing* of what I've been through," Enala cut him off.

Tears sprang to her eyes. Terrible images rose from the depths of her mind. Bile rose in her throat, but it was too late to banish the thoughts now.

She turned on Gabriel. "How *dare* you tell me you know what this is like," the words tumbled from her in a torrent. *"My parents were murdered right above my head!"*

Enala broke off, refusing to look at the man. She ran her hands through her filthy hair, gasping for air between half-choked sobs.

"I listened to them for hours," she continued softly, her voice cracking. "For hours as their tormentors made them scream. I listened to their voices, the endless questions about children, about relatives. In the end, I prayed for their deaths, just so the nightmare might cease," the words were out before she could take them back. She had not even admitted those last thoughts to herself.

Gabriel reeled back before the fury of her words. "I'm sorry."

"Sorry? What does that do for me?" her words dripped with acid. "My parents are gone, dead. I *wished* them gone, yet still they kept me a secret. That didn't last long though and now there are people *hunting me*. I can never go back to my life. What does one, or a hundred, or a thousand 'sorries' matter to me?"

"I have no life to go back to either," Gabriel ventured.

Enala blinked, thrown off track by his words. "What?"

Gabriel's eyes never left the ground. "My home was destroyed by a storm. My parents, my fiancé, they didn't survive," he looked up, steel in his voice. "I may not have lost them as you lost your parents, but don't you *dare* tell me I have no idea of loss."

Enala watched a tear run down Gabriel's cheek. Burdened by her own grief, she had not stopped to think of him. She remembered the basement, remembered Gabriel's tears as they held each other. For the first time she felt a connection to him, a slender bridge spanning the chasm between them.

"I'm sorry," the words came out without thought.

Gabriel laughed. "Ay, sorries we both seem to have in plenty. I guess in the end we're both just two sorry orphans. Friends?" he offered his hand.

Enala found herself smiling. Gabriel had a personality after all. For a brief moment the day seemed a little brighter. She took his hand. "Friends," she agreed. "It seems a long time since I've had one."

"It is a lonely life without them."

"Yes, but not quite so lonely with my parents."

"Ay. We will have to make do with each other now though. Shall we press on?"

Enala glanced at the sun, her anxiety returning. They had been sitting there for close to an hour. Her body ached from the march, but her inner voice reminded her of the danger. The hunters were coming. They would catch them if they stayed still.

"Yes. I lost track of the time. We still have a long way to go," she stood as she spoke, swinging her pack onto her shoulders.

"Where are we going?" Gabriel asked as they moved off.

"Somewhere safe."

They made their way deeper into the trees, leaving the morning sun behind. The stunted canopy hung low over their heads, prickly leaves brushing against their clothing. They caught in Enala's hair, forcing her to pull up her hood to protect herself. It was worse for Gabriel; the low branches meant he had to walk in a half-crouch.

Gabriel's fitness did not measure up to her own and he was soon puffing along behind her. He was also no forester, his heavy footsteps announcing their presence to the forest creatures long before they appeared. The trees rustled in the morning breeze and they heard the soft call of monkeys in the distance. Tiny insects flew at their faces and bit wherever their clothes did not cover.

"You know, 'somewhere safe' doesn't really tell me much. I thought we were friends now."

"We are."

"Aren't friends meant to trust each other?"

Enala grinned, although Gabriel could not see it. "Trust me when I say, it's better you don't know."

Gabriel fell silent. Enala could almost picture his frustration. She wondered how long it would take for him to try again.

He broke the silence a few hours later. "Can you at least tell me how far off we are? This is not an easy trek!"

Enala laughed. The canopy had risen high above their heads now, making passage through the undergrowth far easier. They had reached the floodplains, though they stretched for miles in every direction. "It's a good day's walk through this forest, and it will grow denser again towards the river. We should get there late tomorrow morning, I think," she brushed a leafy branch away from her face and ducked beneath it.

When she released it, the branch swung back and struck Gabriel square in the face. He fell backwards in surprise.

Enala looked back and chuckled. "Sorry, my fault. But you shouldn't walk so close."

Gabriel brushed the dirt and water from his clothing. Standing, he shot her a cheeky grin. "I'll get you back for that one. And *I* don't want to lose you in this forest. I'm a smith, not a woodsman. I'm not used to all these trees, I prefer *roads*."

"Just wait until tomorrow. The trees by the river are younger and the seedlings grow thick beneath them. I doubt the path still exists either, so we'll be fighting our way through."

Gabriel groaned. As they continued deeper into the forest, Enala felt the tension falling from her shoulders. She embraced the music of the bush, feeling its magic all around her. *This* was her home. Let them follow her here if they dared.

Soon the light began to fade and Enala found herself battling to keep her eyes open. They had hardly slept in the last two days, nor during their time spent hiding in the city. In her dreams she found herself running, fleeing pale faced demons with knives dripping blood. Each time she slept, they gained more substance.

Even so, Enala refused to stop until night had fallen. By then the forest was thick around them. There was no way to see the mountains through the canopy, but Enala knew they would be far behind them now. They were closing in on their goal. It would only take a few more hours in the morning to reach the river.

They could not risk a fire, so they sat in the darkness

and feasted on cold beef jerky. The air had grown humid as they dropped into the river lands, leaving them sticky with sweat and their clothes clinging to their skin. Enala almost found herself wishing for the dry heat of the desert. Tomorrow she would savour the chance to bathe in the river.

"Enala, I want to thank you. You saved me, back there in the city."

Enala looked up with a frown. "What do you mean? *You* saved *me*. The wolf would have killed me if you hadn't injured it."

"I wasn't talking about that, but I will add my thanks for the chair as well. No, you saved my soul."

"What do you mean?"

"The wolf, it was given to me by a demon."

Enala's breath hissed between her teeth. Her nightmares leapt into reality. She saw again Gabriel drawing his sword on her. She reached for her knife.

"Easy!" Gabriel raised his hands in surrender. "Let me explain. I think I've earned that much?"

Enala hesitated, before offering a short nod.

Gabriel sighed. "The demon corrupted me. It placed me under some kind of spell, made me something else. My memories were stolen. I'm only just starting to remember."

"That's horrible," Enala could not relax, but the story called to her. *This has something to do with me*, she realised.

"It was my own fault. The demon offered me aid and I was foolish enough to take it. It gave me the wolf, I cannot remember why. It wanted you dead though, ordered me to kill you. But I couldn't do it; something about you broke its spell. *You saved me*."

Enala frowned. "Who was this demon?"

"I don't know," Gabriel shivered, though the air was still thick with heat. "I have never felt such an evil. I cannot think why I was so blind to accept its offer. It was not long after I lost my family. That time is all still a haze."

Enala watched the shadows. *Who am I to these demons?* In a whisper, she asked. "What did it want? Why did it want me dead?"

"I don't know. I think you were an unexpected opportunity though. I was meant to kill an old man – and a young one. Their faces are the clearest images I have left."

"I wonder who they are."

"They are in mortal peril."

Like me, Enala thought. *Maybe they are just as terrified, as confused, as I am.* There was nothing they could do for them now though.

"Your parents were incredibly brave," Gabriel changed the subject.

Enala sighed. "Yes. They gave their lives to save me, hid me seconds before the assassins found them. Somehow they withstood torture to protect me. I doubt I could have done the same."

The leaf litter crunched. Gabriel eased himself down beside her and put an arm around her shoulders. "You were brave too."

"No, I wasn't. All I wanted to do was race up the ladder and save them. But I was frozen, too scared to move."

"It would have broken their hearts if you had. They died in the knowledge they had protected their daughter, that you were safe. There was nothing you could have done for them."

The night pressed in on them. Enala closed her eyes, leaning into Gabriel's shoulder. She found some comfort in his words, though doubts still plagued her. Her parents had raised her to be strong, to never run from an enemy. Yet here she was, fleeing for her life.

You have no choice, she reasoned, *your enemies are ghosts, their motives a mystery. They are stronger and have the advantage of knowledge. There is no choice but to run.*

Still, she wondered what her parents would have done. Their murder screamed out for justice, but she did not have the strength or courage to give it.

Enala could feel the steady beat of Gabriel's heart beneath her head. The earthly scent of his clothes was soothing. She thought of sleep and no longer found it so frightening. She felt safe in Gabriel's arms, his heartbeat a lullaby in her ear.

She slept.

****

Enala woke to sunlight shining in her face. She opened one sleepy eye and looked around. Nearby, a bright red and green parrot hopped along the ground, pecking at the crumbs of their dinner. She lay in Gabriel's arms, though he was still fast asleep. She sat up, smothering a yawn. The bird froze, watching her closely. When she stood, it fled into the sky. With it, the last vestiges of sleep fell away.

She swore softly to herself. They had not kept a watch. Anyone could have come on them, captured or killed them without so much as a fight. She leant down and nudged Gabriel's side. His eyes snapped open.

"We'd better get moving. The day is well under way."

He groaned and sat up. "How did you sleep?"

"Better," Enala had not so much as stirred. Her dreams were already fading away, but she recalled a deep sense of security, one that kept the demons at bay. "Come on, we need to cross the river before lunch."

Gabriel climbed to his feet and pulled on his pack. "No

breakfast?"

Enala considered it, but the risk was too great. "No, we slept too long for that. If they spotted us leaving Chole, they might not be far behind. We've already lost too many hours today."

Gabriel nodded. "We'll make up for it at lunch I guess. Lead on."

Enala checked the sun, then pushed her way into the undergrowth. The bush grew thick here, the branches interlinked to block their passage. She forced her way through the spiky seedlings that tore at her skin and hair. Thorny plants were common on the floodplains, their only defence against the large flightless birds that roamed here.

It was past noon when they finally reached the river. By then they were both sweating in the tropical heat and stinking as though they had not bathed in weeks. Mud stained Enala's blond hair, and her clothes were reduced to tatters.

They had heard the roar of the waters from a long way off, but the river still took them by surprise. The trees stretched right to the riverbanks, their twisted branches hanging out to conceal the dirty water. Unaware, Enala strode right over the edge, her feet sliding towards the raging current. She flung out her arms, her desperate grip finding Gabriel's hand. Her shoulder jolted as he yanked her back to safety.

Enala rubbed her shoulder and moved back to firmer ground. The narrow river was running high from the recent rains, its waters racing past at a frightening pace.

"We need to cross that?" Gabriel asked.

"Yes."

"How do you plan to do that? Can you swim?"

"I didn't live in Chole my entire life. Yes, I can swim. And I think I have a plan."

She moved back into the forest, searching for branches. Her parents had never crossed with her when the river was this high, but she knew how. It would be dangerous, but not as dangerous as staying on this side.

Enala returned to Gabriel carrying two heavy tree branches, one over each shoulder. Each was around the length of her body, heavy and half-rotten. Nevertheless, they would float, which was all they needed.

Gabriel relieved her of a branch when she walked up. "What are these for?"

"Think of them as life savers. They'll keep us afloat in the river," she sat down and started taking off her boots.

"Are you insane? Those currents will drag us under in seconds."

Enala grinned. "We have two choices: cross, or wait on this side to be caught. You can stay if you want," she tucked her boots into her pack. "But I'm crossing."

Gabriel sighed, shaking his head. He sat and took off his boots, placed them in his pack and tied it closed with his sword belt.

Enala hoped the leather packs would keep most of the water out. They would need dry clothes when they reached the other side. She lashed her bag to the branch and glanced at Gabriel. "Ready?"

"Oh, absolutely. This should be a ball."

Enala laughed and threw herself into the water. The river caught her and for a second the wood sank beneath the surface. She started to panic as the muddy water closed over her head, cutting off the world above. Then the wood rose beneath her, hauling her back to the surface. Taking a deep breath, she looked around and kicked for the opposite bank. A splash from behind told her Gabriel was following.

The river raced around her, dragging her downstream. Trees rushed past on either bank. The water swirled around her clothes, icy from its mountain source. Her arms grew numb and the currents threatened to pull her from the log. She took a stronger grip and kicked harder.

Enala had travelled a long way downstream by the time she washed up on the far shore. She clambered up the bank, gasping from the cold, and dumped her pack to the muddy ground. Turning back, she looked for Gabriel.

He was still some distance upstream, struggling with the current to reach her side. He held his branch out in front of him like a kick board, feet churning the water behind him. However, his progress was slow. He looked exhausted.

An ear-splitting roar came from above. The hackles rose on the back of Enala's neck. She shrank against a tree, peering up through the leaves of the canopy. Red scales glittered in the sunlight as the dragon dropped from the sky. The earth shook when it landed, shattering trees like toothpicks. Slitted nostrils widened as it sniffed the air. The great yellow globes of its eyes searched the trees.

Enala slid around a tree trunk, still watching the water. Gabriel had stopped kicking, caught in the depths of the current. Their eyes met.

Go, he mouthed.

Enala shook her head. She would not abandon her friend. The rumble of the dragon's breath came closer.

Go, now!

Enala could see his fear, his desperation. Ignoring him, she started to slip back into the water, prepared to follow him further downstream.

"No!" Gabriel shouted. He started to thrash, sending up a spray of foam.

Enala shrank into the shadows, her eyes drawn to the dragon. Its head had whipped around, eyes locked on Gabriel's floundering figure. He was still in the middle of the river, the open water offering no cover from the dragon's glare. Trapped in the currents, he had nowhere to go.

Tears ran from Enala's eyes. This could not be happening, not again. She stood paralysed, powerless to help. Her hands clenched to fists, her mouth hung open. Cracks spread through her fragile mind, madness threatening. She could not take her eyes from Gabriel.

The dragon took to the air, broad wings carrying it towards her friend. Gabriel watched it come, eyes grim, silent now. With a scream that made her blood freeze, the dragon dove. Its bulk smashed the water, sending a wave rolling across the river. The dragon thrashed in the murky waters, jaws gnashing, claws slashing. Then its great wings began to claw at the air. It climbed above the river, circling still, before it finally disappeared behind the treetops.

Its roar slowly faded away.

Enala watched the roiling waters for a long time, but there was no sign of Gabriel. She sank to her knees. The cracks grew, spreading, and something within her shattered.

Darkness swallowed her. Enala opened her arms to embrace it.

TWENTY

Eric watched the river race by. Leaves floated in the current, while larger objects slid by beneath the murky surface. A cool wind blew off the water, a welcome respite from the humid valley air. Silt and dead leaves hung suspended from the trees on the riverbanks, left behind by the high waters of the past few days.

He shifted in his saddle, aching from the hard ride. The sun was behind them, fading into the afternoon. The stitches pulled tight against his side. His wound was healing well, but Michael insisted they stay in place for another week yet. Inken had done a good job stitching him back up.

He glanced across to where she sat on her horse, eyeing the water. He felt a familiar fluttering in his stomach. The last few days had passed in a daze, leaving him wondering at times whether he was dreaming.

Memories sprang into his mind, too vivid for fantasy. The taste of her mouth, the soft caress of her lips against his. Her hair tickling his cheek, filling his nostrils with her fragrant scent. Her hand on his chest, his own behind her head as he kissed her harder. When they finally separated, he felt as though the earth had shifted on its axis. Inken had smiled at him and winked, then moved away.

When the sun rose, Inken had led their weary party across the desert. She had spotted where Enala and her companion had left the northern road and searched out their tracks east across the sand and stones. It was no easy task. The hard ground left little sign of their passage. It took all of Inken's expertise to follow them across the barren earth and up into the mountains.

Eric paid little attention to the rest of their party. Balistor's wound was not as bad as Eric had thought, for he now rode straight in his saddle. Michael said his shoulder blade had prevented the arrow from penetrating deeper. The doctor himself was quiet, clearly uneasy in their presence, while Caelin rode with Alastair. There was little conversation, the air taut with tension.

A distance loomed between himself and Alastair now. Eric had already forgiven the blow; Alastair had done too much to hold it against him. But he would not be the first to break the awkward silence.

They had not made it far into the forests of the Onyx valley before the gloom forced them to make camp. The trip had been silent and miserable. The gloom was wearing, feeding his doubts as he wondered about his kiss with Inken. They had hardly spoken that first day, too preoccupied by the chase. He had noticed her watching him though, and each time his heart thumped harder.

When their camp was set, Alastair had come and offered to join him in meditation. The darkness masked his face, but Eric had read the apology in the soft-spoken words. He was eager to accept the truce.

Though too exhausted to touch their magic, the meditation gave them both a chance to regain their composure. They moved away from the others, leaving them to themselves. Balistor sat with his back to a tree, eyes closed. The other three sat speaking in soft tones.

Eric crossed his legs and closed his eyes. Slowly, he sank into the familiar trance. His tension began to fade away, as he attempted to set aside the shock and hurt of Alastair's blow. He soon found other thoughts struggling for his attention: Inken's smuggled glances, the soft caress of her lips, what she was thinking now...

He heard Alastair move away, but he remained, struggling to reach an inner calm. It continued to elude him, until at last he opened his eyes, defeated. Inken sat across from him, her hazel eyes watching him with interest. She shot him a mischievous grin when she saw his eyes open. The sight sent his mind spinning, lost in the fiery tangles of her hair.

"What are you doing?" she asked.

Eric stretched his neck, loosening his shoulders in a transparent attempt to appear relaxed. "It's called meditation. Alastair is teaching me to use it to reach my magic, to control it."

Inken leaned in closer. "Can a normal person do it?"

Eric pulled back. "Aren't I normal?"

She gave a wry grin. "Hardly. Most people don't control the weather," she reached across and pulled his head to hers. Their lips met and he could scarcely believe they were kissing again. Her touch was gentle, her lips yielding against his. The sweet tang of orange lingered on her tongue.

"And I don't do that with most people either," she whispered as she drew back.

Eric laughed, his heart still pounding from the kiss. His doubts dissolved and summoning his courage he leaned across and kissed her back.

When they finally drew apart, he furrowed his brow, thinking of her question. "I'm sure there's nothing stopping a 'normal' person from meditating. Come on, I'll show you."

For the next hour, they sat together in the peace of the forest. The exercises were light hearted and playful at first, the two of them sitting close, embracing one another's quirks. Eric forgot about their companions, the past, his quest. Sitting with Inken, he did feel almost normal.

As the night grew later they quieted, each slipping into a more serious trance. Inken had closed her eyes, her breathing slowing. Smiling, Eric did the same, seeking the inner calm that had eluded him earlier. This time, with his doubts crushed, the task was easy. They sat in silence, together but each in their own private sanctuary, beneath the forest roof.

When Eric finally slipped from the trance, Inken was staring at him again. There was a softness to her eyes. "You were so peaceful. The sadness on your face was gone."

Eric shifted, uneasy with her stare. "You should have roused me. How long was I out?"

"Long enough, but it's okay. It was relaxing to watch," she paused. "Eric, I have a question."

"What?"

"Who is it we are tracking? Why does Alastair want to find her so much?"

"That's two questions," Eric teased.

"I'm serious."

Eric sighed. "I know, but I can't give you the answers. It is Alastair's secret to tell, though I can tell you he means her no harm."

Inken frowned at him. He noticed a leaf had caught in her hair and reached across to pick it out before continuing. "I swore to keep this secret. I cannot break that promise, not even for you. But without you we would never have gotten this far. You deserve to know; I'll make Alastair tell you if necessary."

"Now?"

He nodded. They moved back through the forest to where the others sat. As they joined them, Eric noticed Balistor and Michael had already retired. Caelin and Alastair were speaking softly but broke off when they appeared.

"Ah, the young couple returns," Caelin grinned.

Eric flushed and Inken shot Caelin a warning glare. Ignoring the exchange, Eric moved across to Alastair. "Inken wants to know who Enala is."

Alastair nodded without surprise. "I was wondering how long it would take. Inken, your aid has been invaluable. If it weren't for your skills, we would have been killed in Chole. And we would never have found their trail. You have a right to know, as does Michael."

He moved to the doctor and shook him awake. Michael grumbled at the disturbance, but his complaints trailed off when he saw the others waiting. Alastair sat back down, and without embellishment, laid out the tale. Eric was surprised at the casual way Alastair put his faith in the newcomers. He felt a pang of jealousy, his own frustration at being kept in the dark was still all too fresh.

His thoughts soon turned to fear though, the story an unwelcome reminder of the stakes of their quest. He watched Inken for her reaction. Archon was a nightmare whispered of by old men whose grandfathers had fought in the war. Only the Gods rivalled his power. If they failed, if Enala died, they would pay for their defiance. He could not blame her if she turned back now. To stay was to be hunted, to face almost certain death.

Michael's shock was obvious, his mouth hanging open in fear or anger. Inken's expression did not betray her thoughts. She stood, silent, and offered Eric her hand. Drawing him up, she led him into the trees. As they passed beyond sight of the camp, she turned and threw herself at him.

Stunned, Eric almost lost his feet. Pain lanced through his side, but then her mouth was hard against his and it no longer seemed to matter. She kissed him with a new found, almost violent, passion. Eric lost himself in the moment. When at last they broke apart, they stood staring at each other, breathless.

"You're either brave or insane, Eric," she told him.

Eric could not help but smile. "I know. Maybe you could tell me when you work out which it is, because I'm still undecided. Will you help us?"

Inken tilted her head, laughter on her lips. "The other hunters will be looking for me as hard as they are you now. There is nothing for me to go back to. Even if that weren't the case, I could not leave this girl to her fate. She had no choice in any of this," she paused. "And I will not abandon you either."

Then they were in each other's arms, lips locked, tongues tasting, her body pressed hard against him. She groaned and a shiver ran through his body. His arms encircled her, his blood throbbing to the racing thud of his heart. They fell, down, down, down…

Eric sat staring at the river, his face growing hot with the memory. They would have to cross the icy waters. Enala and the man had entered here, of that Inken was certain. There was no sign they had come back out on this bank either – they had to have crossed. He could only guess how they could have done so without horses. Eric prayed they hadn't drowned.

Even if they had survived the swim, the Onyx River marked the Plorsean border with Dragon Country. Few travellers came this way and even less returned from adventures across the border. This was the last territory where the dragon tribes still roamed free and most were not friends to humans. The Blues and Browns had no fondness for people, and Reds were berserkers with no regard for life. The Golds were the only tribe who would not kill them on sight, with some even honouring the ancient alliance made to the kings of old.

Enala had charged headlong into this perilous land, where even armies might have given pause. They had to catch up; every minute that passed was another in which the beasts might find her.

Inken edged her mount into the river. Eric came close behind, bracing himself against the glacial cold. He guessed the waters had fallen since Enala crossed with her companion, receding with the passing of the storm.

Briar carried him deeper and water rushed into his boots. A shiver ran up his legs as it climbed higher, drawing level with his waist. He tightened his grip on the reins as Briar's feet left the riverbed and he began to swim.

There was little he could do but trust the horse to reach the other side. Briar snorted and shook his head, the whites showing in his eyes. Eric patted his neck and willed him onwards, pushing down his own fear. They surged after Inken.

The powerful waters raced around them and even faithful Briar struggled in the current. Eric braced himself; sure the river would pull them under. But the horse prevailed and they reached the other side in one soggy piece.

Eric let out a long breath of relief when he dismounted on solid ground. He led Briar up the bank and began to towel the horse dry with a blanket from the leather saddlebags. Quietly, he whispered his thanks to the horse as the others joined them.

By the time Eric looked up from his task, Inken had vanished. He opened his mouth to call for her and then shut it again. This side of the Onyx was fraught with danger; there was no room for risks. Inken would be checking for Enala's tracks and any noise would only draw unwanted attention to them.

Still, Inken should not have gone alone. It was reckless. The dragons were just as much a danger to her as Enala. He could only hope her skills would be enough to go undetected. Clenching his fists, he waited, anger and fear waring within.

An hour later, Inken had still not returned. Squashing his pride, Eric begged the others to go after her. They waved off his concerns with grim smiles.

"She knows what she's doing, Eric," Caelin told him. "And none of us have the skill to follow her tracks out here anyway. Better we wait another hour at least, instead of getting ourselves lost."

The hour was almost up before the wisdom of Caelin's words were proven correct. Inken appeared from the trees with hardly a sound. Relief swept through Eric, though he struggled to keep it from his face. Time and worry had fed his anger and he wouldn't let her absence go so easy.

"Where have you been?" he attempted to growl, but the words died on his tongue as he saw her face.

"Only the girl made it to this side of the river, and there are signs a dragon landed where she came ashore. Large claw marks and fallen trees. Her tracks head east, but I'm afraid there may be a dragon on her trail."

"There was no sign of the boy at all?" Alastair asked.

"No. I think he may have drowned, or been taken by the dragon. Do you know who he was?"

"No, he is another mystery. We'll have to ask when we find her. Let's go. If the dragons find her first…" there was no need to finish the sentence.

They pushed on, Inken in the lead, until they met up with Enala's trail. From there Inken rode hunched forward, eyes to the ground. She said little, concentration etched across her face, though it was obvious Enala was no longer bothering to hide her trail. She had left clear footprints in the soft ground and crushed undergrowth in her wake.

Eric could understand Inken's concern. Enala may have assumed no one would follow her into land ruled by the dragons. Yet from everything they had seen so far, it seemed uncharacteristically reckless. Was she running from something, or had the loss of her companion been the final blow to her sanity? The devastation this girl had suffered in the last week would be enough to break the toughest psyche.

His eyes swept the forest as they rode, his hands tense on the reins. The trees grew in size as they ventured deeper into Dragon Country, towering over the wary trespassers. Massive tree trunks dominated the forest this side of the river, untouched by the axes of man. The canopy grew higher and higher, blotting out the sun and stunting the undergrowth beneath. The temperatures fell as they climbed from the river valley.

They made good time, following Enala's weaving path through the giant trunks. Even so, the last light of the evening had begun to fade when Inken drew back suddenly on her reins. She leapt from the horse, dropping to hands and knees to inspect the earth.

"Stay back!" she warned.

Eric swiped at a buzzing insect, anxious at the panic in Inken's voice. He glanced at the forest around them, searching for movement. The undergrowth was still. There was not even a breeze to stir the leaves beneath the canopy.

Then he noticed the first signs of disturbance: A crushed fern close to the trail, Bark scraped from nearby trees, Broken branches and claw marks in the soft earth. Something big had crossed Enala's path. Heart sinking, he glanced up and saw the hole in the canopy.

"No, no, no!" Inken hissed. "Where did she go? She's disappeared, It can't be!"

Eric dismounted and moved to Inken's side. He placed a hand on her shoulder. She turned to face him, tears in her eyes.

"She's gone."

TWENTY ONE

The words hung in the air, damning, irrefutable. Enala was gone, and with her, the last hope they had of saving themselves. Their mission had failed before it even began. Eric held Inken tight to him, unable to find the words.

"It's over," Caelin whispered.

Above the leaves rustled in the evening breeze, but beneath the air was still, dead. A horse snorted, pawing at the ground. They did not like the smells here. From the distance came the crash of an animal in the undergrowth, too small to be a dragon.

Eric looked at his companions and saw their despair. Inken slumped against him, all life fled from her face. There were tears in the eyes of Michael and Caelin. Only the two Magickers managed to hide their emotion behind blank faces.

Without even meeting her, Enala had become the centre of their lives. She was the princess they were destined to rescue, crushed by the harsh reality of the world. This perilous land had claimed her. It might claim them too, if they did not leave soon.

"We have to go back," Eric's voice was almost

unrecognisable.

The words struck a chord. Inken winced in his arms and a cloud swept over Caelin's face. Were they truly willing to admit defeat?

"No," Alastair resolved. "We can't give up. Not all the tribes are violent and one may even remain loyal to the kings of men. We must try asking for their help."

No one replied, though Eric wondered whether Alastair had cracked himself. He could not muster any hope from the idea but did not have the strength to argue with the old man.

"What do you want us to do?" he asked.

"The Gold's nest on the coast. They would not have been in this area – the Red or Blues would have found her first," Inken's reply was laced with misery.

"No matter the chances, we have to try. There is no future without Enala," Alastair pressed. "Not for us or anyone else."

Inken shivered. "You know the tales of the coast."

Alastair nodded. "I lived them. That was where the old king Thomas was lost. In Malevolent Cove."

"We would not have to go there, though?" Caelin asked.

"It would be the closest point," Inken answered. "To go around it would take an extra day."

"The place is cursed, no good will come from there," Michael offered.

"Fortunes can be changed, even from ill luck. And an extra day spent in Dragon Country has its own dangers. It is a risk I am willing to take," Alastair insisted. "But it is up to each of you whether you want to follow."

"We can't abandon her," Eric echoed Inken's words from the night before. Beside him, Inken nodded.

Balistor and Caelin agreed.

Eric looked to Michael. His face was stark with fear,

indecision etched across his lips. He still wore the green robes of his order, but this was no place for a priest.

"Elynbrigge asked me to help you, and so I will. But I still think this is folly. The girl is gone."

Alastair closed his eyes and they all saw the doubt there. "I cannot give up hope, Michael. I have searched for too long to surrender now. I will not believe it until I see with my own two eyes."

After that, there was nothing left to say.

****

Firelight flickered across the clearing, casting deep shadows between the surrounding tree trunks. They had left behind the humid valley, climbing back into the cool autumn air. A breeze blew across the open grass, the long blades bending in its wake. The fire barely kept the chill at bay. A pot sat over the flames, a thick stew bubbling inside. A sombre silence had enveloped the fellowship.

Caelin finished chopping potatoes and flicked them into the pot. Eric sat watching, stomach growling as he breathed in the rich fumes. A hot meal would be a welcome change. Balistor had lit the fire when they finally stopped for the night. No one bothered to disagree with the decision. They were all sick of caution.

Eric glanced at the stars glistening in a rich tapestry above. He hoped dragons were not creatures of the night. Darkness had fallen soon after they started out again. No one wanted to risk injuring their horses out here, so they had been forced to make camp in a clearing Balistor had discovered nearby.

"Here, Eric," he looked up as Caelin offered him a

bowl. "And one for you too, my lady," he grinned at Inken.

They accepted the offering with a word of thanks. Eric took a slow sip, enjoying the heat of the spices Caelin had added. A satisfying warmth spread through his stomach, bracing him against the night air.

When they finished he handed back the bowl and glanced at Inken. She sat staring into the trees, thoughts hidden by a grim mask. Her bowl was still half-full, the spoon dangling loosely from her fingers.

Eric put an arm round her waist. "What are you thinking?"

Inken blinked and looked at him "Sorry? I was lost in my thoughts."

Eric kissed her. "I know the feeling. What were you thinking?"

She sighed. "Eric, do you really believe she is alive?"

His good humour evaporated. "Truthfully? No. Her tracks are gone and there were signs of a dragon everywhere."

"So we're chasing a ghost now. Why?"

Eric gazed into her eyes, feeling oddly at peace. "Because we don't have any other choice. Without her, he's already won."

"You're almost as stubborn as the old man, you know," she looked out into the trees again. "Come on, there's something I want to show you."

"What is it?"

"I found it earlier, when I was searching for firewood. You'll like it. Come on!" she stood, pulling him to his feet.

Eric struggled to stand, still exhausted from the day's ride. The movement pulled his stitches tight, but he tried to ignore them. Riding had taken its toll and all he really wanted to do was sleep, but Inken was tugging at his hand and there was no choice but to follow.

She led him into the trees, away from the others. They watched them go, grins on their faces. "There goes the cute couple again," Caelin teased.

Eric blushed, glad his back was turned to them. When they entered the trees, he hesitated, pulling her back.

"What are you doing?" she asked.

He gave sad smile. "It's not safe out here; we shouldn't be going off alone."

Inken's breath hissed between her teeth. He thought she would argue; instead, she stalked past him and back towards the fire. Eric winced and made to follow.

Inken glanced back. "Stay there! I'll be back in a second."

She jogged into the camp, gathered her gear and ran back. Now she carried her bow strung over her shoulder and wore her cavalry sabre at her side.

"Happy now?" she teased.

Eric gave a quick nod, knowing this was the best he would get. It seemed they were going into the woods, whether he liked it or not. Inken shot him a mischievous smirk. She took his hand again and dragged him into the darkness.

He stumbled after her, tripping over the root-riddled earth in the pitch black beneath the trees. He could just make out the dim outline of Inken in front of him; the rest of the forest was invisible. The warmth of her hand in his own was reassuring. She glanced back occasionally, her teeth flashing as she smiled.

Twice Eric almost fell, kept on his feet only by Inken's quick hands. The forest was hazardous in the dark, though Inken managed it far better than him. He kept his ears open, listening for the first signs of trouble. Only the soft hoot of an owl was audible above their own racket.

When they finally emerged from the trees, Eric was

puffing and holding his injured side. The pain vanished when he saw where Inken had brought him. His mouth dropped, a gasp escaping him.

The giant trees opened up onto a patch of low-lying ferns. A soft glow spread across the clearing, lit by fern leaves shining in the dark, their gentle luminescence banishing the night. Tiny insects buzzed between them, and these too radiated with light. A creek threaded its way through the clearing, the currents playing a warm melody against the coarse pebble bed. Steam rose from the running water, leaving a thin fog hovering at eye level. A sweet, rosy scent drifted in the air.

"There was only a faint glow when I found it. I thought you might like it," Inken spoke in a voice hushed with wonder.

"It's... it's beautiful," he had no other words.

Inken turned to him. The scarlet curls of her hair ablaze in the light. She took his hand and drew him further into the ferns. They sat beside the stream, face to face, arms around one another, savouring the closeness of their bodies and the warmth of their skin.

"Eric, I... I want to ask you something," she paused.

He leaned forward, reaching up to stroke her face. Her eyes closed at his touch. She shivered.

"What?" he breathed.

"What do you want, Eric? What are your dreams?"

The question took him by surprise. He looked away. *What do I want?* The question had never really mattered before, not for a long time.

"I don't know," he realised at that moment how tragic it was. "I guess, to help Alastair..."

Inken reached up and entwined her fingers in his hair. She turned him to face her. "There must be something more. You had a life once, before the magic. I know it.

What did *that* Eric want?"

He closed his eyes, unable to meet her fiery gaze.

"He was lost a long time ago."

"I know that's not true. When you were in that trance, I saw him. A man untouched by your curse. Now, *what do you want*, Eric?"

He thought back, trying to remember the boy he had once been, to remember a time before his magic awakened. It seemed a part of someone else's life now, too innocent to be his own. The memories took a long time to surface. Inken waited.

"I wanted to be a *carpenter*," he laughed.

Inken rested her forehead against his. "Do you still want that?"

"I don't know…" he hesitated.

Inken kissed him. "Go on."

Eric drew a shuddering breath. "I want to be *normal*. To finish this business and start a new life. But if we cannot find Enala, what is the point? Archon will tear the world apart."

"There is always a point, Eric. Life is a fickle thing and it must be *lived*. Archon will attack, or he won't. It is no different to the farmer whose livelihood depends on the weather. He knows he may be ruined one day by a drought or a storm, but he battles on anyway. True bravery means pursuing what you want, no matter the obstacles. The world may end tomorrow, but what matters is what we do with the time we have left. Otherwise, we are already lost."

Eric felt a warm fluttering in his chest as she spoke. However, there was still a weight within him. "I can't put the past aside so easily. That nightmare is an anchor dragging me down. I cannot move on until I have redeemed myself."

"And you think saving Enala will do that?"

Eric nodded.

"Oh Eric," she hugged him. "I think you have already redeemed yourself. You are learning to control your power, are doing all you can to prevent the past repeating itself. And you used it to heal Chole. What more can you do?"

"I don't know, but it's not enough."

Inken sighed. "I understand. Maybe there isn't anything you can do to put those ghosts to bed. But you also have to live, Eric."

"I know. And there's something else I want, you know."

"Oh really?"

"I want *you*, Inken."

She stood, eyes locked to his. "Well I'm right here, Eric Storm. So come and get me," she teased, walking backwards towards the stream. As she moved she pulled off her leather jacket, then the shirt beneath. Her leggings quickly followed. She stood there grinning, wearing nothing but the soft curves of her sun touched skin.

"What are you doing?" he asked, eyes feasting.

"Going for a swim," she grinned. "This stream is fed by a hotspring. Are you going to join me?"

Eric sprang to his feet and followed her into the steaming waters.

****

They lay wrapped in each other's arms, eyes closed, the hot water streaming over their naked bodies. Neither had spoken for some time, each lost in their own dreams. A quiet tranquillity had settled over the clearing, as though the world beyond the glowing ferns no longer existed.

A roar shattered the calm. Inken reacted instantly,

leaping up the bank, scrambling for her sword and bow. Eric followed, eyes racking the canopy overhead. The bellow came again, from behind them. *The camp!*

They clambered desperately into their clothes and took off towards the campsite. The darkness fed their panic, the screams from ahead driving them onwards. Each time Eric stumbled, Inken was at his side, helping him up, pushing him on. They raced through the trees, straining to hear, to see what was happening.

Inken emerged first, exploding from the undergrowth into the long grass. Eric arrived a second later, arms raised to protect himself from the low branches. He slammed into Inken's back and almost knocked them both to the ground before he caught himself.

They were just in time. The others stood in the centre of the clearing, weapons at the ready, eyes locked to the sky. Flames leapt across the long grass, dwarfing their tiny campfire. Eric looked up and saw a flash of red as something huge passed across the moon. Flames glittered on scales.

Then the beast was hurtling towards them, the sky erupting in flames, revealing the dragon. Fire licked from jaws large enough to swallow a horse. Bloody fangs flickered in and out of sight. The black orbs of its eyes swept the clearing, lingering on the group of men who dared to trespass here.

It crashed to the ground. The earth shook with the impact, flinging them from their feet. The horses screamed and the thunder of their fleeing hooves echoed in the darkness. Eric spun to protect his wound. He stared up at the beast in horror.

Its massive hide filled half the clearing. It crouched on all fours, claws raking out grooves deep enough to bury a man. Giant wings splayed out on either side, blacking out the moon. Its tail flickered out like a snake. It stank of blood and guts, of death and despair. A blast of hot air struck Eric like a furnace as it turned towards them, tongue sliding out to taste the air. Its scales were the darkest red.

It roared again, fire gushing from its mouth. The grass burst into flames. Inken dragged him back, the heat swamping them. There came a whoosh as the ground caught alight.

Across the clearing, Alastair stepped away from his companions. His cloak spun out behind him, the air shimmering with his magic. His hand swept down. Eric felt the power surging through the air, driving a dull throb into the back of his skull.

The Red dragon shrieked as the magic struck, picking up the beast and flinging it into the trees. The ancient trunks groaned at the impact, toppling backwards beneath the dragon's bulk. The monster thrashed, limbs tearing at earth and wood. The great wings flapped. It bounded into the air and began to circle.

The night shook with the dragon's roar. It folded its wings and dove, fire gushing from its mouth. The trees burst into flames as it swept past. The inferno raced across the grass towards their companions.

Alastair arced out his arms, flinging the blaze back upon itself. Burning wood crackled amidst the flames. Smoke drifted across the clearing, blinding them. Eric bent over, choking on the acrid air. He backed away, straining to hear the whip of the dragons wings over the rumbling flames.

The beast appeared suddenly from the smoke, catching Alastair unawares. He raised a hand in defiance – but too slow. The dragon slammed into the ground, knocking the old man from his feet. A column of fire swallowed him.

Eric's heart stopped. *"No!"* he screamed.

His magic boiled up from the depths of his body. He

did not attempt to stop it. He let it grow, feeding on his rage. The wind stirred. Gusts swirled into the clearing, whipping up the flames. They gathered around him, converging into a thunderous gale. His hair thrashed in its grasp, clothes cracking against his skin.

His vision narrowed until all he saw was the red of the dragon. The stream of fire from its mouth ceased. Somehow Alastair still stood, defiant, his face black with soot. The dragon raised its claws over his head and struck. Alastair held out his hand and the monstrous talons stopped a foot above him. There came a dull thud, as though they had struck wood. The old man's arm began to shake.

Eric unleashed the gale. The air raged around him and then cascaded into the beast. The dragon stumbled back beneath the onslaught. The wind caught in its wings, hurling it towards the trees. The great wings beat down, carrying it within a hair's breadth of the treetops.

The dragon began to turn, but Eric's rage was not finished yet. The winds encircled the creature, crashing against its scaly hide. The power of each blow forced it lower in the sky. Eric gritted his teeth and pressed down with everything he had. Its wings folded and the beast toppled into the forest. The crash echoed through the night.

Eric let out a long breath and released his power. He slumped to the ground, knees quivering, an empty feeling in the pit of his stomach. The brief exertion had drained his weakened body.

Inken grasped him around the shoulders and shook him. "Eric, stop it!"

"What?" he shouted over the whistling wind.

Inken pointed.

Eric looked up. The gales had not dissipated. The wind roared around the clearing, sucking the flames into the air.

A column of fire took shape, whirring around with the circling currents. The trees groaned and saplings were ripped from the ground up into the tornado. They glowed orange as their leaves sprouted flames.

He gaped, frozen by the sight. Inken shook him again, wrenching him from his shock. There was nothing he could do. His strength was gone; he had nothing left to take control of the twister.

"I can't – My magic – Not strong enough," the wind tore the words from Eric's mouth.

Inken's eyes grew wide with fear. Her knuckles tightened on her bow. She grasped him by the shirt and hauled him to his feet. "Then we've got to go. *Run!*" she yelled, trying to signal the others. "*Run for the cove!*"

Then they were running again, fleeing the burning column, the smouldering heat. Gusts of wind sucked at their backs, the inferno close behind, leaping between the trees. There was no trouble seeing the way now. Fire was everywhere. It chased them on hot blasts of air, driven by the tornado's rage.

A roar came from overhead. The canopy exploded as the dragon came crashing down, all teeth and claws. Its wings shredded the bark from trees, its tail whipping out behind it. It landed with a thud, halting their desperate flight.

Eric dug in his heels. His hand lashed out to grab Inken's collar, hauling her back. The dragon stood across their path. Its eyes glowed with hatred. The fire raced along either side of them. The tornado howled at their back.

The dragon clawed its way forwards, tongue flicking out in rapid succession. Then it paused, hesitant to attack. It had been hurt in the battle. A thick branch had impaled one leg and the thin skin of its wings was shredded. Thick blood ran down its scales.

It did not need to attack to finish them. The tornado was closing, its rumbling growing louder. Flames flooded the forest floor around them, taking light amidst the leaf litter. Their skin was already burning in the heat. Through the dragon was the only way out.

Inken nocked an arrow and loosed it at the beast. It hissed through the air, bouncing off the hardened scales. The dragon roared and took another step toward them, its confidence growing.

Eric watched with a sinking heart as Inken drew another arrow. He searched inside himself for a trace of magic but found nothing. Around them the fire roared higher. Only minutes remained to them now. He prayed the others had made it clear.

Inken squinted through the smoky light. This time it took long seconds for her to take aim. Releasing a long breath, she loosed. The shaft arched up towards the dragon's face, plunging into its amber eye. The beast screamed, staggering back. Inken did not pause, another arrow already to hand. She drew back, took sight, and shot again.

The dragon screeched with pain, as the second arrow stabbed through its other eye.

Eric gaped at the shot, but there was no time for pause. The beast had had enough. It dropped its head and charged. Its claws scrambled in the dirt, ripping roots from the earth.

Inken drew another arrow, but Eric saw their opportunity. He tackled her to the ground. They struck and rolled, carrying them from the path of the dragon's rage. The blinded beast charged past into the heart of the inferno.

They sat up. Inken shot him a glare, but he smiled back. They did not speak but climbed to their feet and ran on. The forest around them was alive with flames, leaving them just one way to flee. If they paused, the inferno would overtake them. The roar of the tornado behind them fed strength to their exhausted limbs.

At last they left the flames behind, the growl of the tornado dying away as it drifted from their path. The sounds of destruction fell off into the distance. The forest grew dark again, until all that remained was the flickering of shadows from far off fires.

Exhausted, they collapsed to the ground, clinging to each other in fear, pain, sorrow. The wound in his side began to throb. He had burst his stitches again, but he was too exhausted to care. He hugged Inken to him, taking solace in her touch. He marvelled at her strength, to have found the calm to halt the dragon amidst such chaos. They had been so, so lucky. There was no sign of the others and he prayed they too had escaped the inferno.

They lay in the darkness, silent but for their laboured gasps and half-choked coughs. Slowly Inken's breathing settled into a gentle rhythm. She slept. Eric closed his eyes, willing himself to do the same. Instead, questions raced through his mind. Were they okay? Had they heard Inken's shout?

There was only one way to find the answers. In the morning, they would finish the journey to Malevolent Cove. He no longer cared about the Gold dragons, no longer held out hope for Enala. Alastair's plan had been folly. All that mattered now was gathering the shattered remains of their company and fleeing this land.

Enala was gone.

TWENTY TWO

Malevolent Cove was a dark place. Sheer cliffs ringed the bay, their fragile faces crumbling away into the sea below. Waves slammed into the rocks, white caps churning the murky waters. A maze of reefs lurked below, silent graveyard to many a ship. They stood on the black sanded beach, braced against the storm. Rocky spires spotted the dark sands, their jagged tips like the claws of some buried giant. The air stank of rotten fish and the tang of salt.

They had been waiting for over an hour, searching the forest for sign of their companions. The trees stretched out over the sand, twisted, misshapen things, utterly unlike their towering siblings further inland. Their branches shook in the violent wind, fingers reaching for them.

Eric shivered. The temperature had plummeted as they approached the rugged coast, the humid valley air long behind them. His burning skin stung in the salty air. He was desperately weary; just the thought of the return journey filled him with dread. At least the tornado had driven them east towards Malevolent Cove. Everything else had gone wrong. Now they were stranded here without horses, food, or water.

He glanced at Inken. The corners of her lips curled in worry and her hand lingered on her sword hilt. Fear stared from her eyes, searching the trees. A crash came from the forest. Inken drew her blade. Eric tensed, cursing his lack of weapon.

Caelin emerged first, stumbling from the trees like a dead man. The others followed, one by one, a trail of burnt and bloodied bodies. Alastair appeared last, hobbling and leaning heavily on a branch fashioned into a staff. His grim face lit when he saw them.

"Eric, Inken, thank the Gods! We thought the worst," he limped up to them and embraced them each in a warm hug.

Eric grinned, the worry that had burrowed deep into his heart falling away. He felt a wave of relief. "We thought the same for you."

"It was a close thing, but we made it," Caelin's face was etched with exhaustion.

They sat together on the rough sand and looked out over the dark waters. Eric could scarcely believe they had all survived. He thought of the firestorm lighting up the night and the dragon stalking them from above. How had *any* of them survived? Antonia's cheeky grin leapt to mind and he sent a silent call of thanks to the little Goddess.

Yet even so, the six of them were a sorry sight. The others had not saved any supplies either, although Michael still carried his medical bag. Without food or horses, escape from Dragon Country would be nearly impossible. Eric struggled to keep the despair from his face.

"What is that?" Inken asked.

He looked up to see where Inken was pointing. He followed her finger out to sea, to beyond the waves crashing on the reef. Squinting, he spotted a dark shape moving through the surging waters, drawing closer.

"It's a skiff," Inken said, glancing at him. "Who would be sailing in these waters?"

Eric did not have an answer. They sat and watched the boat grow closer. It raced towards the cove, blackened hull slicing through the waves, wind filling its sails. A figure stood in the bow, wrapped in a thick black cloak.

"What do you think, Alastair?" Caelin asked.

"Nothing good. Prepare yourselves," he answered.

The skiff entered the churned waters of the cove, threading its way between the treacherous reefs. It was clear the man was an accomplished sailor. With the tide high, it would be almost impossible to spot where the water was safe to pass. Still it came on.

They spread out, eyes locked to the dark craft. Inken strung her bow as Alastair and Caelin drew swords. Balistor stood stock still, hands clamped into fists. Eric could feel the man's magic building, but there was terror written on the Magicker's face. Eric shivered. He had never seen Balistor so unsettled.

Closing his eyes, he searched for his own power. Only a drop remained of the ocean he had first glimpsed all those nights ago. He backed up behind the others; unarmed he could only be a liability.

The skiff rode a wave up onto the beach. It crunched onto the sand, settling as the water receded. The dark figure stepped off, heavy cloak alive in the wind. Eric glimpsed two swords poking out from beneath its folds, a black gem glittering on each pommel. His face was hidden beneath a thick hood. He reached up with deathly white hands to pull it back.

Eric sucked in a sharp breath of air. Stark white hair whipped around a smooth grey face. Jet black eyes stared at them, burning with hate. He had no eyebrows or beard, but Eric still recognised the man from his vision.

"*Thomas*," Alastair hissed. He seemed to shrink as the wind whipped the name away.

A whispery laugh carried across the rocky sand, sending ice trickling down Eric's back. The *thing* standing before them was Thomas, the king who had saved the Three Nations, who had defied Archon's wrath. The same king whose descendants had wielded the Sword of Light down the decades. The king who had disappeared on this very shore, all those years ago. Yet it was clear nothing was left of the man he had once been.

The fiend spoke, voice so low they strained to catch the words. "Ah, Alastair. How good it is to see you. You have aged poorly, old friend."

"*Do not call me that!*" Alastair cried.

"Why not? You have called me Thomas, though no one has named me that for an age."

"What did the shadow do to you?"

"Shadow?" Thomas laughed. "The one in the stories? Ha! There was never a shadow, Alastair. He was weak, dying. He let the magic win. He set the beast loose."

"*No!* That is not possible."

The creature cackled again, the sound grating on their ears in a thin mockery of the rich laugh Eric remembered from Antonia's vision.

"Oh it is possible, Alastair. Truly, did you never consider it? I guess not, or you may have searched harder. I knew you would come looking for me. I fled to the north, the magic concealing my tracks. Archon embraced me with open arms when I reached him. My only regret is I did not have the Sword to give him."

"I pity you then. There is nothing left of the man who was Thomas. Not even his magic remains."

"Ah yes. Sadly, time has stripped the earth magic from this frail body. No matter, for the dark magic is more than enough."

"What are you here for?" Balistor demanded.

"Of course, how could I have forgotten? Archon grows tired of failure. His human servants have disappointed him at every turn. They have forced his hand. I have been sent to prepare for his arrival. When he finally marches south, I will ensure there is no one of measure to stand in his path. The Three Nations will fall like autumn leaves."

"You are here to kill us?" Alastair asked.

"Among other things, yes," the demon reached down and slid a sword from its scabbard. It rasped into the air, cold black steel that promised death. Runes shone along its length, the language unrecognisable. The weapon glowed with an aura that seemed to smite the light itself.

The demon charged, sand spraying up behind him. His companions tensed, weapons held at the ready. Eric froze, watching it come with dread. He felt powerless, helpless to aid his companions. Michael stood beside him, his face etched with horror.

The demon closed on them, silent, like death itself incarnate. Inken drew back an arrow and loosed. It sliced the air. Her aim was true, but seconds before it struck, the demon vanished. The shaft embedded itself in the bare sand.

Eric had no time to search for their missing foe. Pain exploded through his back and burst from his chest. He gave a half-choked scream, looking down to see the dark tip of the demon's blade stabbing from his torso. His body shook, a dark sensation lacing its way through his veins, an evil web that sucked away his strength. His knees gave way, but an iron grip on his shoulder held him up. He heard the demon cackling behind him.

Inken screamed, but she sounded distant now, as though miles away. He looked up, searching for her, his vision growing blurred. Five figures stood on the beach, mouths wide as they called for him, but he could not tell them apart. He could not find her.

A boot struck him in the back, pushing him from the sword. Eric slid to the ground, landing with a thud. He coughed, choking on the taste of blood. Agony burned in waves through his body. The dark threads throbbed with an otherworldly pain, filling his mind, scorching away his feeble resistance. He reached for the last drop of his magic, desperate to defend himself, but the power had vanished.

Through the fog, he heard the demon speak. "Such power for one so young. I am glad to take it off his hands," the crackle of lightning followed the words.

Eric cracked open his eyes. The edges of his vision grew dark, but the demon's sword stood stark and clear. Lightning crept along the blade.

The demon stalked towards his companions. He closed his eyes, unable to watch. His breath came in painful gasps. Energy rippled through his body, tearing at his soul, and he had nothing left to fight it. Oblivion loomed. He wished for Inken.

Then Michael was at his side.

****

Inken choked back a sob, her breath catching in her throat. Hot tears ran down her cheeks. A scream built in her chest, crawling up from some dark recess deep within. Her knees shook, the strength fleeing her legs. Instinct was shouting for her to run to Eric, to save him. But the demon stood between them, laughing.

Hands trembling, vision blurred by tears, she struggled

to nock another arrow. She could not find the string and the arrow tumbled to the sand. Inken shrieked with rage, throwing the bow to the ground. Her chest ached, as though a hand of ice had taken hold of her heart. Summoning the last shred of her being, she drew her sabre.

The demon stepped towards them. Alastair leapt, sword lashing out at his foe. The demon's blade swept down to meet it. Steel clashed and lightning jumped between them. Electricity raced along Alastair's blade and vanished into the sleek metal. Alastair sneered and lashed out again.

Caelin raced in from the right. The demon turned aside a decapitating blow from Alastair and lashed out with its boot, catching Alastair in the chest and flinging him backwards. He crashed into a rocky spire and slid to the sand. The demon spun in time to avoid Caelin's wild slash.

The demon turned its sword on the young soldier. Lightning leapt from the blade, but Caelin was already moving and the bolt struck empty beach. The air erupted, the sand boiling where he had stood. Caelin rolled with a smooth grace, his sword striking for the demon's face.

The fiend pulled back, the blade biting empty air. Caelin pressed the attack, but the demon caught the blade with its own. Lightning danced between the weapons. There came a terrifying boom and Caelin's sword shattered like crystal. The blast sent Caelin bouncing across the beach like a ragdoll.

Inken threw herself at the demon, grief boiling in her veins. Balistor charged with her, snarling with rage. The demon turned to meet them, leaving Alastair and Caelin to recover. Or so she prayed.

Black steel flashed for her face. Inken hurled herself aside. The blade sliced through the air, its razor sharp edge shearing off a few fiery strands of hair. The fiend raised its blade again, but a ball of flame smashed into its chest.

Embers exploded, flying in the raging wind. The demon shrugged off the attack and turned to grin at Balistor.

Inken struggled to regain her balance. Balistor launched another fireball, but the fiend's cloak was already aflame and it did not seem to care. Balistor retreated as it advanced on him. Inken saw her chance as the demon turned its back. She sprinted forward and brought her sabre down on the demon's neck.

The blade struck home, and stopped dead. The steel jarred in her hand and a bone numbing shock ran up her arm. The sword slipped from her numb fingers. It was as though she'd struck solid rock, but the blade had not even pierced the demon's skin.

The demon turned on her, flames leaping from its cloak. It lashed out with a fist, striking her in the chest. The blow flung her to the sand. She tumbled across the beach and crashed into a stone pillar. Groaning, she placed a knee beneath her and fought to sit up. A sharp pain lanced through her chest. She gritted her teeth against the pain, the broken rib cutting and grinding. Lurching to her feet, she drew a hunting knife and stumbled towards the fight.

Alastair was back on his feet, wielding his sword two handed with all the power he could bear. Each time the demon blade was there, turning aside his blows with ease. The demon was too fast, too powerful. Not even Balistor's attacks could phase it.

Inken dove in, feet unsteady, searching for an opening. The hunting knife had no reach, but she hoped she might distract it enough to aid Alastair. The demon began to laugh again, its rasping cackle ringing with the clash of blades. Only Alastair's sword was able to touch the black blade, protected by whatever spell had been cast on the weapon.

Alastair jumped back, chest heaving, hands trembling. Inken moved to stand with him, wishing for the strength to help. They crouched low and then sprang forward to attack together.

Lightning arced from the demon's blade, smashing into the sand at their feet. The earth erupted, the force of the explosion picking them up and hurling them through the air. Inken smashed down and slid through the sand. Alastair flew backwards into the ocean and disappeared beneath the waves.

Inken coughed, choking on sand, her body a mess of pain. She rolled onto her stomach and spat out a mouthful of black sand. Her dagger lay a few feet away. Bracing herself, she crawled towards it, glancing across at the demon.

Balistor fought on, his face black with soot. But his powers were useless, the demon advancing through his attacks. Over the roar of the waves and flames, she heard Balistor shout. "Leave them, they're mine!"

Inken closed her eyes, willing strength to her muscles. Her fingers found the blade and clasped desperately at the hilt. It felt better to have a weapon in her grasp, although it was of little use in her state.

The demon raised its sword to the sky, dismissing Balistor with a contemptuous turn of its back. The sky grew dark and flashes lit the underbelly of the clouds. Lightning lanced down with a boom of thunder, spearing the black sword. Another bolt followed, and another, gathering around the weapon as a great ball of energy.

The demon's laughter shook the earth. "You are all traitors and will suffer for it. Farewell!"

Inken closed her eyes tight and braced herself for the lightning's burning touch. She wished for Eric, for one last chance to embrace him.

A roar echoed over the lightning's boom. Inken looked up, eyes wide with shock. A shadow flew overhead, gold scales filling the sky.

The demon's eyes widened. The dragon dropped, streaking towards it, its giant mouth open to bare a hundred fangs. It slammed into the demon, talons tearing to send it flying. The gathered energy flashed away, the blasts leaving glassy marks in the sand where they struck.

The fiend spun in the air to land on its feet, sword held out before it. It dropped to a crouch, a snarl on its pale face.

Inken stared, unable to believe her eyes. The dragon towered over them, twice the size of the Red that had attacked last night. Its wings spread wide as it prepared to take flight, casting the beach in shadow. The massive tail lashed out, shattering rocky spires like toothpicks. Its diamond eyes glared at the demon. Smoke snorted from the slits of its nostrils. On its back sat a girl with golden hair.

Her clothes were torn and her skin streaked with dirt. She grasped the dragon's neck with one arm, legs gripped tight to the scales. Her sapphire eyes glared down at them, fury written across her face. With her spare hand she pointed to the demon and screamed.

White-hot flames leapt from the great jaws, far greater than any Balistor had summoned. For the first time fear showed on the demon's face. It dove from the path of the flames, unable to stand before its cleansing heat. The dragon came after it, claws ripping up the black sand. There was no escape from its rage.

Fire encircled the demon, forcing it to turn. Its sword slashed out, a bolt of lightning lancing for the girl. Inken's breath caught in her throat. The girl flinched back, but golden wings rose to protect her. The lightning shattered on the thick scales.

Then the dragon was attacking again, flames licking at the heels of their foe. The demon fled across the sand, chased by an inferno that left a path of glass in its wake. The dragon charged after, clawing its way into the air. The great wings beat down. It roared.

The fiend swung around, sword raised. Lightning twitched along its length and flashed at the dragon's unprotected stomach.

Flames rushed to meet it. The forces collided mid-air and exploded outwards. The shockwave whipped sand into Inken's face. She squinted through the grit and saw the flickering blue lightning succumb to the all-consuming fire. The demon disappeared into the conflagration.

A hideous scream filled the air. Within the inferno she saw the outline of a figure writhing against the flames. The dragon kept on, relentless.

A flash split the sky, blinding the onlookers. Inken scrunched her eyes closed, but it seeped through to burn her anyway. Pain flashed through her skull. The light vanished as quickly as it had appeared.

Inken opened her eyes, her vision slowly returning. The flames had died away. The dragon stood back on its hind legs, its great head staring at where the ground had turned to molten black glass. All that remained was a trail of glassy footprints burnt into the sand, heading for the forest. The demon had fled.

Inken looked up at the dragon and the girl.

Enala stared down at her.

TWENTY
THREE

C aelin pulled himself to his feet. The dragon loomed
over the beach; scales gleaming, fangs bared, eyes
glaring. Caelin ignored it. Turning, he sprinted for
the sea. The surf roared up to meet him as he dove over the
raging waves. The salty water stung his eyes as he searched
for Alastair.

He bobbed to the surface moments later, Alastair slung
over his shoulders. Straining beneath the weight, he dragged
himself back to shore and up the beach. Dumping the old
man to the sand, he collapsed beside him, gasping for
breath. Alastair gave a hacking cough as he fell, water
gushing from his mouth.

Balistor moved to his side. "Is he okay?"

Caelin nodded, shivering in the brisk sea breeze. He
glanced again at the dragon and the girl who rode it. It was
an astonishing sight and he could not help but appreciate
the irony. After all they had gone through to find her, it had
been Enala who had saved them.

"I'm going to talk to her," he said to Balistor. "Look
after him."

He walked towards the dragon. The golden scales glistened in the morning sunlight, blinding him. Its giant head turned to watch him come, eyes alive with intelligence. Its jaws cracked open, revealing rows of dagger length teeth. A gust of wind carried with it the stench of rotting fish.

Caelin shivered. Alastair's blade lay on the sand nearby. The dragon growled when he reached down to scoop it up. He lifted it slowly, an arm raised in submission, and slid it into his empty scabbard. Showing his empty hands, he continued forwards.

His gaze drifted to where Eric lay. A pool of blood stained the sand around him. Michael and Inken sat at his side, but even from this distance he could see the gaping wound. He fought back tears.

Summoning his resolve, he focused again on Enala. The girl glared down at him, following his approach. Her blond hair fluttered in the breeze and he noticed now the copper lock dangling across her face. Dark circles ringed her eyes.

When Caelin reached the dragon, he dropped low in a bow. It had been a long time since anyone had visited the tribes, but he knew the courtesies expected.

"Who are you?" Enala demanded.

Caelin frowned, his curiosity mounting. It was common knowledge that even the Gold dragons did not allow people to ride them; even during Archon's war it had been a rare occurrence. He wondered how Enala managed it.

Even so, he knew the correct etiquette. Ignoring the girl, he addressed the dragon first. "Dragon, my name is Caelin, Sergeant of the Plorsean army. I know the name of the one you carry, but may I enquire as to yours?" he offered.

Air hissed from the dragon's nose in what might have been laughter. "Well met, Sergeant. I am Nerissa."

"Nerissa, excuse my curiosity, but why do you bear this

girl?"

Again the snort of laughter. "Her parents and she often visited this place. Her blood is old. She may ride with us, for we still honour the pact we made with her ancestors. She and I have flown together many times."

Caelin nodded. Nerissa spoke of the pact the old kings had made with the dragons to fight Archon. King Thomas had been the orchestrator of that pact. The dragon had confirmed Enala truly was related to the ancient king.

"Who are you all? Why are you here?" Enala spoke through grated teeth. The fire in her eyes dared him to defy her again.

He bent his head in apology. "My apologies. These are the hunter Inken, Magickers Balistor and Alastair, and Alastair's apprentice, Eric," he pointed to each of them in turn. Then he looked up at the girl. "And we are here for you, Enala."

The girl stiffened. The dragon dropped into a crouch, a low growl rumbling up from its chest. Sand crunched beneath its claws as it stepped towards him. A tongue of flame licked the sand.

Caelin raised his hands in surrender, fighting back the instinct to draw his sword. "*Wait!* We mean you no harm, Enala."

"That is *all* anyone wishes for me," her lips curling back in a snarl.

"Please, let me speak. We came here to help you!"

Enala paused, nostrils flaring. She leaned closer, though she sat high above him. Her gaze seemed to look right to his soul. "How did you plan to help me, Caelin? When you cannot even save yourselves," she gave a cruel laugh.

Caelin's cheeks flushed, but he pushed on. "There are others hunting you, Enala. Archon wants you dead."

The laughter died. "Archon?"

"Yes."

"What would he want with me?" there was fear in her voice now.

"You are a threat to him. You are the descendent of Aria, sister to King Thomas. And you are the last one who can wield the Sword of Light."

Enala's eyes widened. "What?"

"You must come with us, Enala. The Three Nations need you."

Her eyes hardened to crystal. "There is nothing for me there now. Everything and everyone I ever loved is gone. I am safe here with Nerissa. So, Caelin, why should I care?"

Caelin gaped. He had come too far to care for the ravings of a selfish teenager. Whatever Enala had been through, he would not allow her to abandon her nation.

"Why should you care?" he shouted. "Because people will die. Because without you there is nothing to stop Archon unleashing his terror on our world. Because if you don't, a thousand other children will lose their parents, just as you have."

Enala stared down at him, her face expressionless.

****

Balistor looked up at the arrogant young girl. She sat there on her dragon: beautiful, brave, naïve. Did she really believe she would be safe from Archon here? Archon had the power to turn a dragon to dust if he chose. There would be no escaping him once he came, and so long as Enala lived, she was a threat to his plans.

Balistor smiled. So she had to die. He felt a surge of pleasure looking at the girl. They had finally found her. Her death would redeem him in the eyes of his master. The only obstacle left to surmount now was the dragon. Fortunately, he had a piece of dark magic that might just have the power he needed.

He looked down at Alastair, lying so weak at his feet. The deception had been easier than he'd expected. How desperate the old man had been for help. No one had even questioned his story.

His anger flared. Why had Archon sent the demon? Things had been under control. He could not believe his master could sentence him to death so easily. There was no treachery in caution. Besides, it was not *his* fault things at the inn had gone so wrong. Two people had been responsible for that. The first was whichever foolish hunter had shot him in the back. A small wound, but it had prevented him from burning the lot of them alive in the haystack. By the time he had recovered, they were a long way from his hired help. There had been no choice but to go along with the fools.

The second was Inken, and he would ensure she endured a long death as punishment for her betrayal. He smiled, pausing to appreciate her heartbroken sobs. It was a satisfying sound.

"She's the one," Alastair coughed, a smile on his lips. He closed his eyes and drifted into unconsciousness.

Balistor's thoughts returned to his present problem. Two threats remained to his plans. The dragon he was sure he could best. Then there was Alastair. The old man's strength was phenomenal and he did not think it would take long for him to recover. It seemed whatever he faced, Alastair found a way to triumph.

Not this time, he decided with a smirk. *The girl's sweet throat will have to wait.*

Balistor drew his sword.

****

Inken's eyes burned. Her throat was hoarse from crying, her shirt soaked with tears. She sat on the soft sand cradling Eric's head in her lap. His eyes stared up at her, flickering with whatever waking dream had taken him. A shiver ran through his body. She placed a hand on his forehead and found his skin cold with sweat. When he coughed, red foam dripped down his chin.

She wiped the blood away with her sleeve. "Please, Eric, stay with us."

Michael laid a hand on her shoulder. He had done his best to stem the blood, but they all knew the wound was mortal. "I can give him something to ease his passing, Inken."

"*No!*" she screamed at him. "No, no, no!" she sobbed.

Michael shrank back from her wrath and she instantly regretted the outburst. All she wanted was for someone to hold her, to tell her everything would be all right.

Eric coughed again, eyes scrunched closed in pain. When they opened, he caught her gaze. "Don't worry, Inken," he gasped. "It's… going to be okay."

Inken leaned close and kissed him. "Don't you leave me," she whispered.

Eric's eyes slid down the beach. His skin was a pallid grey, his lips blue. He smiled. "We found her, Inken. Everything's going to be okay."

Inken couldn't bring herself to smile back. The demon's blade had pierced Eric's lung, leaving him to drown in his own blood. The wound was beyond any doctor's skill to heal.

Eric's grin faded away. He struggled to raise an arm. A spasm shook his fragile body, a groan rattling up from his chest in a gurgling cough. Red flecks stained her shirt. Amidst the seizure, she made out one word. "*Alastair!*"

Inken shook her head in confusion. She turned to look at the rest of their fellowship.

Down the beach, above the raging surf, Balistor stood over Alastair. His sword was in his hand. She watched as he raised it above his head.

"*Caelin!*" she shrieked.

****

Caelin heard his name over the roar of the surf. He looked up, saw Inken pointing at him. No, *not at him.* Behind him. He spun, fuelled by the terror on her face.

Balistor loomed over Alastair, sword poised above the fallen Magicker. He had frozen at Inken's cry, a look of hesitation on his face. Their eyes met. Balistor grinned. The sword lanced down.

Time seemed to stand still, freezing the scene in Caelin's mind. He heard the crash of a wave on the beach, the great rushing breath of the dragon, Enala's gasp, Inken's painful sob. He saw the hate in Balistor's eyes – the hate he should have seen long ago.

A spark of sun pierced the clouds above, catching on Balistor's sword. For a second it seemed the traitor held the Sword of Light itself. Then the blade plunged home, burying itself in Alastair's chest, and the light died.

Alastair lurched against the blade, one last gasp escaping him, and then slumped to the sand. Caelin thought he heard the whisper of a word, but the wind whipped away all meaning.

Balistor wrenched back his blade and began to cackle. Blood dripped from his sword tip and a pool was already gathering around Alastair. His laughter carried across the beach, fuel to Caelin's fury.

"*Traitor!*" he drew the sword he had gathered from the beach.

Balistor walked towards him. "Traitor? *No*, I don't think so. Spy would be more apt. I never served your king, only Archon. Thankfully, you're a gullible fool, Caelin."

Caelin gritted his teeth, resisting the urge to attack. Nothing made sense here.

"Who are you?" he hissed.

Balistor smirked. "Perhaps Inken might recognise me," he waved a hand. His purple robes darkened to black.

"You!" Caelin heard Inken hiss from behind him. He did not take his eyes from Balistor.

"Still cannot guess, Caelin? I am the one who hired Inken and her hunter friends, the one who has been hunting you. And this time, you won't escape."

The pieces began to click together. "All this time?" he choked.

Balistor continued his march up the beach, growing ever closer. "Yes, although I had intended to be done with you all at the inn. An unfortunate series of events messed up my plan, Inken's interference most of all," his eyes swept across to where Inken crouched. "And believe me, Inken, you will scream for mercy before you die."

Inken growled. "Not if I kill you first."

Balistor laughed, ignoring her threat. "Still, things have worked out quite well. You have helped to shame a rival of mine and led me straight to the girl."

"And do you think this girl is going to die so easily?" Enala growled at him. Nerissa's jaws stretched wide, showing row upon row of teeth to emphasise her words.

Balistor only grinned. With his free hand he reached into his cloak. Caelin stepped towards him, but Balistor's hand hissed back out, flames licking from his fingertips and rushing for him. Caelin threw himself back. The sand exploded at his feet, sending sand sizzling through the air.

"Stay back, Caelin. Your turn will come," his hand disappeared into the cloak again, drawing out a glass sphere.

Caelin stared at the alien object. Dark mist rolled within, clawing at the glass with smoky fingers. A sickly green glow seeped from within and a dreadful humming rung in his ears.

"I've been waiting to use this for a long time. Here, Enala, a gift from Archon," he tossed the ball in her direction.

The globe tumbled through the air. Nerissa reared back, the globe shattering against her head. A muffled explosion rung out. A black cloud rushed from the glass, engulfing the dragon's head. Nerissa roared in fury, rising up on her hind legs. She clawed at the dark fog, head shaking as she tried to dislodge the cloying magic.

Enala lost her grip amidst the dragon's struggle. She screamed as she tumbled from Nerissa's back, hitting the sand with a bone-rattling thud. Winded and gasping for air, she struggled to find her feet.

Above, the darkness writhed about the dragon's head. Nerissa's claws slashed and tore at it, but the cloud was like a living thing, reforming with each attempt. It clung to the dragons face, robbing her of sight, of smell, of air.

Her movements grew more violent and distressed. The great head shook, jaws opening to bellow her defiance. The greasy poison poured down her throat, cutting off the sound. She stumbled across the sand, wings clawing, struggles growing ever weaker.

Caelin could only watch in helpless terror. Enala sat frozen beneath the beast, staring in despair at her dying dragon.

A sudden stillness took Nerissa, the last of her strength fading away. She began to sway. Then she was falling, falling straight towards Enala.

Caelin was already moving, sand slipping beneath his feet, a desperate sprint to reach the girl in time. Enala did not move, did not seem bothered by her impending death. She looked up at the dragon, on her knees, and watched the massive body descend.

He leapt beneath Nerissa's shadow, bounded to Enala, and tackled her from the path of the dragon's fall. The ground shook as the beast struck, sending up a wave of coarse black sand. Caelin shielded the girl against the dragon's dying throws, the razor sharp claws coming within inches of them.

As the dragon stilled Caelin picked himself up, leaving Enala where she lay. Nerissa had fallen a couple of feet from where they had landed. The great beast lay like a statue, still as stone. The evil smoke had vanished. The glassy globes of the dragon's eyes stared up at him, blank and devoid of life.

Enala opened her eyes and saw Nerissa lying there. Caelin watched a wave sweep through her tiny body, a great shuddering jolt, as though something within had shattered into a thousand pieces. Enala rolled into a ball and began to sob, the quiet whispers mere hints of her sorrow.

Caelin had no time to worry about her. He picked up Alastair's sword and stood over the helpless girl, waiting for Balistor to come.

The traitor walked up onto Nerissa's stomach, grinning as he gave them a mocking clap. Caelin gripped the sword tighter, swallowing his rage. The Magicker looked down at them, his smile dismissing Caelin as a spider would a fly. Yet Caelin would not back down. He would fight to his dying breath to protect the girl.

"Well done, Caelin. For a second I thought I had dealt with a few birds with a single stone. As ever, you do not fail to impress. Sadly though, it is time for this mockery to end," flames raced along his arms.

Caelin braced himself and brought up Alastair's sword. Fire filled the air, racing towards him too fast to avoid. He flinched back, the sword raised before him. The flames struck Alastair's weapon, and vanished.

Caelin blinked to clear his eyes, staring at the sword. He ran a finger along the steel and found it cool to the touch.

Balistor's breath hissed between his teeth. "Ah, Alastair's sword. It will be a nice souvenir."

"Come and get it," Caelin grinned. He slipped into a fighting stance. A swordsman he could deal with.

Balistor drew his own blade and touched a hand to it. Fire leapt down its length and spread along his arm, then to his chest until it covered his body in a blazing suit of armour. Heat radiated off him in waves, forcing Caelin back. He squinted against the flaming light and braced himself.

"Do you think those flames will stop my blade?" he mocked.

Balistor made no reply. Caelin would not have heard him over the snarling flames anyway. His foe's sword flicked out, leaving a burning glow trailing across his vision.

Alastair's sword caught its edge and turned it aside. Metal clashed as Balistor swung again. Embers sprayed across Caelin's face, forcing him to raise an arm to protect his eyes from the smouldering rain. He slid backwards, sword slashing out to cover his retreat.

Balistor pressed the advantage, heat radiating out before

him in a stifling cloud. Smoke cloyed the air, making it a struggle just to breathe. Sweat trickled down Caelin's face and into his eyes. His sea soaked clothes were already beginning to dry from the fire's touch. Even so, he blocked each blow with cool efficiency. His mind focused, driven by thoughts of what failure would mean for all of them.

Yet Balistor was gaining ground. The heat sapped Caelin's strength, his attacks already becoming more and more feeble. Alastair's sword protected him from direct attacks, but it could not be everywhere. Each time the blades met flames erupted between them, the cinders leaving scorch marks on his skin. Embers had set his shirt aglow in several places and his body screamed with exhaustion. Between the attack last night and the demon, he had nothing left to give.

Inken appeared from nowhere, arrow nocked to her bow. Before either could react, she loosed. The arrow came within a foot of Balistor before a tongue of flame lashed out to catch it. The shaft fell to the ground as ash.

Balistor lashed out with his blade, forcing Caelin back, then spun and hurled a wave of flame at Inken. It struck her in the chest, throwing her to the ground. She spun through the sand, fighting to beat out the fire catching on her shirt. When the flames finally died, she collapsed to the beach, overtaken by the pain.

Caelin turned in time to block a decapitating blow. Heat swamped him, driving him back. It was like fighting in a furnace. The flames sucked all moisture from the air, leaving his skin burned and lips cracking with each gasp of breath. The burning sword tore through the air. Caelin leaned back, the blade ripping through the space he'd just occupied. He spun on his heel as it passed, his own weapon seeking flesh.

Balistor wrenched back – but not fast enough. Alastair's

blade streaked through the flaming armour, catching flesh. The stench of burning blood quickly followed. The wound only drove Balistor harder. His blade struck at him, faster now, leaving Caelin defending desperately for his life. Pain rippled down his arm as each blow struck.

Then Balistor's blade caught on his own, sweeping beneath his guard. The burning sword tore across his chest, burning as it went. Caelin screamed as pain seared through his body, forcing him to his knees. Balistor raised his weapon to finish him. Caelin rolled backwards, coming to his feet outside his opponent's reach.

Balistor laughed. "And now the mighty Caelin flees. Did I not tell you how useless a sword is amongst Magickers?"

Caelin staggered, heat burning deeper into his chest. He gritted his teeth, fighting to keep his feet. *I cannot fail*, he yelled within the confines of his mind. But nor could he stand. His legs crumpled and he fell to his knees.

Balistor laughed down at him. "Ah, the great swordsman humbled. I am glad to see the day," he placed his sword against Caelin's neck.

Flame licked at his flesh. He flinched back, hands reaching down to scoop up a fistful of sand. Balistor raised his sword and Caelin hurled the sand at his foe's face. It disappeared through the mask of fire.

Balistor reared back with a scream of agony. His sword fell to the beach and his hands reached for his face. Another nightmarish shriek echoed off the cliffs and he toppled to the ground. His fingers clawed at his face as though his eyes were afire.

Caelin did not stop to question the turn of luck. He stepped close and put an end to the traitor's cries. The flames died as he wrenched back his sword. He gasped at the sight of what lay beneath, reeling back in shock. The sand he'd thrown had liquefied in the flames, covering

Balistor's face with molten glass. It had congealed in his mouth and eyes, the skin beneath blistering, his eyes blood red. Caelin's stomach lurched at the smell of burning flesh and hair. He turned away in horror.

He looked around at the bloody battleground the beach had become. The dragon's body loomed large in his eyes, Enala still catatonic beside it. Beyond Alastair lay alone on the red sand. Further up the beach, Inken had managed to crawl back to Eric's side. The breeze blew across the black sands, carrying with it the stench of ash, the reek of their ruin.

His eyes drifted back to Enala. She was the one they had sought, the one who would save them all. Yet in saving her, they had paid a toll beyond what anyone had expected. Who was Enala but a young, inexperienced girl? How was she to stand against the powers of Archon?

Was she really worth this?

TWENTY FOUR

Waves crashed down on the black shores. Night slipped ever closer. The light of the evening star hung on the horizon, its light beckoning them into the dark. Eric would not live to see the sunrise.

Michael watched the young couple, his heart breaking. Not for the first time he wished the Goddess had gifted him with the magic to heal. All his adult life he had studied the art of healing, but his skills were next to useless when compared to those with magic. He could do nothing for Eric.

It amazed him the boy still lived. Through sheer courage he fought on, eyes locked with Inken's. The girl would not leave his side. Young love, if anything, was fierce. Even so, it would not be long now. He closed his eyes, fighting back tears. *I told them*, he raged to himself. *I told them it was folly, but I never imagined…*

Michael looked back at them. Eric had to fight for every breath now. Liquid rattled in his chest, blood drowning his lungs. He had patched up the wound, but the bleeding continued within. He did not have the skill to repair such damage.

"Michael, help!" Inken cried, desperate.

The girl's voice tore him from his despair. He moved to them and together they shifted Eric onto his side. His breathing eased, but a moment later he began to cough again. Michael saw the terror in Eric's eyes.

He glanced across at Inken. Her eyes were red from crying, but there were no more tears. Her face showed the burns and bruises of battle. Her eyes pleaded with him for help.

There was no hope he could give her. "I'm sorry, Inken. I don't think it will be long now."

"No," she whispered.

Michael moved away, unable to bear her grief. He saw the accusation in her eyes. *Why?* He looked over at Enala, the girl who had drawn them across all these miles. She sat stone faced, hands around her knees, rocking back and forth. She had not spoken for hours, only stared at the dead dragon. No one could break her from the trance and Michael was not game to try again.

He moved into the trees and sat down. A cloud of insects rose to greet him. He ignored their tiny bites, struggling to immerse himself in the sound and smell of the earth and forest, to reconnect with his element. It seemed an eon since he had left the temple. He missed the simplicity of his life there, the rareness of death.

Today's slaughter made no sense to him. "Why, Antonia? Why did this happen?" he asked the forest.

"Because I failed," a tiny voice spoke from behind him, heavy with sorrow.

He turned his head. A young girl walked forwards, bathed in a faint green light. Her feet crunched on the hard leaves, her violet eyes staring at him from beneath a fringe of silky brown hair. Faint freckles spotted her cheeks and her lips were twisted in sadness. She looked nothing like the paintings in the temple, but there could be no mistaking her. This could only be Antonia, Goddess of Plorsea.

Michael fell to his knees, head bowed and arms out before him. His heart raced. *Elynbrigge told the truth!* He could not believe it.

To his surprise Antonia began to sob. "Get up, you fool. Please, no more."

He looked up. There were tears on the Goddess' cheeks. He noticed now the rips and scorch marks on her blue dress. Exhaustion hung beneath her eyes. She staggered towards him and started to fall.

Michael leaned forward and caught her before she hit the ground. She seemed to float in his hands, the fabric of her dress slipping through his fingers like mist.

Antonia sighed, looking up at him. "Thank you," she whispered. Her eyes closed. He thought she slept, until she spoke again. "I'm too late. This wasn't supposed to happen. Damn you, Archon."

She ran her hands through her hair, fingers twisting the long strands in frustration. Her voice was weary. "He attacked, testing what remains of the banishment we cast. He was only probing, toying with us – *but his strength!* We could hardly hold him back. And while we fought him, his demon snuck through our net. He knew, he planned it all," her voice cracked, but whether from rage or grief he could not tell.

Michael sat speechless. He held her as though she were the greatest of treasures. It felt like blasphemy even to touch her. He shivered, taking in every aspect of her features.

Then he remembered Eric, lying in such pain, so close to death. Yet Antonia was exhausted, at the end of her strength. Dare he ask?

He summoned his courage. "Antonia, there is a boy, Eric. He is dying. Can you save him?"

Antonia drew herself up, pulling from Michael's arms. "Yes, of course. It's not over yet. Take me to Eric, Michael. He I can save."

His heart skipped a beat. "Truly?"

Antonia stalked past, dismissing the question. Her movements were steady now. She had shrugged off her fatigue, new purpose feeding her. Michael stumbled after, too stunned to watch where he put his feet.

Eric and Inken lay close to the tree line. Inken still knelt beside him, but Eric's eyes had closed. Michael's chest clenched in terror. Antonia walked up to them. Inken spun when she heard her footsteps. She reached for her hunting knife when she saw the strange girl.

"Don't worry, Inken. Everything will be okay," Antonia's hand reached out, her hand brushing across Inken's forehead. She slumped to the sand, fast asleep.

Antonia looked at Michael. "This may take some time. There is more than just Eric's physical injuries to heal. Help Caelin build up the fire and find some food. He will be hungry."

She turned her back and leaned over Eric. Reaching down, she placed both hands on his chest. Her eyes closed and light seemed to leap from nowhere to bathe them both. The air hummed with power.

Michael drew a deep, shuddering breath and turned away. He moved to help Caelin.

****

Eric was lost. Whichever way he turned darkness rose to meet him. Shadowy creatures danced just out of eyesight. His heart raced with fear. He whirled and ran, unsure where he fled but knowing he must escape. From behind came the clack of claws on stone.

A tide of anger washed around him. He felt the shadows hunting him, tasted their bloodthirst. Hatred seeped through his core, though he knew it was not his own. It fed his terror, driving him through the dark.

His legs felt like lead. Pain blossomed in every muscle, but he could not stop. A strange certainty gripped him – if he stopped the hounds would catch him, and his life would end. He pushed his aching body onwards.

His surroundings raced by, unchanging. He saw no trees or boulders or landmarks, no sun to distinguish his direction – just the ever-shifting darkness. And the barking of the hounds, growing louder. He fought to find someplace to go. Somewhere in this nightmare there must be salvation. An image of Inken rose within his mind; he clung to it and ran on.

Ahead a shape loomed from in the darkness. Despair trickled through him. A cliff rose above, stretching out to eternity in either direction. Its sheer face stared down, defying him. He reached it within moments. His hands clasped at the cold stone, shaking with fear. There was no going on. His body could not go any farther anyway. In despair, he turned and looked out into the empty darkness.

Except it was not empty. Sounds of movement came, deep growls emanating from just out of sight. Glowing red eyes appeared from the gloom. The shaggy bodies of the wolves followed, one by one from the shadows. The demon's slaves.

Eric watched them come, preparing himself for the end. There was no fight left in him, nothing for him to give. The last glimmer of hope fluttered away. They had him, and his friends were a long way from here. He leaned back against the cool stone and closed his eyes.

The wolves howled. Eric shivered and scrunched his eyes tighter. He waited. Claws scraped. They barked as they leapt.

A flash of light burst through Eric's eyelids. He squinted against the glare and saw a shining figure stalk through the darkness. Tall and shimmering with power, robes of pure white spilling out around him. By the light the man cast, Eric saw one wolf already lay dead. The others shrank back, growling.

Eric's stomach clenched as the figure turned towards him. Alastair smiled, his face filled with warmth, the lines of age vanished. Their eyes locked. Alastair looked back to the wolves and raised a hand. Light shone out. The wolves leapt back, but too slowly. As the light touched them, they collapsed without sound.

With the beasts vanquished, Alastair moved to Eric's side. He raised a pale hand and placed it on his head. Warmth spread through his body. "You are safe now, Eric. Antonia has healed your wounds – life awaits you."

"And you?"

Alastair's smile faded. "My time is over, but yours is only just beginning. Enjoy it; fill it with love and family and friendship. Do not repeat my mistakes. I wish you well," he began to fade away.

"Alastair, wait!" Eric cried out, desperate.

"Yes?"

"*Thank you?*"

Alastair smiled, and vanished.

Antonia walked from the gloom. She offered him a pale white hand. "Life beckons, Eric."

****

Eric sucked in a breath of sea air. His hands went to his chest and found the tear in his shirt, but the skin beneath was whole. He looked up. Around him was a dome of light, shutting off the outside world. Beside him sat Antonia, dried tears on her cheeks. She forced a smile.

"You saved me," it was not a question. "Thank you."

"I wasn't the only one there, Eric. I would have been too late."

"Is he still here?"

She shook her head, voice breaking. "No, he's gone now."

Eric nodded. The dome faded, slowly revealing the world without. He could hardly bear the thought of returning to it without Alastair. "I'm going to miss him, Antonia."

"We all will," she whispered. She wore her fatigue like a cloak.

"You're tired."

Antonia sighed. "Archon is mustering an army. It is taking all our strength to keep his magic from the Three Nations. Soon the last of our protections will fail, and his demons will be free to wreak havoc on us."

Eric shot up. "The demon!"

She laid a hand on his shoulder. "It has fled."

"Why did it come here?"

"I believe Balistor had a way to inform his master about your plans. Archon attacked us, creating a distraction for his demon to sneak through and come for the girl."

Eric looked away, his hand absently feeling where the blade had pierced him, remembering the icy chill of the blade. "What did it do to me?"

"It carried a *Soul Blade*, a creation of Archon's. When it inflicts a wound to a Magicker, the victim's magic is absorbed into the blade."

Eric shivered. "That's not all though, is it? I felt something from the blade... infect me."

"Yes. Your magic is intertwined with your soul. The blade allowed the demon to borrow your power, but it cannot last without your soul. So the blade sends its magic into its victim. That dark magic harries the spirit, breaking down your will. Eventually, it engulfs everything you are, and the *Soul Blade* swallows the soul."

Shuddering, Eric thought of the wolves hunting him through his mind. If it had not been for Alastair, they would have taken him, consumed him.

"Does this mean my magic will return?"

"Yes, it will replenish itself where the *Soul Blade* cannot. Its power will be gone by now. The demon will need a fresh victim," she smiled. "And I have replenished your magic with my own strength."

"Thank you," he hesitated. "Was it truly Thomas?"

Antonia's face twisted with pain. "His body, yes. Such an awful fate, but I will put an end to his suffering," she stood.

"Where are you going?"

"Nowhere, yet," she offered him a hand. "Come, I believe there are some people waiting to see you."

Eric smiled and stood. A fire burned further down the beach, ringed by his companions. They stared into the golden flames, backs to the night. He could hear the faint whisper of their conversation. They moved towards them.

When they were just a few steps away, Inken turned her head. Her eyes widened, a grin splitting her face, then she was up, sprinting towards him. There was no avoiding her as she tackled him to the ground.

His breath whooshed from his lungs as they landed in a tangle. He coughed and then started to laugh. "Nice to see you too, Inken!"

She pinned him down and planted a kiss on his lips. There were tears in her eyes. Her breath was warm on his cheek. "Don't you *ever* do that to me again, Eric, or I swear I'll… I'll…"

Eric pressed his mouth to hers, silencing the threats.

When they broke apart, Inken bowed her head to Antonia. "Thank you, Goddess."

"It was my pleasure, and please, call me Antonia. Come, let's return to the warmth of the fire."

Inken nodded and pulled Eric to his feet. They re-joined the others.

Caelin rose and slapped him on the back. "Welcome back to the world of the living, my friend."

"I'm glad you're healed," Michael offered.

Eric returned their greetings, noticing Enala still sat hunched by the fire. Her face was steel and her eyes did not seem to have registered him at all. He moved across to her and held out his hand.

"Hello, Enala. My name is Eric, it's nice to finally meet you," he introduced himself.

There was no response. Frowning, he turned to the others.

Antonia answered the unspoken question. "Enala has retreated from the world, from the pain. It will take more than magic to bring her back. But that is a worry for tomorrow."

Silence fell. Despite his recovery, grief still hung over them. He looked at the miserable band, filled with a chilling anger. He forced it down.

Antonia stood. "I should leave now. The demon must be found and destroyed."

"Wait! What do we do now?" Michael asked.

"You put your dead to rest. Use the boat, he always

liked the idea of a burial at sea."

Eric climbed to his feet. "Stay, Antonia. You knew Alastair better than anyone. Say your farewells with us. Besides, you're exhausted."

Antonia gave a sad smile. "I have already said my goodbyes, Eric. And the demon must be stopped – before it finds more power. But I will leave you each with a farewell gift."

She raised a hand. Light seeped from her skin. It crept to Caelin first, his burns vanishing at its touch. The rings beneath his eyes faded away. Then the light spread, to Michael, and Inken, and finally Enala. Only the girl did not seem to notice her bruises healing.

They raised their hands in farewell. Antonia vanished into the forest.

****

Alastair's emerald eyes stared up at him. His skin was grey, devoid of life. Eric could not bear to look at him. His thoughts turned inwards, to remember the man Alastair had been. The man who had laughed with him, who had offered silent comfort against his despair. The man who had told him of his magic and protected him from its darkness. Most of all, he remembered the man who had been his friend.

The wisps of his grey hair and beard blew on the gentle ocean breeze. The wrinkles of his face had receded, restoring his lost youth. He looked to be at peace. Yet Eric's heart was breaking.

Inken stood beside him, offering her silent comfort. The others ringed the black skiff in which they had placed Alastair's body: Caelin, who had killed the traitor, and

Michael, who had helped Eric save his mentor just a few days ago.

Eric's eyes burned. He reached down and squeezed Alastair's cold hand. His heart ached. It was hard to convince himself this was not still some horrible nightmare. Alastair was dead. During the short time they had known each other, the man had carried him through so much. He had bestowed on Eric the gift of knowledge, the ability to control his magic. Not once had he asked for anything in return.

He felt the debt all the same. Alastair had given his life in the fight against Archon. It was up to them to carry on that fight. He would not rest until the Three Nations were safe again.

For now though, it was time to say goodbye.

Eric stepped up to the black skiff. His eyes brimmed as he placed his hands on the hard wood. The tears spilt, running in torrents down his face. Inside he was breaking, but he had a job to do, final words to say.

He looked down at his mentor. "Thank you, Alastair, for all you have given us. Farewell."

His grief broke free and he began to sob. He started to push all the same, his friends stepping in to help. The skiff crunched on the sand and into the ocean. There the fierce currents took hold. There were no waves tonight, but the water lapped at the sides. It drifted out into the bay.

Inken nocked an arrow to her bow and lit it in the fire. Her hands shook, but they steadied as she drew back the bowstring. Firelight sparkled in her damp eyes. She loosed.

The arrow arced out across the waters, a tiny shooting star. It fell, striking Alastair's final resting place. The wood and tinder they had stacked the boat with blazed into light. Flames reflected off water and heaven.

No one spoke. Eric felt an arm around his waist. He

looked to Inken, saw his grief reflected in her eyes. They stood and watched, offering one last silent farewell to the great man.

"What now?" Inken whispered.

"We live."

EPILOGUE

Antonia yawned, her eyelids beginning to droop. She shook her head, fighting the fatigue. She walked on with hands outstretched to brush against the vegetation as she passed. The trees leaned towards her, branches and vines reaching out like arms to embrace her. The thick tree trunks groaned. Their voices whispered in her head, told her their story, of the demon's passage. It would not escape.

Her pace slowed as the chase stretched on. The day had taken its toll and all she wanted now was to rest. The call of sleep beckoned. The thought scared her; she had not needed to sleep in decades. She could not afford to now.

Antonia pressed deeper into the forest. Feeling her weakness, the trees offered their own strength. She took a drop, but with winter coming, she knew they had little to spare.

The demon had not stopped to recover from its battle. She had already covered miles and her prey still showed no sign of stopping. The forest was broken and battered from its passage. The trees whispered of the demon's pain. The dragon had hurt it badly. That would make her task easier.

Her bare feet caught on a rock, sending her tumbling to

the ground. Cursing, Antonia sat up. This method of travel was far too time consuming for her liking. *If only I could rest!* She closed her eyes, just for a moment, gathering her strength. Her spirit was weary, her limbs lethargic.

Her thoughts turned to her brother, Jurrien. She wondered how he was coping after their ordeal. He possessed a greater stamina than her own, though he had borne the brunt of Archon's initial assault.

She let out a long breath, bracing herself to push on. Yet sleep still beckoned, so tempting, so needed. She relaxed again, wriggling sideways so her back was against a tree. She would rest for an hour and push on when she woke. The demon would not get far.

Her breathing slowed and her thoughts began to drift. She slept.

****

The demon watched from the shadows. He wondered how long the Goddess had been sleeping. It had taken him most of the night to circle back and morning was fast approaching. He had to act quickly.

He slipped forward, smiling in anticipation. Archon's plan had worked better than they could ever have imagined. The Goddess herself had come after him, and she was exhausted in both mind and magic. The battles of the last few days were too much, even for her. She should have rested before giving chase. The mistake would cost her dearly.

Silent as death, the demon slid between the trees. Antonia slept on. He pulled one of the *Soul Blades* from its sheath and drew closer.

The Goddess's chest rose and fell in steady succession. Her magic had shrunk to a dim spark, fluttering with each breath. The *Soul Blade* would pierce both easily. Smiling, he raised the sword.

Antonia's eyes flickered open. Her mouth opened in shock. The blade flashed down. It met a second's resistance as the God magic rose to defend her, but the black magic sliced through like butter. The blade slid home.

Antonia screamed, stiffening against the cold steel. Her eyes widened, her fingers clawing at the *Soul Blade*, cutting on the sharp edges. Her legs thrashed, unable to reach him. Her body fought to heal itself, but with the sword in place the magic could not save her. Light flashed from her body, burning his eyes. Each flash quickly died, sucked into the dark depths of the *Soul Blade*.

The Goddess' struggles began to weaken. Her hands were bloody from their fight with the sword, her dress turned red. She screamed again, as though the sound itself could move him. The demon drank her pain, savouring the taste, the sweet essence of her fear.

Slowly her magic began to fail. Powerful as she was, the God magic could not sustain her mortal body forever. Her struggles grew feeble, her fingers slipping from the blade. Her purple eyes stared into his, her chest heaving with tiny gasps. He could feel her magic raging against the sword's power, fighting him with every inch of her will. He held on.

At last, her eyelids slid closed. A final breath hissed between her teeth and the Goddess of Plorsea gave herself over to death.

And her spirit went screaming into the *Soul Blade*.

HERE ENDS BOOK ONE

OF

THE SWORD OF LIGHT

TRILOGY

THE ADVENTURE CONTINUES

IN

BOOK TWO:

FIRESTORM

NOTE FROM THE AUTHOR

Thank you for reading my very first novel, Stormwielder. I hope you enjoyed it! This has been my pet project for several years, and I feel absolutely honoured by each and every person who has read and enjoyed the tale. And don't worry, there's plenty more to come ☺.

Reader feedback is a huge part of the writing and publishing process, and all reviews on Amazon would be very much appreciated.

Signup to my newsletter for updates on my new releases, exclusive giveaways, and special contests for fans. Oh, and **I also frequently give away limited numbers of free Advance Review Copies (ARC) of upcoming books**, so you'd better signup quick. ☺ You can find the link below:

aaronhodges.co.nz/newsletter-signup/

41342804R00178

Made in the USA
Middletown, DE
09 March 2017